W9-CTM-864

RECEIVED

JUL 0 0 2022

By

NO LONGER PROPERTY OF
SEATTLE PUBLIC LIBRARY

More Critical Praise for Michael Zadoorian

for *The Narcissism of Small Differences*

"'You shut up and went to work because people were counting on you,' writes Michael Zadoorian in *The Narcissism of Small Differences*. This is perhaps the best description ever of the Detroit attitude, exemplified by protagonists Joe and Ana, a couple at the crossroads, utterly compelling as they try to move up—and stay together—in the world's most blue-collar city. Zadoorian's glittering prose will often make you laugh, but it's his gusto and unfailing eye that pull at your heart in this fantastic novel."
—Scott Lasser, author of *Say Nice Things About Detroit*

"When you have spent a life living apart from the mainstream, carving out a niche of artful individualism, it's good to find that you are not alone after all. Michael Zadoorian's *The Narcissism of Small Differences* shows you that there are kindred souls in all the cities of the world who struggle with the same failures and successes. It's like discovering your family."
—Sven Kirsten, author of *The Book of Tiki*

for *Beautiful Music*

• A 2019 Michigan Notable Book, presented by the Michigan Department of Education and the Library of Michigan

• Adult Fiction Winner for the 2018 Great Lakes Great Reads program, presented by the Great Lakes Independent Booksellers Association

"Danny Yzemski tunes out a dysfunctional family with Frank Zappa and Iggy Pop, shaking his countercultural fist at The Man in this eight-track flashback of a novel set in 1970s Detroit." —*O, the Oprah Magazine* (Top Books of Summer)

"*Beautiful Music* is a sweet and endearing coming-of-age tale measured in album tracks." —*Wall Street Journal*

"For Danny, cracking the seal on a fresh piece of wax and dissecting cover art and liner notes are acts of nigh religious experience that unveil to him a community of fellow rockers across Detroit . . . It's in these small moments—a lonely boy experiencing premature nostalgia—that Zadoorian shines." —*Washington Post*

"A fantastic book . . . A very compelling read."

—*Stateside* (Michigan Radio/NPR)

"I read *Beautiful Music* compulsively until its end, captivated by the sympathetic character of Danny. I was left with the satisfying, 'Wait a minute, this wasn't really about music at all' feeling that I demand of music writing. But then I had to admit that it really was about rock, its power to heal and transcend. Zadoorian had an easy book to write. His refusal to write it the easy way makes all the difference."   —*Razorcake*

"[Zadoorian's] third novel—*Beautiful Music*, about a radio-loving teen's transformation through music during the early '70s in Detroit . . . [is] rich with Detroit details (Korvette's, Bill Bonds, Iggy Pop), [and] follows Danny through racial tensions at high school, his changing body and his imploding family life."   —*Detroit Free Press*

"Zadoorian takes us back to Detroit in the 1970s, which was still throbbing from the 1967 rebellion, and was in the throes of the energy crisis and the sexual revolution. Protagonist Danny Yzemski finds that growing up in such times can be . . . complicated. But with a little help from Iggy Pop, the MC5, and Led Zeppelin, he finds just the boost he needs to survive—and even grow a bit."   —*Detroit Metro Times*

"A delightful trip down a memory lane in the '60s with a soundtrack folks of a certain age will all recognize."

—*Lansing City Pulse* (Best Michigan-Inspired Books of 2018)

"*Beautiful Music* is touching, hilarious, and heartbreaking, much like the gamut of emotions you may have felt the first time you heard your favorite song. And much like that first, mind-opening musical experience, you'll return to certain passages within this novel because like the perfect song, it hits all the right notes—something you can feel deep in your gut."

—*Michigan Quarterly Review*

"[A] raucous bildungsroman . . . Zadoorian touches on white flight, iconic radio stations, and the racial history of Detroit, but remains rooted in [protagonist] Danny's transition out of his shell. With its echoes of works by Nick Hornby and Stephen Chbosky, Zadoorian's ebullient novel is full of energy, pain, growth, and great music."   —*Publishers Weekly*

"[Zadoorian is] skilled at capturing the feeling of release that music can provide ('something snaps in your heart and a jolt of pure happiness shoots through you better than all the dope in the world') as well as the anxiety the novelty of that experience can produce in a sheltered kid

". . . A likable bildungsroman that cannily evokes how music transforms teenage identity." —*Kirkus Reviews*

"This affectionate, nostalgic novel about a sometimes-troubled teen is a crossover delight with appeal to both adults and teens." —*Booklist*

"Zadoorian captures the inner and outer life of Danny Yzemski with perfect pitch . . . When Danny unwraps a new album, the reader experiences the feel and look of it, the smell of the liner, hears the hiss and pop when the needle first makes contact with vinyl . . . *Beautiful Music* is a novel that lingers." —*Santa Barbara Independent*

"If you grew up in the age of transistor radios, powerhouse rock stations, record stores, first love and last kisses—you will love Michael Zadoorian's new novel, *Beautiful Music.*" —*Lansing City Pulse*

"[A] knockout . . . Exceptionally entertaining . . . If you haven't discovered Zadoorian's books, you're in for a real treat!" —*Lansing State Journal*

for *The Leisure Seeker*

• Now a Sony Pictures Classics film starring
Helen Mirren and Donald Sutherland

"Zadoorian's pace is deceptive, it's restful. But unexpected scenes jump out at you. Come to the end and you'll say, 'Oh my God.'"
—Elmore Leonard

"*The Leisure Seeker* is pretty much like life itself: joyous, painful, funny, moving, tragic, mysterious, and not to be missed."
—*Booklist* (starred review)

"In this affecting road novel, an elderly married couple leave their Detroit home and take off in their camper for one last adventure together . . . An authentic and funny love story." —*Publishers Weekly*

"A bittersweet fable of the golden years likely to offer consolation to readers who've ever known anyone old or have plans to get old themselves."
—*Kirkus Reviews*

"Michael Zadoorian's bittersweet story about two runaways who are in their 80s and in failing health could be a lovely film." —*USA Today*

"I hoped for a book that would make me laugh during these tight times, and I was rewarded." —*Los Angeles Times*

for *Second Hand*

• An ABA Book Sense 76 Pick

• A Barnes & Noble Discover Award Finalist

• Winner of the Great Lakes Colleges Association New Writers Award

"*Second Hand* may feel like a gift from the (Tiki) gods."

—*New York Times Book Review*

"A charming, comic novel." —*Marie Claire*

"Wonderful . . . a novel about finding value in the most unlikely places."

—*Tampa Tribune Times*

"Anyone who has found delight in a thrift store, captured glee in finding that perfect scarf or that retro chair, will delight at this novel." —*Booklist*

"How can one capture the spirit of this wondrous book in so few words? Marvelous observations about secondhand items and life in general . . . Readers will thoroughly enjoy this book and will be sorry when it ends."

—*Library Journal*

"Astonishingly mandatory and compelling . . . frequent fascinating and insightful meditations on the nature of stuff."

—*San Francisco Bay Guardian*

for *Lost Tiki Places of Detroit*

"[The stories are] sometimes wildly funny and more than a little crazy, yet they have a heartbreaking affection for the battered lives they portray."

—*Ann Arbor Observer*

"These newly envisioned stories of Detroit come at you without apology for the gritty language of the city, the racism, the madness of everyday life. The whiff of 'presence,' of being there, grabs at your throat."

—*Northern Express*

"These are stories that grab you, shake you and slap you upside the head." —*Lansing City Pulse*

"Zadoorian knows the streets and side streets and alleyways of his city and its surround; better, he knows the humor, the sadness, and the sometimes hidden beauty of life in the Rust Belt."

—Paul Clemens, author of *Made in Detroit*

Michael Zadoorian

The Narcissism of Small Differences

BROOKLYN, NEW YORK, USA
BALLYDEHOB, CO. CORK, IRELAND

This is a work of fiction. All names, characters, places, and incidents are the product of the author's imagination or are used fictitiously. Any resemblance to real events or persons, living or dead, is entirely coincidental.

Published by Akashic Books
©2020 Michael Zadoorian

Hardcover ISBN: 978-1-61775-818-8
Paperback ISBN: 978-1-61775-817-1
Library of Congress Control Number: 2019943615

All rights reserved
First printing

Akashic Books
Brooklyn, New York, USA
Ballydehob, Co. Cork, Ireland
Twitter: @AkashicBooks
Facebook: AkashicBooks
E-mail: info@akashicbooks.com
Website: www.akashicbooks.com

For my friends

Boxed in, pulled together, touching my tomb with one hand
and my cradle with the other, I felt brief and splendid, a
flash of lightning that was blotted out by darkness.
—Jean-Paul Sartre

"Tell me exactly what happened. Did you do any heroic act?"
"No," I said. "I was blown up while we were eating cheese."
—Ernest Hemingway

1

Detroit

2009

1

The Two of Them

"Are we weird?"

Joe closed his eyes and quietly sighed. Not another one of these conversations. "I don't know, Ana," he said, his voice belying a complete lack of enthusiasm in this subject. "What do you mean by weird?"

She was sitting on the floor of the living room of their town house, leaning back against the couch. She scooted her knees up until they were under her chin. "I don't know. *Weird.*"

Joe was perched on a sixties lowboy chair directly across from her, paging through the latest edition of the *Detroit Independent*, the local alternative paper for which he wrote. He had wanted to look over the piece he had written on the works of Donald Goines, Detroit's bard of blaxploitation, but instead he was doomed to have this conversation. "Look, you tell me what weird is and I'll tell you if we're it."

"I don't know."

He folded the newspaper and tossed it in a vintage black wire magazine rack. "Okay, what's up?"

"I don't know. I just feel like we're weird."

"Really?" he said. "I don't know what to tell you, but trust me, we are definitely not weird. There are lots of people who actually live different, crazy, interesting, *weird* lives—they go live on ashrams or tour with Sun Ra tribute bands. They go off the grid. They travel the world seeking knowledge. They go tripping on *yage* with a shaman in the Amazon. We, on the other hand, have jobs. We live in the suburbs. We go to Target, for fuck's sake. We are *not* weird. We are nowhere near weird. In fact, it makes me sad to think of how not-weird we are."

Ana's turn to sigh this time. "I disagree. First off, Ferndale isn't some affluent suburb. We're a mile from Detroit. We're an inner-ring city. And I don't know if what you have could be considered a *job*."

He was going to ignore that last comment. "Fine, okay then, I guess we're weird." Maybe this would end if he just agreed with her.

"People think we're weird because we've been shacked up for fifteen years." Ana wasn't letting him get off that easily.

"That's not weird, Ana. That's monogamy. Very common and nonweird."

"It's a little weird."

Another loud exhalation. "Is that it? You want to get married?"

Ana peered at him over her glasses, brow canted above the smallish cat-eye frames, as if he had just casually suggested a murder-suicide pact. Joe usually thought she looked wonderful in glasses until she did that.

"No," she said. "Why in god's name would we need to get married?"

He shrugged. "I don't know. Because that's what most people consider *normal*?"

She laid her head back on the cushion of the couch and gazed at the ceiling. "Hm."

"People have an extremely low tolerance for weird. They

think everything that's not exactly like them is weird. Trust me, we're disgustingly normal."

"Please stop talking, Joe."

"What? What do you want me to say? Truly, if we are what passes for weird, then the world is in big trouble."

She sighed again. "I don't know. Just forget it. I'm going upstairs to read."

After she left, Joe had an unsettled feeling in his stomach, a burning that only a couple of beers would help extinguish.

2

The Law of Random Sync

Ana did not know why she was saying these things. She didn't used to worry about being weird. Weird used to be a good thing, something she aspired to but never really achieved. So why was she complaining about feeling weird? She really just felt like complaining about *something*. It was true that she didn't feel normal. She felt in-between, in a boring, helpless, semicontented, semidisgruntled place. Neither here nor there, in a sort of no-woman's-land of the psyche.

Maybe she felt this way after ten years in a cramped two-bedroom town house in Ferndale (getting more cramped by the day, what with Joe's pack rat tendencies seemingly getting worse as he got older, making her worry that the two of them would someday be found dead after some sort of Collyer brothers hoarder avalanche). Maybe it was her still bringing in the bulk of the income for the two of them (which, admittedly, was irritating her more and more these days). Maybe it was the fact that Joe seemed to be walling himself off from her lately—out boozing with his friends or spending long periods of time in the study or falling asleep on the couch and not coming to bed until it was practically time to get up. Either that or getting up so early, there was little chance for face-to-face time, no time in bed, no time to talk about what was going on in their lives.

Ana missed when they used to cobble together a dinner out of what was in the fridge or pantry, open a bottle of cheap wine, light a candle, and sit at the table all night, just talking. It seemed like years since they had done that. And most every night had been like that at the beginning, at least when they weren't going out to some show or event or to meet up with friends.

There had been a lot of things going on back then. Maybe it was just their youth or that particular moment in Detroit or the fact that she had just gotten started in advertising and going out every night was just what everybody did at that time.

It was how she and Joe had met—a party at a photographer's loft in Eastern Market, someone with whom Ana had just shot one of her very first print ads.

The photographer, Michelle, had set up a makeshift set so she could shoot Polaroid portraits of all the guests. Ana had sat down on the so-tacky-it-was-fabulous crimson crushed-velvet couch from Lasky's in Hamtramck, to wait for her friend Lena (now married with a sweet brood, living in the far suburbs, at what felt like 108 Mile Road) to join her. Lena was taking too long, so Michelle the photographer told Joe, who was standing nearby, to sit down next to Ana. Joe looked around and behind him as if she couldn't possibly be talking to him.

"I'm sorry? Excuse me?"

"Sit down next to her," said Michelle, who was obviously accustomed to arranging people and personalities for photographic purposes.

Joe continued to bumble and stammer. "Oh, I, um. Okay." He plopped down on the other side of the couch.

"What's your name?" said Michelle.

"Joe," he said, blushing furiously.

"Okay, Joe," said Michelle. "Move over closer to Ana."

Joe scooted over, looking worriedly at Ana, as if he was concerned about violating her personal space.

"That's better. That's it. Now look interesting."

The resulting Polaroid revealed Ana covering her mouth in faux shock and Joe with eyes frozen wide and mouth slightly agape. A photo that when viewed now, with its slightly faded color and mottled edges, gave that moment and the life together that followed a retro feel, a strange, anachronistic sense of midcentury spontaneity.

When Joe saw it, he said in a deadpan, "Well, I definitely look interesting."

Ana nodded, trying to keep from laughing. "Yes. Very *interesting*. You look freshly taxidermied."

Joe glanced up from the photo and smiled at her.

Lena still hadn't appeared, so they walked over near the bar to look at Michelle's fine art photography (gritty but respectful portraits of the men and women who sold fruits and vegetables at the market) that was mounted and displayed there. After five minutes of talking to this sweet young man, with the floppy dark hair and furry secondhand cardigan, who was talking too fast, so excited about everything—about photography, music, art, and suddenly, obviously about her—Ana was already feeling something. She felt relieved. Yes, definitely relief. Was that strange? Was that actually love she was feeling right then, five minutes after meeting the guy? Probably not. It was too easy to look back at these things through a soft-focus romantic lens and think that, yet at that moment she had known she was capable of loving him.

Those first months were a lot of going out—events, performances, art openings, raves, poetry slams—whatever the hell was going on back then, they were there. Joe was quite the man about town. She liked that he was invited to everything and that he wanted to go everywhere and experience things and write about them. *We've got to see this band here, that play there, the book-release party over here.* They were together all the time.

But even with all the going out, there was also a lot of staying in, a lot of laughing. They genuinely seemed to amuse each other. Even when Joe wasn't in a good mood, he was still pretty funny. She came to appreciate his mild curmudgeonliness, his brand of gentle grouchiness. She found it amusing how he loved being in a dark, deserted, chilly movie theater on bright summer days, when everyone else was outside enjoying the beautiful Michigan weather. When she asked him about it, he said, "Sunshine is overrated. It's like the climatic equivalent of a conventionally attractive blonde. You're obligated to think it's pretty." He stifled a smile, then held his index finger up to make one of his proclamations. "I refuse to be subject to the tyranny of so-called *good* weather!"

Oh, and there was a lot of sex. A lot of pretty darned amazing sex. When she would stay over at his place (which, while cluttered with books and CDs and VHS tapes and vinyl and cassettes and zines, was always surprisingly clean) on the weekends, sometimes he would blow off all the events he was invited to and they wouldn't leave for forty-eight hours. They would eat carryout, watch movies, listen to music, lie in bed and read (he always had something good around that she would come to appreciate—Dawn Powell, Terry Southern, Carl Van Vechten), and make love. They couldn't keep their paws off each other during that time.

Ana was just getting started as a junior art director, and while working on her very first television commercial, she heard a term from a producer that she couldn't help but to apply to her and Joe: "the law of random sync." Which meant that when you put a piece of existing music up against a rough cut of a commercial, sometimes, just once in a while, everything accidentally matched perfectly. All the beats were there, the music changed at just the right points in the edit; even the energy was right, as if the music was scored specifically for the commercial. Yet it wasn't. It was all pure chance, but everything fit just right.

That was the way it felt between her and Joe, physically and every other way. They had randomly been thrown together and somehow everything fit.

And now, it had certainly been months since they'd had sex. That was one she didn't know how to explain. That was one she kept coming back to when she thought about the big birthday coming up. Was this it? After forty, no fucky? She knew it didn't have to be like that, but it sure felt like it was shaping up that way.

The only fun she'd been having lately was at work, which was strange since work hadn't been fun in a long time. Detroit advertising was hurting. The car companies were fleeing the agencies of their birthplace. Luckily, Ana was working at one of the few places in town that wasn't dependent on the automotive business. New accounts had actually come into the agency recently. Nothing fancy—vacuum cleaners, office-supply superstores, spark plugs—but she and her partner were doing good work and actually getting stuff produced. In a few days, she was going to LA for a week, which sounded pretty wonderful. Getting out of Detroit in January was its own kind of blessing for anyone struggling through an endless, lightless, near hopeless Michigan winter.

3
The Midlands

Joe bundled up and headed out into the bitter January cold to the Midlands, a bar whose name obliquely referred to what Ana had mentioned about Ferndale: the town directly bordered the city limits at 8 Mile Road, but it was a town that was not quite Detroit, with its 138 square miles of abandoned buildings and unrelenting poverty and deserted, pheasant-strewn urban plains; but nor was it the whiter, wealthier, more insular suburbs of the north. Ferndale was in-between, an interzone amalgam of white and black, gay and straight, blue collar and no collar, that had enjoyed a brief period of gentrification a few years earlier, but was now suffering along with the rest of the state after the collapse of the auto industry. The new condo complexes and manufactured lofts hadn't quite gotten a chance to get built. Thus the bad economy and suddenly sinking property values had made it possible for people who would normally be forced to move out—working musicians, teachers, public radio employees, and the few artist types who had amazingly figured out how to make a living doing their thing—to hang on awhile longer.

The Midlands had somehow managed to open its doors during that flourishing, fleeting period between creative-class boon and real estate boom. It was too nice to be a dive, too rough-hewn industrial to be uptown, with its burnished plywood booths and polished concrete bar, its walls full of local art, taps full of local beers, and jukebox full of local bands. The place was family friendly early in the evening, yet lousy with slouching scenesters after eleven o'clock. Joe preferred the time in-between.

Once settled at the bar, Joe shed his Carhartt but kept his beanie on, which he'd been doing more lately since his hairline started its slow but steady decampment northward. Still recovering from the icy walk, he treated himself to a microbrew, a Bell's Two Hearted Ale (after that he'd switch to a mass-produced and decidedly cheaper Stroh's), and began to read his book, *Revolutionary Road*. After a short while, his stomach started to calm as the beer worked its magic on those troublesome centers of his brain. Joe loved reading about fucked-up bourgeois types. And the novel felt like even more proof that even what was deemed "normal" wasn't necessarily good.

He couldn't stop thinking about their conversation. Weird indeed. It *was* disgusting how normal he and Ana were. Of course, their families didn't think so. He knew that there was much shaking of heads, aggravated exclamations of, *Well, I just don't know*, among the respective parents. Living together for fifteen years without matrimony, procreation, or a mortgage bewildered most Michigan parents. To them, he and Ana existed in some state of suspended maturation, and would do so for the rest of their selfish, soon-to-be-middle-aged, progeny-free lives.

He started to read the next page, but was distracted by a flyer on the bar.

THE MIDLANDS PRESENTS CHIN TIKI NIGHT!
OUR ANNUAL RITE OF SPRING
POLYNESIAN CELEBRATION
ZOMBIES—MAI TAIS—PU-PUS—
HULA—FILMS—VENDORS
EXOTICA MUSIC BY DJ DAVE DETROIT
MARK YOUR CALENDARS!

It was for the Midlands' yearly spring Chin Tiki party. Where the local bohos shed their winter parkas, donned aloha shirts, grass skirts, and coconut bras to ironically celebrate the arrival of spring. It was a big thing in Ferndale. A few years ago, Joe had written a feature on Detroit's burgeoning underground tiki culture and had completely fallen under the sway of the whole wonderfully ridiculous idea of it. Looking at the flyer, he couldn't help thinking of what fueled the popularity of tiki culture in midcentury America: the repression and conformity of the times, i.e., being too normal. It was a way for gray-flannel types to shed their inhibitions, go native, and get weird—uninhibited boozing, semierotic dancing to faux-exotic music, gaudy flowered shirts, sticky finger foods, unclad maiden flesh, and phallic tiki idols. At one point, Detroit had three Polynesian palaces, but when the city started bleeding honkies after the '67 race riot, all of them eventually closed. Only one building was still standing, albeit shuttered: the Chin Tiki, after which this shindig was named.

Joe had gone for the past two years. It was always filled with interesting people: artists, musicians, performers, writers, filmmakers, zinesters, photographers, drag queens, performance artists, aging punk rockers, sundry eccentrics, all people whose normalcy Ana might call into question.

Joe often felt a little outclassed because so many of them seemed to be doing so much—performing, making art and music, getting grants and fellowships—while he was still a mere freelancer for the *Independent*, as well as some websites and a few other (now dwindling) print publications. Jealousy aside, it wasn't unusual that he would end up interviewing people from this crowd, which resulted in substantial pieces that actually made Joe feel like a real writer.

After getting his creative writing degree, he had actually aspired to the life of a freelancer. Journalism had seemed like a great way to support himself, so he could have the time to write short stories, though it never quite worked out that way. After three years of constant rejection by small literary magazines, he finally did get something accepted. The *Bellwether Journal* liked his story, which wasn't so much a story as a collection of humorous fragments about a suicidal man with a big nose, a kind of cross between Gogol's "The Nose" and Fitzgerald's *The Crack-Up*. He was thrilled about the story's acceptance and told everyone at work about it, but it turned out that people who worked at Blockbuster Video weren't all that interested in his literary achievements. Which turned out to be a good thing when the magazine went under before his story was published.

The following year, *Terraplane Review* accepted his story "Detroit Pastoral," and then a month later quietly closed its doors. After he killed one last quarterly, the poor, innocent *Kerfuffle*, Joe, without really even acknowledging it, just stopped working on his cursed stories. He considered writing a novel, but then thought about all the people who would be left unemployed and homeless if he happened to put down a major publisher. That was what he told himself, at least.

About the only writing successes he'd had were the "New in Video" capsule reviews for the *Independent*. (Finally, his credentials from clerking at Blockbuster were paying off!) While he wasn't about to become the next Lester Bangs or Roger Ebert, it was a start and the editor encouraged him be funny or snarky in the reviews. He began hanging around the office when he wasn't doing shifts at the video store, taking any writing job they would give him, no matter how shitty. Eventually, he became the utility guy, the one they could always count on to write *something*. When they got a new editor, he liked Joe's tastes in what he called "kooky, artsy, kitschy stuff" and decided that his talents resided in mining the depths of old and weird pop culture. He offered Joe a short column every week where he would recommend obscure or forgotten books, videos, music, and anything else of interest to him. Joe grabbed it, even though it was just slightly more than no money. For the past fifteen years, he'd been doing different versions of the same column, albeit with the occasional name and format change. It wasn't really all that popular, but he did have a following, considering Detroit's taste for the arcane, the old, and the crumbling. And since they weren't paying him very much, they just kept letting him do it. Later, when they needed content for their website, the column was exiled there, which became a good thing as the digital version soon outpaced the actual newspaper.

These days, though, he had gotten lazy, doing the occasional feature, but mostly churning out his column as well as 500- or even 200-word reviews. It was as if everyone else's dwindling attention span was actually making him dumber.

Joe read a little more. He had just started his second beer when his friend Chick walked up to the bar.

"Hey," said Joe, closing his book, placing it on the bar facedown. "What brings you here?"

"Just thought I'd stop in for a quick one."

"What's up?"

"Boned. The Man is sticking it to me again."

Joe laughed. This was pretty much the story of Chick's life, according to Chick. The Man was forever sticking it to him.

"Our friends out on the coast?"

"Who else but fucking Hollywood?"

Chick was an odd bird, at least for Detroit. He was a screenwriter, and not for small independent films or short art flicks. Chick wrote blockbusters and sci-fi fantasies and animated films. And he wrote them for big Hollywood studios. From what Joe knew of them, he was quite good at it. Actually, Chick was one of those friends that Joe had written about. The "Local Boy Strikes It Rich in La-La Land" sort of angle. Not that his friend had ever mentioned any figures, but Chick had sold a number of scripts, many for "mid-to-high six-figure advances." Joe had read this on various film biz websites (while experiencing a curious emotional ad-mixture of envy, contempt for Hollywood, and pride for his friend). None had ever been produced because Chick wrote the kinds of high-concept projects that were expensive to actually make, so the studio cowards were always spending a lot of money to buy the script so nobody else would get it, and then somehow everything would fall apart, much to Chick's frustration. Basically, he would make a truckload of money, then nothing would happen.

Chick looked at Joe's beer. "What are you drinking?"

"Stroh's."

Chick made a face. "Ugh. How can you drink that swill?"

He motioned to the bartender. "I'll have the Two Hearted."

The beer appeared almost immediately before the bartender walked away. She was a tall woman, with blue-black hair and a tattoo on her back, just above the exposed low beltline.

Chick shook his head, as if disgusted. "That girl is fire. She's killing me. Jesus. That tattoo probably says *do me* in Celtic."

"So talk to her."

"A woman like that would have nothing to do with me. She's too cool for me. Too tall for me."

"Too cool? Because she has a tramp stamp? Might I remind you that you're a rich screenwriter in a town where no one is a rich screenwriter?"

"That doesn't matter. I'm still this." Chick frowned, splayed his hands, and gestured at his body like it was something he had picked up at the dollar store.

"What? You're fine. Look at you, you work out and everything."

"Typical short-man syndrome. You can't get taller so you go wider."

Joe laughed. "What are you, like, 5'7"? Isn't that supposed to be average?"

"They say it is, but it isn't. You have no idea what it's like because you're tall. You tall fuckers get all the breaks. You don't even deserve to be tall. You practically slouch. It's wasted on you. Why couldn't I have gotten some of your tallness? But no. Joe Keen, height hog."

Joe shook his head, half laughing.

Chick took a long sip as he watched the bartender. "Oh my god. Would you look at her? She's killing me."

Ana, who surprisingly found Chick quite amusing, once

told him that he had "the most objectifying male gaze" she had ever seen. Chick's reply was, "Thanks!"

"You're worked up tonight. Heard something on a script, I take it?"

He gave Joe an exasperated stage frown, then exhaled loudly. "No. They're taking forever to respond. Bad sign. I'm never going to get a movie made."

"Maybe it's time to bite the bullet and move on out there," said Joe, deciding to goad Chick. They both knew what he was doing, but Chick was happy to play along.

"Yeah, I'm going to go live out in Hollyweird with those nutjobs and their fucking Bentleys. That's a great idea. Some friend you are, Keen." He peered over at Joe, mock-disgusted, trying to keep from laughing.

Joe shrugged innocently. "Just a thought."

"You son of a bitch. I don't even know why I'm sitting with you."

Seeing Chick was raising his spirits considerably. Oddly enough, Chick was probably the most "normal" of all Joe's friends. Chick watched sports, even wore the occasional article of athletic apparel, unabashedly loved big action movies and mainstream music, didn't read many books, and didn't care about art. He also had seen every episode of *Seinfeld* at least ten times. All Chick really wanted was to be married and have a family. To be normal. That, and to have a movie made.

The not-so-normal thing about Chick was his persona of the grumpy, dissatisfied, chauvinist misanthrope who often made inappropriate remarks in mixed company, but who was in reality a sensitive guy. The problem was that he was so good at playing the misanthrope that sometimes people forgot that it was just a persona and got angry with him.

Actually, it was pretty easy to forget that you were dealing with the persona. You had to constantly remind yourself that there was more to him. Joe had once told him that he was like Andy Kaufman, the comedian who invited everyone in the crowd to beat him up. Chick was pleased at the comparison.

Joe had seen it happen many times before: a group of politically correct liberal men and women all taking verbal potshots at Chick for one of his simple but incendiary comments like, "Why's everybody so down on porn? I *love* porn!" or, "How can you not like Ted Nugent? 'Wang Dang Sweet Poontang'? That's my jam!" Chick would put it out there and then just enjoy the fireworks. It seemed to be the only way he could be the center of attention and be comfortable with it. He could deflect the abuse (and also deflect the attention he got from being the guy who sold screenplays for major coin in Hollywood) and even make it funny.

"What are you doing here by yourself, Keen? Seems kind of dipso of you. Sitting at a bar, drinking, reading your fancy-pants novel for all the world to see, like Johnny Intellectual." He put on an upper-crust lockjaw accent and tipped up his pinky finger. "Look at me! Crown Prince Sonny Boy is *reading*."

"Are you done?" said Joe.

"Not quite yet," said Chick. "Shouldn't you be at home snuggling with the little woman? Excuse me—snuggling with the common-law little woman, planning your next antiestablishment FU gesture?"

Joe lowered his head to the bar, laughing. "All right. Uncle. I give up. You win."

Chick, pleased with himself, held up his hands and tilted his head forward in a slight bow. "Thanks, I'll be here all week. Be sure to tip your waitress." A beat. "So why *are* you here? I have no life. What's your excuse?"

Joe raised his upper lip. "Eh, Ana's in one of her moods. She's decided that we're weird."

"So what's news about that? You *are* weird."

"Actually, I told her that we're disgustingly normal. There's nothing more normal than being with the same person forever."

"You're angling for a threesome, aren't you? Bring a little spice into the house. A little *strange*. Huh? Am I right?"

Joe glared at Chick until he stopped.

"Sorry," said Chick, sheepishly. "This happen often?"

"It's been happening more lately. I think its because she's coming up on her fortieth birthday."

Chick's eyes widened. "Holy shit, really? I knew you were older than me, but I had no idea you guys were *that* old."

Joe shrugged. "Yeah, well. No kids. We're not grossly overweight. Oh, and also age-inappropriate clothing. You'd be surprised how much it helps."

"So what's the problem? I thought you guys had it whipped. You two are the only couple I know that actually seem happy."

"Us? Really?"

"Yeah. Aren't you?"

"No, we're happy, I guess. It's just that sometimes Ana seems to want something . . . I'm just not sure she knows what it is."

"You sure she doesn't want a kid?"

"I don't think that's it." Though Ana had always made it very clear that she wasn't interested in having children, this had still been a recent nightmare of his. That she would suddenly want to become a parent at the age of forty. He had seen a few of those older new parents around the neighborhood. They always looked haggard and out of breath.

"Would you ever want one?"

Joe shook his head slowly. "Nah, I just never felt the calling."

Chick took a sip of beer. "I don't think men feel it like women do. Men just want to go spread their seed across the land."

"Probably true, but it seems like you should feel something. Even a little. I mean, I know *you* want a kid, right?"

"Absolutely."

"There you go."

"Yeah, but first I have to get someone to put up with me. I mean, come on, who could love me? I'm hideous."

Joe laughed, then smacked his friend's arm with the back of his hand. "Stop saying that. You're not hideous."

"I'm going to die alone. You know it, I know it."

"Yeah, you're probably right."

Chick shot him a look, then sighed loudly and took a sip of his beer. "Going to the tiki thing?" he said after a long silence.

"Who knows? That's months away. Spring may never come to Michigan. They're just going to find us all preserved in a giant ice floe a thousand years from now." Joe sighed. "Probably. How about you?"

"Sure, I'm going, I've got nothing else to do. I told you, I have no life." Chick downed the rest of his beer, stood up, and laid a five on the bar. "Ah well. I'm gonna head home. They're showing *Kiss Me Deadly* on Turner Classics."

"That's such a great movie. Maybe I'll do the same."

"You're welcome to come by."

"Nah, I should get home."

Chick creased his forehead, pursed his lips, and nodded. "Yeah, that would be less *weird*."

Joe shook his head. "Bastard. Way to use information spoken in confidence against me."

Chick smiled. "Next time you'll know better." He raised his hand and headed toward the door.

And just then, the turn of the conversation made Joe wonder about his life. While he was going to tiki parties or concerts or indie films or DIY craft fairs or gallery openings or literary events, most people his age were concerned with things like their kids' soccer games and parent-teacher conferences. Their children ate up their lives. He did not know much about parenting, but he knew it was really hard work. Most parents, he felt, were just trying to survive. (Someone at the paper had once said to him, "If my kids are alive at the end of the day, I feel like I've done my job.") It seemed like he knew so many parents who had given up what they really wanted to do in order to provide for their children. The fact that they didn't mind that enormous sacrifice was amazing to Joe. Even admirable. Yet it wasn't what he wanted for himself.

Maybe all the things that were whispered about childless couples were true, he thought, that they were selfish and shallow, emotionally arrested, incomplete adults. Maybe those people were right. But what about he and Ana, or their other childless friends? They all supported themselves (question mark after Joe), had relationships and friendships, not to mention cars, furniture, rent or mortgages (more question marks after Joe), and led what appeared to be essentially adult lives. But then how come he often didn't feel like an adult? Was that because he had no child? Or was it because people perceived him as one because of that very fact?

Perhaps the advantage of kids was that they made you feel your age. You looked at little Zoe or Seamus and saw that five, eight, twelve, sixteen, twenty years had passed and you knew that you were old. Which raised the question: was it all that great to know you were old? Was it so wrong to deceive yourself for as long as possible? (Like the helpful way we deceive ourselves into forgetting that we're going to die in order to get through the day.) It seemed to him that a little childlike self-delusion really came in handy sometimes.

Joe picked up the flyer again, which was now ringed with welts from the pint. Should you be going to tiki parties in your forties? Was it possible to maintain ironic distance for that long, or should you have outgrown it by then? How long before you needed an irony supplement?

Still, he got the distinct feeling that his peers, many of whom were younger than him but already feeling old and out of it, weren't going to give up a goddamn thing. Children or not, they would happily take irony into old age and off to the graves with them.

When he got home, Ana was waiting for him. Joe could pretty much tell as soon as he walked through the door that she wasn't mad anymore. She looked up from her book (Calvin Trillin's *American Fried*) and smiled, just slightly, her eyes softer now and a little sad.

"Hey, I'm sorry," she said as he approached. She took his hand and guided him toward the couch, next to her.

"That's okay."

She tilted her head, then let out a long breath. "I don't know what my deal is sometimes."

"I wish I knew. When you're like that, I just start to assume that the problem is me."

"You're not the problem." She paused. "At least not this time." She smiled at him. "I don't know. I think I'm just freaking out because of my birthday."

"That's weird, I was just saying that."

Ana let go of his hand. "You were talking about this with someone?"

Oh shit. "Uh, I sort of mentioned it to Chick. I saw him over at the bar."

Ana's head fell forward and she stared at her lap. "Damn it, Joe. Can't we have a private discussion without you broadcasting it all over town? You have to go around telling everyone that I'm going to be forty?"

He tried not to sound too defensive, but it wasn't working. "Since when do you care? It's never bothered you before. Anyway, I didn't broadcast it. I was upset and I was talking to my friend."

Ana got up from the couch. "Fine. Forget it. I'm going to bed."

Joe leaned back in the couch until he was lying down. He put a pillow over his head and stayed that way for a couple of minutes. Finally, he groped around on the coffee table until he found the remote.

4

Be Careful

Thursday morning, Ana pretended she was dozing until Joe got up to make coffee. After he moved into the study to work, she roused herself out of bed. It was still only eight fifteen. She could take a quick shower, throw on enough makeup to make herself presentable, a little product on the hair (the short do—a boon to womankind), and still get to work by nine fifteen or nine thirty. It would be fine. Loose starting times were one of the many insubstantial but pleasant perquisites of working at an advertising agency. You hardly ever left the place on time, so no one really cared when you came in.

Mostly, she just didn't feel like talking to Joe. She was still pissed at him for blabbing her age all over town and pissed at herself for caring and for being such a big baby about this whole birthday thing. Everyone was getting older. It was ridiculous and vain and silly to worry about such things. She was ashamed for being so girly about it.

After she showered and got dressed, she walked over to the door of the study. Ana could hear the vague clatter of computer keys as she approached and it made her feel less annoyed at him. There was something about Joe seated at his desk, writing, that she had always liked. He was bundled up in yet another old sweater. She thought again of that vintage cardigan he was wearing that night they met, long since worn through at the elbows and discarded.

Joe had made the room into a work space a few years back. It was meant for both of them: just a lightly bashed-up Paul McCobb fifties maple desk set for their Mac, an old Plycraft imitation Eames lounge chair and ottoman, as well as shelves for all their many books and LPs and CDs and DVDs. It was a place to work or write or read or use the computer, as well as somewhere to go to get away from the other, when it was necessary.

"Hey," he said, still concentrating on the screen in front of him.

"What are you working on?" she said from the doorway.

"Eh, just some reviews for *Out of the Attic.* Couple of old CDs—Spade Cooley, Mildred Anderson, some Krautrock sampler, Babs Gonzales's memoir, DVD of *Two-Lane Blacktop,* reissued Nick Drake."

Ana stepped into the room and walked up behind him. "Ohh, I love Nick Drake."

Joe nodded, still staring at the screen. "Ah yes, Nick Drake. Supertalented, once-obscure sixties Brit folkie, now ruined by advertising." He looked up at Ana slyly, waiting for her response.

Ana rolled her eyes, put her hands around Joe's neck, and playfully squeezed his windpipe. "Yes, that's right. It's so horrible. Millions of people actually know how great he is now because his music has been used in—ack!—commercials."

Joe nodded, half smiling. "Exactly. *Ruined.*"

Both she and Joe liked to play this game. "Not so much ruined as appreciated."

"Oh, I see," said Joe. "If by appreciated you mean exploited."

"That's right, Mr. Arbiter of Taste. I forgot—now people like you can no longer feel special for enjoying his music because he's not obscure anymore. Because an artist can only be good if other people don't know about him. Preferably, he dies poor, alone, and forgotten. Oh, and of an overdose."

Joe sighed blissfully. "Absolutely. It's the perfect storm of cool. Artists are much better that way, there's no doubt about it." Suddenly, his eyes widened in false indignation. "Wait a second, are you calling me pretentious?"

Ana patted his unshaven cheek. "Of course I am, dear. And I notice there are plenty of your precious little obscure bands who are quite happy to have their music in commercials."

"Sellouts."

And so it went. Both kind of kidding and both kind of serious. Joe resumed typing.

"I hope you're being *pithy*," she said, chiding him as he wrote. He had once used that word and she never let him forget it.

Joe didn't move his eyes from the computer screen, but she saw him smile. "Always down with the pith," he said.

Ana pulled her purse up over her shoulder. "Okay, I'm taking off now."

The clicking continued for a few seconds, then stopped. He looked up at her. "All right. Be careful."

Ana leaned forward to kiss him on the lips. "You going to be around tonight?"

"Yeah, I think so," he said, adjusting his glasses. "Why?"

"Thought maybe we could go grab a bite to eat or something since I'll be out of town. A little guilt dinner."

"I don't have a lot of cash right now, Ana."

"It's okay, I'll get it. I said it was a guilt dinner. I'm abandoning you here in the tundra while I go frolic on the coast."

Joe eventually nodded. "Okay, that'd be great then. Thanks."

"I feel bad for leaving you here to take care of everything. See you tonight." She gave him another quick kiss. "I love you."

He grabbed her hand as she leaned down to him. "Love you too," he said dolefully, and she knew he was thinking about last night's argument about nothing. "See ya."

As she headed for the door, Joe gave a little wave and turned back to the computer. "Be careful," he repeated, after she had headed down the stairs, put on her long down jacket, and opened the front door to leave.

It was always the last thing he said to her every morning when she left for work. There was something comforting about it to Ana. As if he worried that she wouldn't come back. She loved that about Joe, that he thought about things like that.

On the way to work, she suddenly felt a lot better. She put in a Beth Orton CD and was singing along with "Stolen Car," until she remembered that she had left her stupid laptop at home, still in its padded bag, having meant to do some work last night. Instead, the meltdown with Joe had pretty much taken up the whole evening.

Ana turned the car around in a bank parking lot. She rolled her eyes at how familiar it felt to her. She wondered how many parking lots she'd turned around in over the last twenty-four years of her life since she started driving. The bad thing was that Joe's sense of direction was even worse than hers. Most couples she knew had at least one person who was good at directions, but not her and Joe. The two of them with a map was a pathetic scene that usually ended with an argument. Thank heaven for GPS.

At home, not wanting to disturb Joe, she quietly used her key and pushed open the heavy wood door. That was when she heard the sound of a woman gasping for air, a kind of panting. It alarmed her.

"Joe?"

The sounds got louder for a moment, then immediately stopped. From the front door, she walked up the stairs, stopping at the door of the study, where Joe was at the computer, clicking screens away while fumbling with something in his lap. Finally, he just slammed shut the top of the computer.

"What's going on?" she said.

"Nothing," he snapped, putting both his hands up on the desk, his posture impossibly straight. "What do you want?"

"Take it easy. I just forgot my computer." Something told her not to step into the room, so she crossed the hall toward the bedroom where she had left her Mac, next to the dresser. She heard muffled cursing from the other room and it was starting to occur to her what she had witnessed. She wasn't sure whether to laugh or be upset.

Joe appeared at the doorway. "Hey," he said meekly.

Ana looked at him. His cheeks were burning red and his eyes were everywhere except on her.

"What's going on?" she said.

"Nothing."

She almost laughed. "Right. Nothing. You can't even look at me. You were masturbating, weren't you?" She said it, but not with horror or derision in her voice. She said it as if she had just figured it out, which she had.

"Um."

"Jesus, Joe. What was I gone for, like, five minutes?"

He looked up at her sternly, and then shrugged slightly. "What difference does that make? I thought you were gone."

"I don't know. I just thought a person would give it a couple of minutes, that's all."

He exhaled. "I'm *sorry*."

"So what were you looking at in there?"

He frowned at her.

"Seriously."

"No," he said angrily. "I don't want to tell you that. Stop it." He headed back into the study.

Ana followed him. After a few steps, he was confronted by the scene of the crime. He turned to face her again. She was genuinely interested. What was pushing his buttons these days? It sure wasn't her. "Come on, seriously. I want to know."

Joe sighed loudly. "Jesus, Ana, I don't know. Internet stuff. Porn."

She stared at him, her head tilted. "Joe, I'm not an expert in porn, but I know it tends to be fairly specific. It's okay, I want to know."

He scratched hard at his jaw, just below the ear. "You're freaking me out here, Ana."

"Come on. Really. Please?"

Joe looked at the floor, eyes wide. "I can't believe this."

"Joe."

He exhaled loudly and crossed his arms even tighter. "Fine. *Cum-hungry* MILFs, okay?"

"What?"

"You heard me."

"I guess I did. What's a . . . MILF?"

Joe squeezed his eyes shut. "Just never mind, okay? Jesus, I'm sorry. This will never happen again."

"Ha! Come on, what's a MILF?"

"How can you not know this? You work in advertising."

"We don't advertise porn, Joseph. Tell me."

"I'm going to tell you, then I'm going to leave the house."

"Fine."

"It's an acronym. It means Mothers I'd Like to Fuck."

She tried not to look aghast. "What? These are women who look like your mother?"

Joe shook his head violently. "No! Jesus! It's just hot women in their thirties and forties."

Ana brightened slightly. "Oh. Well, it could be worse." She was trying to keep from laughing. She wondered if she should be more upset about this, but it wasn't like some big surprise that Joe masturbated. They used to talk about things like that, what got them off, what was sexy to them. They used to have phone sex when she was out of town. She used to masturbate a lot more than she did these days.

"Ana, stop being this way. Stop being so understanding. Yell at me or something."

"All I'm saying is that it could be worse. Could have been golden showers or bestiality, but it's not. It's women my age."

Joe looked up at her. "Um. These women don't look any-thing like you."

Ana closed her eyes, took a breath, then opened them. He was just standing there with his arms crossed. "You as-shole." She hefted the soft tote that held her computer and flung it over her shoulder.

"Ana."

"Fuck you. Go jerk off, you pig."

"Ana. *Shit.*"

She pushed past him through the doorway and headed toward the stairs. Behind her, she thought she heard the sound of a zipper.

5

The Detroit Way

It was good to get out of the house. Café Limbus wasn't too crowded during the day, so it was a decent place to work. At night, it was filled for open mics, hootenannies, and poetry readings, and during the weekend, there were popular vegan brunches, which Joe mostly avoided. Though he wasn't Vegan Intolerant like Chick, it was still a tad crunchy for his tastes. During the day, though, it was just crowded enough that you didn't feel like the only loser in the coffeehouse. By the time the waiter dragged himself from the huddle of smokers out on the sidewalk and loped over to his table to take his order, Joe had his laptop set up.

Tall and brutally thin, the waiter had long dyed-black hair twisted into shanks and tufts of varying lengths, and, of course, endless tattoos. All ink from fingertips to neck. Joe couldn't really distinguish what any of the tats were, but it had the effect of his body being turned inside out, as if the guy were wearing arteries, capillaries, and tendons on the outside. It was many more tattoos than Joe normally preferred on a food-service professional. He ordered a large black coffee and the waiter disappeared in a vapor trail of nicotine fumes.

Joe felt weird as hell about what had happened. He was relatively sure that Ana wasn't going to leave him for it, but it made him realize the precariousness of his situation. The fact was, when he really thought about it, she had a lot of much more valid reasons to boot him out than wanking to Internet porn—most of them financial. Ana paid most of the rent, most of the utility bills, and bought most of the food. He would kick in maybe a quarter of the rent and bills (on a good month), pay for his own cell phone, and was the house's main purveyor of alcoholic beverages, which should be noted was a fairly sizable amount, since they both loved to drink. That was it though. He got a small stipend from the paper for his column. His income was also supplemented by whatever he got from freelance feature writing and reviewing at various low-paying pubs and websites. (Then there was the dirty little secret of selling the review copies of everything that he received. Everyone did it, but no one admitted it. Some months, he made more money doing that than by writing. Unfortunately, everything was now starting to switch to digital.)

Awhile back, he'd had a steady gig working for the *Detroit News* as a second-string film reviewer (kids movies, trashy comedies, B horror films, and anything else the regular film critic was too cultured to watch). It was a good feeling, paying his share of the household expenses. Although Ana usually didn't complain about her disproportionate share of the bills, he could tell she was pleased that he was finally pulling his weight for a change. Then after a year or so, there was a change in management and he was suddenly out. It had happened just as he was getting used to the extra cash.

The fact that he wasn't paying his way somehow made today's situation all the more embarrassing. It wasn't that he felt bad about jerking off. He, like most men he knew—married, single, gay—pretty much considered it a normal thing to do. He felt bad about getting caught. Maybe he felt bad getting caught while Ana paid for the Internet access.

He also felt guilty about the pornography part. Certainly part of him liked it (it wasn't hard to figure out which part), but another part of him found it grotesque. Basically, he considered himself a fairly enlightened modern male, but most of the porn out there was not so enlightened. In his queries on the Internet, he had found none of the "couples friendly" material that was alleged to exist, supposedly erotic to both men and women. (At one point, he was thinking of getting some of this mythical pornography for him and Ana to watch together as a sort of turn-on, something to rekindle the fire and all that pathetic nonsense, then he chickened out.) No, what he saw out there during his research was anything but couples friendly. It certainly wasn't woman friendly—hell, it wasn't even man friendly. A lot of it was just mean. It didn't look like fun, but the women were usually trying to act like it was, which just made it sad. He didn't understand why anyone would subject themselves to this sort of thing.

Of course, he did know the reason: money. That was the main reason for everyone doing things they didn't want to do. He was sure there was other stuff too: bad childhoods, bad parents, bad relationships, bad pornographers, and, well, stupidity. Stupid men and stupid women. That was the main thing you saw in pornography—all the plenteous and wondrous degrees of stupidity in all its glory. All the men thinking they were so smart and all the women just doing what they had to do. Joe hated the men in porn and felt sorry for the women, but it didn't seem to stop him from looking at it.

The waiter arrived at the table with Joe's coffee. Besides the tattoos, he also had all the requisite epidermal punctures—lip, nose, brow, cheek. It was a lot of hardware. Joe considered asking him if his face ever got tired of carrying that around all day. He thought of a book from the fifties that he had reviewed in *Out of the Attic* a few weeks earlier called *The Dud Avocado*, where the main character, a young woman living in Paris, refers to a group of expatriate nonconformists as "so violently individualistic as to be practically interchangeable." Was that why this guy looked familiar? Then it came to him.

"Hey, man," said Joe. "You in a band?" *Of course you are. Why am I even asking?*

The illustrated man nodded somnolently. "Yeah, dude. I'm in a couple. The Stuckists and Merkins of Death."

"Right," Joe said, nodding back. "Yeah. I've seen the Stuckists. You guys are really good. Didn't I just hear that you all got signed?"

"Ye-huh." He set down Joe's large Ferndale blend, then took out a cloth and smeared a small blotch of spilled sugar and coffee around on the table.

"That's awesome. No offense, but why are you still waiting tables?"

The waiter pursed his lips and cocked his head. "Got to make a living, dude. I ain't no rock star yet."

"Pretty close."

"Maybe in Rotterdam, but not here." He gave Joe a smirk. "Anyway, I ain't gonna blow all my cash, then get dumped by the record company for not selling enough units. I know too many people that's happened to. So I work here when we're not rehearsing or touring. Keeps my head straight."

Joe couldn't help but smile. "I guess you're right. Still, good for you. Congrats."

"Whatever, thanks. Need anything else?"

"No, I'm good. Thanks."

"Rock on."

That last comment by the waiter was made at a level of irony that Joe almost couldn't hear anymore. Dog-whistle irony. It was something that was happening more and more these days. Humor he couldn't quite laugh at, cultural references that he wasn't quite getting anymore. Was he getting to the point where he just wasn't understanding the younger generation? Oof.

Then there was the comment about how working in a coffeehouse "keeps my head straight." So funny. This was one of the things Joe loved about Detroit. Even the creative folks, at least the ambitious ones, the people who were getting their work out there, their music or writing or art, hardly ever quit their crummy day jobs. The only people who did were musicians who had to because their bands were touring Europe all the time. Places like Berlin and Dusseldorf and Amsterdam absolutely loved Detroit music and pretty much everything to do with the place. Strange: to most of America, it was fucked-up Detroit, a forgotten manufacturing wasteland with decaying buildings, and the murder capital of the nation. But to Europe, Detroit was the embodiment of überurban, echt-industrial, protoapocalyptic, rustbelt cool. (At least it was to the extremely well-paying Euro culture magazines for which he sometimes wrote about the Detroit scene.) Europeans were way more hip to the positive things going on in Detroit, the music and art and history, the grit and spirit of the people—and even if they sometimes overappreciated the aesthetics of blight, they at least understood the way the whole place somehow inexplicably got under your skin.

Even if a Detroit band made it big, you'd still hear them

say things like, "I haven't forgotten how to deliver pizzas," or "I could go back to doing upholstery work if I had to." It was that twisted Midwestern work ethic, the factory-rat DNA that threaded through Detroiters, embedded by generation after generation of immigrants who put their heads down and ground it out in a loud, grimy, windowless place for thirty or forty years, because that was just *what you did*.

There weren't discussions about happiness or fulfillment or self-actualization. You shut up and went to work because people were counting on you. Then, after all those great-grandfathers and grandfathers and fathers and mothers who toiled silently (and often bitterly), came the spoiled generations after, the ones that went to college, that thought it was their right to be happy at a job.

That was Joe, of course, who had deluded himself into thinking that he could actually make a living as a freelance writer. He used to think it was okay not having that much money, always buying cheap beer and thrift-store clothing. It was officially part of his lifestyle. It was part of Ana's too, at one time. Now, here in his late thirties, being poor didn't seem like so much fun anymore. (During his brief tenure at the *News*, he had developed a taste for microbrews and top-shelf booze. He started drinking above his station.) He was tired of saying things like "I don't have a lot of cash right now" to Ana. He was tired of being a mooch. He was getting the feeling that Ana was tired of him being a mooch too.

She had been making good money for about seven years now, though it may have been longer. Lengths of time deceived him these days. Awhile back, he had started automatically adding three years to any casual estimate of elapsed time. Thus, if it felt like something happened two years ago, it was probably five. If it seemed like six years ago, it was definitely nine. And these days, he had noticed that three years wasn't quite enough. He'd started adding five just to be on the safe side.

Which meant that Ana has probably been making good money for close to twelve years. Lucky thing too, because by now, he would probably be living beneath the 8 Mile Road overpass, cadging rumpled singles from passing cars, like the guys he would encounter coming home late from seeing bands at the bars in Hamtramck. Two thirty in the morning, and there they were, with their six coats and three hats, their overstuffed shopping carts, and their greasy, creased-soft, cardboard *GOD BLESS* signs, staring blankly at you at the traffic light. These days, Joe had been giving them the stray dollars that he'd find wadded in his bar pockets. He'd look them in their eyes, all rheumy and broken, so as not to seem like one of those people who didn't think of them as humans. He didn't like it, though, the time that one of them wanted to shake his hand. Joe did it, but couldn't get the little bottle of hand sanitizer out of his glove box quickly enough once he was down the street.

Which was another thing—when did he become one of those geezers with hand sanitizer in his glove compartment?

6

The Daughter
She'll Never Have

If Ana had met Adrienne Kaminski at a party, she would have run fast and far. She would have thought the woman was completely obnoxious. It was true that Adrienne made a big impression. She was loud, especially when she laughed, she wore clothes that were too tight, showed too much, and were possibly too young for her, and maybe even her hair was a shade too red, but the fact was, Adrienne pulled it all off. Mostly because the woman just didn't give a fuck. Adrienne had attitude for days. Maybe it helped that she was 6'1", but that didn't always add up to feminine confidence. Other tall women Ana had known had leaned toward the slouchy, as if ashamed of their height. But Adrienne rocked hers like a plus-size supermodel. (When she got off an elevator, guys would invariably look down at her feet to see if she was wearing high heels, as if that could be the only explanation.)

Luckily, Ana never got the opportunity to run away from Adrienne at that imaginary party. They were pushed together as an art director/copywriter team at the agency five years ago when Ana started. Aside from copywriting, Adrienne was the half of the team that was happy to do the talking in presentations (Ana talked, but wasn't all that happy about it), and the selling, and the pushing, and the calling of bull-shit, if need be. And often, the need did be. "They force me to be this way," Adrienne would say. "They can call me a bitch, but I do not care." Sometimes they did, but not to her face. They knew better. Adrienne Kaminski was not afraid to throw down against man or woman.

After working together for a few weeks, Ana found that she and Adrienne had a lot in common—seventies folk-rock girl singers, screwball comedies of the thirties, a love of midcentury graphic design, and even some of the same secret shameful reality TV shows. And certainly they shared a taste for wine. Yet Ana especially liked how she could tell Adrienne something and the woman would keep her mouth shut. This was a rare and wondrous thing in people, and even rarer for people in advertising. Adrienne gave her partner credit for ideas even when Ana wasn't in the room. And the woman believed in good work, which was something that got a lot of lip service in advertising, but the desire to do it was the first thing to die with most creatives. If they ever had it in the first place.

Ana had known they would be friends the first time they went out to lunch together, when Adrienne grabbed the chromed handle of the glass door leading to the parking lot, stopped, made a face, then slowly lifted her hand to her nose. She spit out the word "Fuck!" She then pushed through the doors and started wiping her hand in grass near the flower beds that lined the parking lot.

Stunned, Ana walked up to her and asked, "Uh, Adrienne, what are you doing?"

"Some nasty motherfucker just spritzed a gallon of Paco Rabanne or some such shit on himself," she said. "Now my hand stinks of account executive!"

The sight of Adrienne, tall as she was, on her knees in a pencil skirt running her hand in the grass to get the stench of AE off was all it took. Ana pulled a wet wipe from a packet in her purse, handed it to Adrienne, and they were off. This also set the tone for their relationship in many ways as well. Ana was often taking care of Adrienne, mothering her, making sure she was eating right, not drinking too much, and using condoms. (She did not wish for a repeat of the time that she was Adrienne's ride and waiting room plus-one at the women's clinic in Southfield.) Adrienne usually had a crush of the moment, often geeky cute musicians or willowy art boys who were initially stunned by the attention of a woman like her, only to be later shattered by their abrupt dismissal. Adrienne was attracted to artistic talent, but she also tended to lose interest when those same men displayed what could be called an artistic temperament (i.e., moody, neurotic, and insecure). She had no stomach for prima donnas. Still, Ana enjoyed hearing about her escapades, although Adrienne had a tendency to offer up a tad too much graphic detail.

"You're like the daughter I'll never have," Ana was fond of saying.

Which was another thing that bound them together at work—their respective childfree existences. The creative department, while never as fecund as the rest of the company, had just recently gone through a spate of pregnancies like Ana had never experienced. It seemed like all the women were getting pregnant—married, unmarried, early twenties, middle-aged, it didn't matter.

It got to the point where Ana was getting the look. The forlorn, swollen-bellied, cocked-headed *Shouldn't you be doing this too?* look, when she'd run into a couple of the knocked-up women in the coffee room where they were refilling a hand-thrown cup with kukicha or sipping a decaf soy chai latte, talking about how special it was being pregnant. To be fair, she had heard them bitch about the discomfort and hormonal mania too, but even those comments were couched in language that reveled in *the wonder of it all*.

"It's so awesome," one would say to Ana, the other nodding avidly. At which point Ana would smile sweetly, fill her thermal cup with fully leaded dark roast, and clear out tout de suite. She didn't dislike those women; she was happy that they were happy. It was just that they couldn't seem to be happy that she was happy *not* having kids. As if once they'd conceived, they could no longer conceive of the idea that every woman wouldn't want the same thing as them.

"It's that water purifier," proclaimed Adrienne about the epidemic. "I'm not drinking out of that fucking thing anymore."

Yet what were she and Adrienne doing today? Reviewing the casting for children for the spot they would be shooting in a few days. They needed a kid for a nonspeaking role. It was simple stuff that required minimal attention. They just had to lock themselves in a conference room where they wouldn't be interrupted. They just needed a nice, normal-looking Midwestern kid to be part of a nice, normal-looking Midwestern family.

"God, this is terrifying," Adrienne said with a strained voice, as she stared at the laptop screen, finger poised over the touch pad, ready to instantly skip ahead once Ana gave the go-ahead to do so. "How these parents make these perfectly cute kids so hideous is beyond me. Look at this child. Poor thing has one of those horrible Hollywood Little Lord

Fauntleroy haircuts. He's been brainwashed to smile after he says anything. That kid's already been so messed up by his parents. He hasn't got a chance at a normal life."

"And we're helping to exploit him," said Ana, only half kidding. "We ought to be ashamed of ourselves."

Adrienne laughed. "I'd be happy to exploit him, and so would his parents, except he can't act his way out of a dry cleaner's bag."

"Next," said Ana. Adrienne clicked forward.

"Ouch. Ana, I do believe that child is wearing makeup."

Ana nodded. "Moving on," she said.

Adrienne fast-forwarded the DVD to the next audition. On the screen appeared a blond, blue-eyed child, so beautiful, so perfectly coiffed and styled as to be almost otherworldly. It was like looking at a video of a rare wood nymph. Beautiful, but eerie.

Adrienne had a similar reaction. "No thank you. No *Children of the Corn* in our commercial. Mind if we move on, A?"

"Yes please."

Adrienne clicked the fast-forward button. "You okay? Usually casting is much more cruel fun than this."

"Eh." Ana fell back in her chair. "I just . . . *eh*."

"What?"

She thought about chewing Joe out for blabbing personal matters to his friends, then decided that she didn't care. "Weirdness at home, that's all."

"Everything okay? You want to talk about it?"

She did, but she didn't. "Too embarrassing."

Adrienne took her hand off the touch pad and looked pointedly at Ana. "Now you fucking have to tell me."

Ana threw her mechanical pencil onto the stack of casting notes and exhaled. The noise she emitted might have been either exhausted sigh or annoyed growl. She grimaced, not wanting to say it, yet knowing she would.

"Ugh. I left him at the house this morning, then I realized that I had forgotten my laptop, so I had to turn around and go home."

"Uh-oh."

Incredulous, Ana looked at her. "What? You know what I'm going to say?"

Adrienne raised an eyebrow, made a fist with her palm up, moved it back and forth as if she were shaking dice, but that was not what she was pantomiming. It was a gesture Adrienne was known to make often, especially when she knew that they were going to be wasting their time on a project.

"How did you know?" said Ana.

"What? I know that scenario, come on. So what's the big deal? He's a man. He can't even help himself. They do it constantly. They're like dogs except they can't lick themselves, which is a good thing because if they could, they would never stop."

"So it's nothing?"

"Unless he's not saving any for you. Then it's a problem. How are you guys doing in that department?"

Ana did not speak.

"Well, that doesn't sound good. Okay. How long as it been?"

Ana stared at the frozen close-up of a child on the television. "Months."

"Holy shit. I'm getting way more play than you."

Ana smiled blandly. "Yes. Thank you for pointing that out. It never once occurred to me while you were regaling me with tales of three-times-a-night Darryl."

"Sorry."

Ana reached out to touch her friend's hand. "Don't be. There's nothing to be sorry about. It's not your fault the man I live with would rather jerk off to MILFs than fuck me."

Adrienne put a hand over her mouth in fake horror. "I don't think I've ever heard you say anything like that. It's kind of shocking."

"Yeah, isn't it?" Ana looked for something to do with her arms besides fold them, fumbling them a bit on the conference room table, then folded them anyway. "I guess I'm starting to get over the shock. Now I'm just getting mad."

"Ruh-roh," said Adrienne in the manner of Scooby-Doo.

"I mean it. What's going on here? This is fucked up."

"Ana, it's not that fucked up. This stuff just happens. People are together for a while and—"

"What? Familiarity breeds contempt?"

"No. Familiarity breeds familiarity. Entropy. Come on, you've been with Joe for a long time. You guys are used to each other. Those women he's looking at are just different."

Ana folded her arms tighter against her body. "That's pretty much what he said . . . You know, it's not even just that. It's just gotten harder for us to, you know, be intimate with each other these days. It's harder to make the commitment. We're both so fucking moody and high-strung. He'll come to me and I can tell he wants to do it, but I had a bad day here or there was something on the news that pissed me off or I just don't feel like being touched." Ana glanced up at Adrienne, who was staring at her. She did not like the pity she saw in her friend's face. "I'm sorry. This is pathetic, isn't it?"

Adrienne tried to smile, but it just looked like she was displaying her teeth. "Little bit, yeah."

"Am I like a walking cautionary tale for not ever being in a long-term relationship?"

"Come on, it's not that bad."

Ana thought she was lying. Right now, Adrienne was probably thinking, *If I ever get married, this will never happen to me.* She was probably right.

Ana reached over and unpaused the DVD. "We should get back to this." She watched the little redhead thespian on the screen in front of her. His parents had obviously coached him to play up his lisp. The child was not at all natural and he was simply talking to the casting director. You could see that he was just trying to please everyone. She wanted to kill this poor kid's parents.

"Adrienne, please fast-forward before I have to pull my eyes out and stuff them in my ears so I don't have to look at or listen to this abomination."

"Ah, now you sound like you."

"What? Mean and bitter?"

"Yes. That's my girl. Look, maybe you just need to shake things up."

"What are you suggesting?"

Adrienne laughed, but Ana got a feeling that she wasn't going to say what she was thinking. Sometimes Ana got the feeling that maybe Adrienne was against the whole concept of monogamy.

"I don't know, lady. Only you know how."

"Hm. I don't think I like the sound of that."

7

Ruin and Other Porns

L ater in the day, Joe was back home, doing some research. He was thinking of pitching a long piece to his editor at the *Independent* about *The Paris of the Midwest Is Crumbling*, a blog devoted to the photographic chronicling of the many deteriorating and abandoned buildings in the city of Detroit. It was one of Joe's favorite websites and he'd wanted to do something on it for a while. It also crossed his mind that something like this could be a great piece for the *New York Times* (they seemed to be paying a lot of attention to Detroit lately), or maybe even a book, some sort of collaboration.

The creator of the website, a Brendan Sanderson, would enter these old buildings to photograph their dilapidated interiors. There were incredible images of aged and decaying theaters, hotels, apartment buildings, restaurants, auto plants, churches, office buildings, many of them left over from the halcyon years of automotive industry—the forties, fifties, and sixties—when the city was still flush and glutted with people and money and power.

Joe was looking at photographs of what was left of the Michigan Theater building, a grand old movie palace from the twenties that had been slated for demolition in the late seventies for a parking lot. In fact, demolition had begun when the contractors realized that it was integrally connected to the building next door. One couldn't go down without pulling down the other. So an interior parking structure was constructed inside the shell of the old theater. Pretty shocking to see a Pontiac parked underneath an Italianate ceiling or an SUV snugged beneath the proscenium where they had projected Valentino films in the twenties, where Sinatra had crooned in the forties, where Iggy and the Stooges had bled eardrums in the seventies. When film crews shot in Detroit for movies or television, they invariably ended up there. The image of parked cars surrounded by crumbling grandeur appealed to auteurs as the perfect symbol of the decline of a once great metropolis.

At home, the image was pretty much a cliché, the quintessence of everything that locals considered "ruin porn," the vacant exploitation of Detroit squalor and "grittiness" for fluff—Hollywood films that needed the perfect postapocalyptic environment, street cred for gangsta indies, or as background fodder for European fashion shoots or J-pop videos—all with no thought to the people who lived in the city and considered it home. To a lot of people in America, the fleeting image of an abandoned building just seemed to fulfill every idea they already had about Detroit—that it was a place uninhabitable for humans. At least that was what Brendan Sanderson had to say about the subject. He photographed these sites out of respect for them, with historical context and editorials that spoke of what it meant that these formerly sacred sites were now moldering. He was also active in historic preservation and trying to shame the owners of these decaying buildings to properly secure them, rejoicing when he was no longer able to trespass onto them.

There were also photographs of the colossal old Packard plant just off of East Grand Boulevard that had been abandoned since the fifties—building after building, forty-seven in all, chockablock with broken windows, rusted girders extracted by scrappers, derelict equipment, rubble-scattered factory corridors, tumbling walls, collapsing roof-lines, essentially a sprawling thirty-eight-acre architectural exoskeleton. Joe had once gone to a rave there in the late eighties and remembered thinking even then that the place was spooky, but cool. He didn't actually remember much of the evening (a significant amount of alcohol and marijuana had been consumed), only fragments—the orgiastic thump of insanely loud techno music (had it been Richie Hawtin?), ecstatically dancing people, the swelter of the room, and the lights of the city that had looked so beautiful that night, there from a window of an abandoned factory.

Joe lingered on the curious image of a graffitied dump truck hanging from a fourth-floor ledge and thought that wandering around in the place now sounded both intriguing and terrifying. Then he heard Ana's key in the front door and flinched, surprised by the sound and the breathless whoosh of dread that rose suddenly in his lungs and gut. *Well, this is going to be interesting.* He decided that he would just try to act normal when he saw her. What else could he do? He heard her stamping some snow off her boots and putting her coat away. So he decided to get up, head downstairs, and meet her in the kitchen, where she would surely be pouring herself a glass of wine.

Yet when Ana saw him coming down the stairs, she turned to walk up to the bedroom, passing him on the narrow staircase without a word.

Joe figured that this was going to be even more excruciating than he'd expected. "Hi," he called out to her back, as she headed toward the bedroom. Ana said nothing.

Joe turned and started after her, but then decided he wasn't quite ready for that yet. Instead he just stood there, leaning against the banister. "How was work?" he said as loudly as he could without yelling. He heard the airtight thump of the bedroom door as it was briskly pulled shut.

Joe headed toward the kitchen, knowing that she would eventually come down for that glass of wine. It wasn't so much that he was looking to force the matter. He just wanted to get it over with. Already embarrassed and exhausted, he flopped down on a chair at their dinette set, the one they had picked out together at a local resale store when they first moved in together. He sighed as he traced the yellow teapot inset on the tabletop with his fingertip. Moments later, he heard Ana's cushioned footfalls on the stairs. She walked into the kitchen, wearing jeans and slippers and a fleece track jacket zipped to the neck. She walked past him to the cupboard, got out a wineglass, then opened the cupboard door under the sink and pulled out a half-full bottle of cabernet. She poured until it was damn near to the rim of the glass. Not a good sign.

"Do you still want to go out to eat tonight?" he asked cautiously. Ana took a gulp of wine and peered blankly at him over the top of the glass. "*What?*" he said, as if he didn't know. The silent routine was wearing thin.

Ana took another sip, put down the glass on the kitchen counter, leaned back against the sink. "Oh Joe."

Here we go. "Oh Joe *what?*"

"What am I going to do with you?"

Joe had never felt more like a little boy, even when he

was a little boy. "I dunno," he said. Not I *don't know* as an adult might have said it, but I *dunno*.

Ana sighed.

"I feel really stupid," he said.

"Yeah. Me too."

"Why do *you* feel stupid? You didn't get caught . . . doing anything." He'd almost said *masturbating*, but didn't quite feel like saying the word just then.

Ana moved her tongue over her upper teeth, and then stopped. "I know, but still. Somehow I've managed to make this feel like my fault."

"That's stupid."

"Don't tell me what's stupid."

Joe closed his eyes momentarily, took a breath. "I'm sorry. It's just that it's not your fault. It's all mine. I was the one doing it." He crossed his arms. "I guess we'll have to duct-tape oven mitts to my hands when you're not here."

Ana crimped her lips so she wouldn't smile, and it made him wish that he could have thought of something just a little bit funnier to say. She walked toward him and stood by the table. He wished that she would just sit down.

"Yes, I agree that part was your fault," she said. "But that's not what I was talking about. This really isn't about *that*. Things have just gotten awkward lately."

"How so?"

"I don't know. They've just gotten awkward."

From where he was sitting, he could see the window over the sink. Outside there was snow, lots of it. They had gotten another inch or two that day, and everything looked white and clean and simple outside, so unlike the conversation he was currently having inside. "Yeah. I don't know why either. We're just doing what we've always done."

"Maybe that's it. Maybe we've been doing this for too long."

"Ana, what are you saying?" He didn't like where this was going. About once a year, Ana would get into a mood and decide that maybe they should split up. It had been happening since they got together. This was the first time in many years that it actually felt serious.

"I don't know," she said. "I just don't know."

Joe didn't know what to say either, so he just said the first thing that occurred to him: "I think maybe you're just hungry."

He wasn't sure how she'd react to this, but she lowered her head and chuckled, probably because it was such a dumb thing to say. He was actually quite good at saying the right dumb thing. It was one of his talents. He thought of Andy Warhol calling something *exactly wrong*.

"Oh, do you think that's it?" she said, trying not to smile.

He nodded matter-of-factly. "Yes, I think you're just hungry."

"Right," she said, rolling her eyes. "That's it, Joe. I'm just hungry." Shaking her head at the absurdity of his statement, she glanced over at the old restaurant menus they had framed on their kitchen wall, with their happy chefs, dancing chickens, and mile-high pies. Joe couldn't tell if it was for effect or coincidence. "Oh shit. I *am* hungry—I totally worked through lunch. Maybe we should just get something to eat."

"I told you." He was smiling now, glad that he had broken the spell and gotten through to her. "Don't forget, you still owe me a guilt dinner," he said, immediately regretting it.

She peered over her glasses at him.

Joe cleared his throat theatrically. "Even though, uh, I'm currently the guilty one."

They went to Loui's in Hazel Park for square pizza and antipasto salad. It was where they went when they were both feeling depressed. It was absolutely delicious high-fat food that never failed to cheer them up. The decor of the place didn't hurt either. Pink walls splashed with glitter, and clusters of old Chianti bottles hanging everywhere. Somewhere among the hundreds of bottles hanging from the walls of Loui's was one from their third date, magic-markered with both of their names.

"I feel so much better," said Ana, after two plates of meat-and-cheese-heavy antipasto salad and a piece of pizza.

"Me too. Are you going to have another slice?"

"I'm waiting for this one to settle. Let's see if it turns into a cheese bomb in my stomach."

"Trust me, it will." He started to cut a slice in half, and then decided to just take the whole thing. "When are you leaving for LA?"

"Sunday afternoon. Monday we'll scout locations. Tuesday we'll go for a pre-preproduction meeting. On Wednesday the client will be in and we'll do our final prepro with wardrobe. Thursday and Friday are the shoot. I'll probably fly back Saturday, unless I decide to surprise you again and come home Friday night."

"I'll keep that in mind." He liked that they were joking about this a little. It made him feel like they were getting past it somehow.

"Joe?"

"What?" he said, cutting into his pizza with a knife and fork.

"Why are the MILFs so different from me? What's the attraction?" She drank her last sip of wine, but continued to hold the glass with both hands.

So much for that. He set down his utensils next to the plate and exhaled through his nose, hoping he didn't sound as exasperated as he felt. "Oh god, Ana. I don't know."

"Why did you say that then?"

"Say what?"

"You know, that those women don't look anything like me."

He groaned. "I don't know why I said that. It was like you were being too understanding or something. It freaked me out."

"Just tell me, Joe."

"Ana."

"You're making me mad. Just tell me."

"I don't know! Because they don't. They aren't you."

Ana firmly set the wineglass onto the table where it made a loud noise. She raised her voice. "What is it? Is it because they're *cum hungry*?"

"Everything good here?" said the waitress, an extremely large woman, like all of the Loui's waitresses, who just at that moment had decided to stop by to make sure they were well taken care of. Joe watched her face contract and redden when she realized what she had walked into. Before she could scurry off, Joe ordered another boomba of Labatt.

"Well, is it?" said Ana, still loudly and apparently oblivious to what had just happened with the waitress.

"Please lower your voice." He held up his right hand, folded at the knuckles, then lowered it, as if notching down her personal potentiometer.

"I don't want to."

"If you do, I'll tell you, all right?"

A pause. "Okay, tell me," she finally said, her voice gentler now.

"They're just different, all right? That's all. They're not you. They're all fixed up, all overbeautified and surgically augmented and tarted up."

"What? Am I so disgusting?"

He sighed. "No, of course not. You're not disgusting at all. I think you're beautiful. I love the way you look."

"Okay then. So it is because I'm not cum hungry?"

"Good god, would you shut up about the cum hunger?"

"Now you're the one yelling."

"No I'm not!"

"Come on, is that it? You want more blow jobs? Why don't you just say it?"

He couldn't believe he was having this conversation. "Excuse me? More blow jobs? There'd have to be any at all before there could be *more*."

"Go fuck yourself, Joe."

"I tried to, but you interrupted."

"You're an asshole."

"Fuck you."

His beer arrived. The waitress left the check and just about ran away from the table.

Ana shook her head. "I'll be glad to get away from you for a week."

"You and me both."

Joe drank the beer off in one long draft, then leaned back into the red Naugahyde banquette, ready to get the hell out of there. He stared at the check, then at Ana, but she was lost in her rage. They sat there for two long minutes. "Do you want to go?" he said finally.

"Yes, I do."

"Are you going to get that?" he said, nodding toward the check in its worn black vinyl folder.

Finally, she understood why they were still sitting there. Ana shook her head, sighed loudly, leaned forward, and picked up the check.

"I'll get the tip," Joe said, after she put down two twenties.

"Think you can manage it, Rockefeller?"

They didn't speak again before Ana left for Los Angeles.

2

8

The Little Visitor

Was she the only Midwesterner who felt this way in Los Angeles? Was it just her, or was the climate exactly the same every day, every time she visited? It was bizarre to Ana, this unvarying spook-weather, hour after eerily comfortable hour of vapid sunshine bleeding into one generically beautiful day after another. Of course, it was a relief to her light-deprived, iced-over Michigan constitution, and she certainly didn't surging through her home state, but this was just plain strange. But then, Michiganians were always thinking that the gods were conspiring against them when it came to weather—why would she be any different?

All of which was not to say that it wasn't quite fabulous to shed her parka and scarves and boots and walk around in jeans and flip-flops and a Detroit Technology T-shirt. (She would definitely not be wearing an eighties hair-metal concert tee, despite the fact that they were currently considered fashionable in LA. Oh, what a surprise to realize that the embarrassing musical choices of her youth had quietly turned ironic.) When in LA, she felt the need to represent her hometown. As paranormally pleasant as it might be here, she would never want to be mistaken for an Angeleno. Of course, with her Middle West nasal twang, decidedly unfake boobs, ghostly pallor, and the stray extra pounds distributed here or there (mostly there), that would probably never happen.

All that aside, she was pleased to be there, except for the situation with Joe. She was sorry for how things had gotten entirely out of hand with their argument. She was holding up fine, considering she had never gone this long without speaking to him. Ana knew that the fight was not entirely about the wanking incident. With a little distance between them, she could see that there was more going on than that. Certainly, she was tired of supporting Joe, but even more tired of him being snotty about it. If she had wanted a sullen teenage son, she would have had one the old-fashioned way. She didn't need to both pay the bills and be resented for it. Still, Ana missed him and hated that they were fighting.

Adrienne could tell something was up, even though Ana had judiciously avoided the subject so far, even on Sunday after a few too many gimlets at the Standard bar after they got in. The subject had been easy to avoid in the crew van scouting locations yesterday (car sickness keeping her woozy and nauseous as they bounced across the Valley), all the way up to today, until they were having breakfast at Hugo's before heading to the production company office in Santa Monica, where they would meet up with their producer, Joan, who was staying down there.

"You've been pretty quiet, lady. What's going on?" said Adrienne, dangling her fork in Ana's general direction.

"I have?"

"Yes. Very quiet. You haven't exactly been a boatload of fun. Frankly, you're snuffing my glow. You're harshing my mellow."

Ana playfully tinked away Adrienne's fork with her own. "Really? Am I chumping your flava?"

"Yes. You are fading my gingham. Knock it off."

Ana dropped her fork, then reached over to pat Adrienne's left hand. "I'm sorry, Ade. I thought I was being pretty good."

Adrienne put down her fork as well. "Oh, I'm mostly kidding. You're being okay. You just seem a little off or something. What's up?"

"I'm still fighting with Joe."

"*Dude.* Really? Is he still being a whack-job? Emphasis on the whack."

"I guess so. But it's not just him. Or that . . . I don't know what it is."

Adrienne picked her fork back up, then put it down and reached for her glass of grapefruit juice. "How long have you guys been shacked up? Tell me again."

It was starting to get embarrassing to Ana to admit how long it had been. She thought about how she and Joe had run into an old neighbor recently, at an estate sale. They hadn't seen Mark in at least ten years. When he saw the two of them, he said, "You guys are still together? Wow. How long has it been?" He said it in such a condescending way, as if they were somehow emotionally retarded simply because they were still together. She couldn't quite understand why it had bothered her because the guy had always been a jerk, but it did. Rationally, Ana knew there was nothing wrong with being with someone for a long time, but it now just made her feel old to say it.

"Fifteen years."

Adrienne drained the glass, plucked a pip off her tongue, and looked at Ana incredulously. "Well, fuck *me.*"

"I thought you knew how long it had been."

Adrienne put down the glass, picked up her napkin, and held it to her mouth as if to mask her astonishment. Then Ana realized that she was just burping. Adrienne threw the napkin on the table. "I knew it was a long time, but I didn't realize that it had been *that* long."

"Well, it has."

"Dang."

Ana's nostrils flared slightly as she glared at her friend. "Okay, you can stop being so surprised now."

"I'm sorry, it's just that I forget how domesticated you are."

"God, Adrienne, I see you every day of my life practically. We're together at least nine hours a day. I probably see more of you than I do of Joe. You could try to remember a little bit more about me."

"I know. I'm sorry, I probably just repressed it. Take it as a compliment. You just don't seem that old and boring and married."

"I'm not married."

"Not officially, but you are."

"Yeah, I know." Ana looked tentatively at Adrienne. "So I don't seem old and boring?"

"No, you're fun. Not today, but usually. You're not like some of those people we work with. The ones who have been married for ages and are so ridiculously boring—"

"Like Dawn? She says she can't even stay up past nine. She falls asleep trying to watch a movie."

"The weird thing is that she's proud of it. She practically brags about it. You are certainly not like that."

Ana smiled at her partner. "All right. You've redeemed yourself."

"Have you talked to Joe since we got here?"

Ana examined what was left of her fruit plate and shook her head. "I haven't talked to him in like three and a half days."

Adrienne grimaced. "Yikes."

"Yeah, I know. We got into a big fight the night of the, you know, the *thing*, and we haven't spoken since. All weekend. He didn't even tell me to be careful when I left. He always says that whenever I go anywhere. I hardly even saw him. He was working at the Limbus every night." Unexpectedly, Ana felt herself near tears. This had been happening a lot lately, just not in front of other people. She was having a hard time breathing.

"You should call him. It's obviously bothering you. Fuck it, just give him a call. You'll feel better."

Ana's eyes were welling up by this time. "I know," she managed to say. "You're right."

"Why don't you go do it right now?"

"You think?"

"Yes. Just go outside and give him a call." Adrienne pulled a packet of tissues from her purse and handed it over. "Here, loser."

Ana plucked a tissue from the packet and tried to blot her eyes without making too much of a mess of her mascara. "Okay. Thanks, Ade."

"Now go. I'll take care of the check."

Ana blew her nose. "Be sure to put both our names on the receipt."

"Yes, Mom. *Go.*"

Outside, there was another swell of tears. Ana hadn't had a sobbing fit like this in a while. She tucked her cell in her pocket while she pulled a couple more tissues from the packet. That was when she saw people heading toward the front door—some insanely young, ridiculously attractive, miniskirted LA girls, so she scurried into the parking lot behind the restaurant. After a set of yoga breaths next to someone's giant black BMW, she felt more composed. She pulled out her phone and called. It rang twice, and then Joe picked up.

"Ana?" His voice cracked as if it were the first time he had spoken today.

"Hi."

"Are you all right?" Of course he would think there was something wrong. The worried tone of his voice intensified what she was already feeling.

"I'm fine. Everything's okay. I'm just . . . I'm sorry we got in the fight."

"Oh god. Me too. It's been so awful here without you and knowing that you're mad at me. I'm sorry about everything."

"Me too. It really got way out of hand."

"I love you, Ana. You know that, right?" A sizzle in the line.

"Of course. I love you too."

Ana wiped her eyes with the now-damp, black-streaked wad of tissues from Adrienne. There was a long pause, which felt like a kind of relief, but then it was as if they had nothing else to say to each other.

"How is it there?" said Joe, finally.

"It's okay. The weather's nice. It's sunny, of course. I'm standing outside right now next to someone's massive Beemer."

"Isn't it impossible to *not* stand next to one out there? It's snowing here. Goddamn, is it snowing."

"We just had some breakfast before we head over to the production company."

"That's good. You guys do anything when you got in?"

"We had drinks at the hotel bar. The place is so cool it's almost unbearable. I felt like my head was going to explode from the coolness."

"Well, don't hook up with any actor-slash-waiters."

"Yeah, right. Those guys look at me as if I'm not quite as good-looking as their grandmother." Joe laughed and she remembered how much she enjoyed making him laugh. "They do have GILFs here, you know. I've been doing research."

"Great," said Joe, chuckling. "Good to know."

It was so strange: how could being out of town for less than forty-eight hours give her an acute appreciation of this person she'd been with for so long? Sometimes after being away for a few days she'd miss Joe so much it felt like a physical longing.

"I'm glad you called," he said.

"Me too. Why don't I give you a call tonight? You going to be home?"

"Yeah, should be."

"Okay, I'll talk to you then."

Ana hung up and stood there for a moment until she noticed a man with long blond dreads wearing an ill-fitting sport coat and creased jeans glaring at her. "What?" she said, not sure what was going on.

"Please get away from my car."

"What? Huh?"

He kneeled and examined the paint on the door right near Ana's butt. "Were you leaning on it?"

Ana wanted to speak, but was too flummoxed by the proximity of his head to her ass. That was when Adrienne walked up.

"What's up?" she said.

"I think she was leaning on my 750i." He exhaled on the black lacquer and wiped it with the sleeve of his sport coat.

Ana, still a little spooked, just shrugged at Adrienne.

"Not you. *Her*," said Adrienne, grabbing Ana's arm and pulling her over, all the while staring stonily at the man, who was still crouched down next to his car. "*Oooooh.* You gonna call the Surface-Scratch Division of the LAPD?"

The guy looked up from the glistening metal and frowned at her as if he had just then realized, *This amazon is not at all sympathetic to my plight.*

Adrienne started to lead Ana toward their car. "Blow me, Bob Marley," she yelled over her shoulder.

Ana said nothing as she settled into their white Malibu rental for the drive to Santa Monica. Adrienne was driving, like she always did.

"You okay?"

Ana nodded. "I'm fine. He just kind of freaked me out."

"What a tool. Dreads. So hilarious on a white dude. Fucking trustafarian twat." She paused and her voice relaxed. "Everything cool with Joseph?"

"Yeah." Ana admired Adrienne's ability to transition so quickly from scorn to concern. "Everything's fine. I'm glad I called. Thanks."

"Knew you'd feel better." Adrienne steered the car onto Santa Monica Boulevard. "I checked my messages while you were outside. Looks like we're going to have a little visitor while we're here."

Ana looked over at her. "Uh-oh. Our periods?"

"No, Bruce Kellner."

"Bruce is coming to our shoot? What for?"

Adrienne's fingers flared from the steering wheel for a moment. "I have no idea why. But I don't have a problem with it."

Ana shot her a sidelong glance. "Really. Hmm . . . Well, I know why you don't have a problem with it."

"What are you saying, Ana?" said Adrienne, her voice steeled with false indignation. "Is it because he's so good-looking, is that what you're saying?"

"That's exactly what I'm saying."

There was a faint smile on Adrienne's face as she watched the road ahead. "Okay, you'd be right. I've totally got a boner for him."

"I would not mess with that, Ade."

"Oh, like you wouldn't if you weren't in a *committed relationship*," she said, dragging out the last part to make it sound disgustingly respectable. "Come on, you know he's totally doable. It doesn't hurt that he's also in charge of the creative department."

A light-blue Maybach suddenly cut in front of them. Adrienne hit the brakes. "Fucking douchebag!" she yelled, displaying her middle finger against the windshield. A window powered down in the rear of the Maybach and a well-manicured, tastefully bejeweled black hand emerged, returning the finger.

Ana loved Adrienne, but she did sometimes grow tired of the confrontations, the swearing, the bluster that came with spending time with her. But the scene in the parking lot with Adrienne rescuing dumbstruck Ana—that was the other side of it. Despite the drama, she always knew Adrienne had her back.

"Bruce is our boss," said Ana. "And isn't he married?"

"I think he's recently divorced. I'm not sure though."

"Yeah, I bet he likes to keep it that way. Vaguely unattached."

Adrienne pushed the button to open one of the rear windows. A cool rush of air entered the car and riffled a few loose strands of hair behind Ana's ear. She smoothed them back with the tips of her fingers.

"Eh, I don't know," Ana continued. "I just don't get why everyone goes so crazy over him. I mean, he's nice-looking and everything, I guess. There's just something about him, I don't know. It's like when he enters the room, he walks in crotch first."

Adrienne laughed. "That's it exactly. That's what I like. But he doesn't wear it out there in a sleazy way. It's like he just can't help it. Plus, he's got the power thing. He's one of those guys that just seems totally comfortable running everything."

"You have thought about this way too much."

"I'm just agreeing with you," Adrienne said, both innocent and insincere at the same time.

After the conversation with Joe, it felt good to talk about work, about something not very important. "Come on, Ade, you've heard the same stuff as me. It always seems to involve some hot young art director."

"Maybe that's because he actually does work now and then, unlike most creative directors. Maybe he's just working with—"

"The hot young art director?"

"You know. Benefit of his experience. He *is* very accessible. Not one of those CDs that you can't even get in to see."

Ana glanced over at the Troubadour as they passed. "Hmm, maybe *too* accessible. Remember Leiah? How she suddenly and mysteriously soared up through the ranks?"

Adrienne considered this. "I did hear a few rumblings about a thing."

"That said, Leiah is a great designer. God forbid anyone should think that's why she's successful."

Adrienne nodded absently. "True."

They were both silent for a moment. The more Ana thought about it all, the less she liked the situation. "Why the fuck do they suddenly think we need to be supervised? Because we're both women?"

"Take it easy, Steinem."

"Seriously, I'm insulted."

"It could be perfectly innocent," said Adrienne.

"You think?"

"Sure. He's probably thinking that since we are a two-woman creative team, his chances of having sex are doubled."

"You asshole," said Ana, laughing.

"It's win-win, as we say in FranklinCovey training."

Years back, the agency had forced everyone to participate in a 7 *Habits of Highly Effective People* program. Everyone except the most brainwashed AEs thought it was total bullshit. She and Adrienne took every opportunity to deride the program, making all that business dogma sound as dirty as possible.

"You're right," said Ana, giving in. "He's Beginning with Your End in Mind."

"So you're saying you want him to Make a Deposit in Your Emotional Bank Account?"

"Unless it ends up somewhere else."

The two of them couldn't stop tittering after that.

Adrienne reached over and petted Ana's shoulder. "You see? You are fun. I love it when you're filthy."

Ana held up her right hand with the thumb folded over her palm. "I will try to be more filthy more often."

"I wish you would. Anyway, you know he's gorgeous."

Ana sighed. "I know. I just think he knows it too. And I guess I think men who aren't quite so sure of themselves are nicer to be around."

They stopped at a light. Adrienne looked over at her, completely bewildered. "Good lord, woman. Why would you ever think such a thing?"

"I don't know, I just do. He's too used to all the women adoring him."

There was something inexplicably appealing about Bruce Kellner. Ana would hear women in the office (even the pregnant ones) say things like, "I get to present ideas to Bruce today!" then sigh like schoolgirls. She had heard that whenever Bruce would go to pitch new business, the admins would be swooning after he left the building. But it wasn't just women, men liked him too. All the male creatives raved about what a good guy he was. Ana had once seen him charm a roomful of auto-part store owners who she thought were complete louts. (Maybe that was because they had pretty much ignored her and Adrienne.) Those gearheads walked out of the conference room loving a pretty wacky TV campaign that no one thought could be sold.

Lately, it seemed as though Bruce had been paying extra attention to her and Adrienne. She had noticed that whenever she was in a meeting with him, he seemed to funnel a lot of comments directly to her, as if to let her know that she was an important part of the group. The first time it happened, she had been thrilled. Then, later, it bothered her that she had been thrilled.

She fancied herself as having better taste in men than someone like Bruce Kellner, some $200-haircut, designer-suit-with-no-tie-wearing, smooth-talking creative-director type. Ana's tastes ran more toward men who were considered "interesting looking" by most women. Like Joe, who was definitely rocking the arty nerd look. True, these days it was a slightly balding, horn-rimmed, middle-aged arty nerd, but she still found it appealing (along with other women she knew). He was also interested in things other than advertising, thank god. Someone like Bruce made her appreciate what she loved about Joe. That he was funny and kind and smart. How he wasn't afraid to be vulnerable around people, especially men. (She had witnessed a fair number of times when some seemingly macho frat-boy type would suddenly start talking to Joe about John Cheever's stories or Gil Scott-Heron or the French new wave, as if he was so relieved to reveal this side of himself that he didn't have to be a *guy*-guy for once.) Yet Ana was concerned that in the past few years, Joe seemed like he had lost some of his confidence. He used to be a bit cocky, especially when it came to his writing. He had opinions and wasn't afraid to express them, damn the consequences. Now it seemed like what he did was practically the equivalent of copywriting. He summarized things, wrote bullet points, recommended products. Sure, those products were great music and books and movies and whatever, but still. It was like he had lost something—his passion, the need to care.

It was quiet in the car.

"So when's Bruce coming in?" asked Ana, just to say something.

"Oh, he's in."

"He is? Already?"

"Yeah, he's waiting for us over at the production company."

"Hm."

9

Gentlemen

It had been sitting there on his desk at home all day Tuesday: a giant pile of CDs, books, and DVDs, as well as all the accompanying promotional materials (often more important to Joe's work than the actual music, books, and films) that he needed to sift through to write capsule reviews. "Short-Attention-Span Review" was for a different publication, *Rent*, a culture magazine that reportedly was on the verge of killing off the print edition in favor of going completely online. (Joe knew that this meant anything was possible, including an e-mail that informed freelancers that in the future, the magazine would no longer be able to compensate them. *But we'd still love to have you write for us.*) When he told someone that he wrote reviews for the magazine, he tried not to put little air quotes around the word *reviews*, but it was still hard not to do it in his head, for what he wrote were not so much reviews, but précis. Thumbnails. Synopses. *Scut work.* The bummer of it was that he spent so much time trying to make money by writing about what other people created that the idea of creating something of his own was fast becoming strangely insurmountable.

As for this day, he still hadn't gotten around to doing any of that scut work. Instead, he had spent it eating cereal and watching a film noir box set that he had reviewed weeks back. Just after he finished watching *Gun Crazy* ("Two people dead, just so we can live without working!"), Joe turned off the TV and started the long trudge upstairs to the study. He just hadn't been in the mood for it. The irony of the name of his column was not lost on him today.

At about six p.m., when Malcolm texted him to see if he felt like going out for a drink, it felt like the governor had granted him a stay of execution. Joe was all too happy to text back *yes* immediately. He told himself that he needed a break even though he had hardly gotten anything done. Malcolm worked with Ana, but he was more Joe's friend than hers. He was an art director at the same agency she'd worked at ten years ago and wound up moving to her current agency two years after she hired on. When Joe first met Malcolm, it took him awhile to get used to his dandy-ish manner: the tousled hair and the stylish, flashy clothing (part couture, part vintage) that made him look like the lead singer of a twee band.

Yet once Joe got to know him, the two of them had become great friends. Joe had found that it wasn't always easy to develop close friendships with ad people. When a group of them gathered (he had been witness to many such evenings out, mostly agency going-away parties at bars, when Ana or Malcolm toted him along), their conversations were often sharp and funny, well peppered with references to obscure music or cult films or brilliant but unappreciated television shows. They raved about certain graphic designers and artists as if they were gods. In their offices, they fetishistically passed around glossy Taschen books devoted to arcane ephemera like nineteenth-century circus posters, fifties men's magazines, or seventies steak houses as if they were samizdat. In many ways, they were his kind of people.

Yet there was something else he saw in them, something unsettling, a soiled shared knowledge, a rarefied attitude with its own argot of condescension that he suspected was often found in people who made their living manipulating the masses.

It was as if they were saying, *We are not like the people to whom we sell things.* Often they didn't seem anywhere near as evolved as they fancied themselves. Sometimes they were just people with bigger paychecks, bigger egos, better clothes, and too much cynicism for their own good. Of course, Ana wasn't that way. Mostly. And who the hell was he to talk? When it came to his opinion of humanity in general, he was no Johnny Sunshine, that was for sure. Malcolm though. Malcolm seemed to understand people on a different level, perhaps a bit more than he cared to at times. Joe had never felt condescension from him about anybody. In fact, whenever Joe couldn't quite get a handle on someone, he would ask Malcolm, who viewed everyone in a filterless way, seeing things that might be thought of as faults as simply fascinating traits. It was detachment in a way, but mostly a positive one. Malcolm simply believed that it was easier to like someone than to dislike them. Yet Joe also remembered one of the first real conversations that he had with him (after a few beers, of course), when Malcolm had revealed that he had a strange talent. He said that after getting to know someone he could tell the truth about them.

Joe was fascinated by the idea of this. "What do you mean, the truth?"

"Oh, stuff they might not realize about themselves. What they might not want to know or have never wanted to admit to themselves."

"Wow. That's like psychological kryptonite," Joe said.

Malcolm nodded solemnly, as if it were a curse that he was doomed to carry with him forever, like some character from Greek mythology.

"Do you ever use it on people?" Joe asked eagerly.

He nodded again. "I've used it eleven times."

Hearing that had both enthralled and unnerved Joe. "I find it alarming that you know the exact number of times you've used your deadly power on people."

Malcolm said nothing to this.

Joe did not feel as though he were lying. "So what's it like?"

Malcolm's eyes tightened. "It's kind of horrible, actually."

"Really? Well, I'm envious," said Joe. "There are some people I'd like to use that on."

Malcolm shook his head. "No, you wouldn't. Once you say something like that to someone, you can see in their face how deeply you've hurt them. It's a bad feeling. It really is."

Since then, he had never seen Malcolm use his power on anyone, but for whatever reason, Joe had never once doubted that he could do it. Afterward, he kept wanting to ask Malcolm about his own secret truth, but always chickened out, afraid of what he would hear.

Tonight at the bar, Malcolm was already waiting at a table, along with Chick and Todd, Malcolm's cousin, who was friends with all of them. Todd was the only one who actually lived in Detroit, in the Woodbridge district, one of the areas that was currently becoming a kind of artist enclave. Todd was very committed to living in the city. He helped build a community garden hut with an edible roof and did free music workshops with the kids in his neighborhood. He was also an engineer for a local sound studio, wrote soundtrack and commercial music for a production house, and was a player in various bands that had formed around some of the crazy ethnic mash-ups that were not uncommon in Detroit. If anyone needed an oud, koto, bouzouki, duduk, or shamisen virtuoso for their Albanian/Japanese/Armenian avant-folktronica band, Todd was their man. Joe admired Todd's commitment and musicianship, but also felt like a no-account suburbanite around him, since he and Ana had once lived in the same neighborhood in Detroit right after they started living together. They gave up and ran off to the burbs after their apartment was broken into for the second time. Joe was also amazed that Todd had figured out how to practice his art, support himself, and be a decent human being all at the same time. Joe had tried so hard to hate him initially because that would have made everything so much easier, but damned if he could.

"When did Ana leave for LA?" asked Malcolm.

"Couple of days ago."

"That's cool," said Malcolm. "I didn't talk to her. She excited? Is it a good spot?"

"I guess. I don't know. We didn't really talk about it that much."

"Oh, okay," Malcolm said, leaving it alone.

There was silence at the table. Joe looked around. "We didn't really talk that much before she left." More silence, which made Joe keep talking, even though he knew that he should shut up. "We were actually kind of fighting."

"You were in the doghouse the other night too," said Chick.

Joe nodded wearily. "Yes, I remember. Thank you."

"Dibs on Ana if they get divorced," blurted Chick. Everyone looked at him in disbelief. He shrugged back at them all. "What? I'm just kidding. Besides, he's not even married."

Finally, Joe shook his head and laughed. It was some-times all you could do with Chick. "I don't know whether to slug you or to tell Ana and have her do it."

Malcolm turned to Chick. "You'd be better off with Joe slugging you. I've seen Ana go off on someone."

"It was a joke. She's a great girl, that's all. You don't know how lucky you have it, dude. Funny. Nice. Hot."

"A surprising order of importance," said Todd.

"I know," said Chick. "I didn't even mention her rack. Plus, she can cook."

Joe remembered the time when he and Ana had Chick over for dinner. A simple chicken and wild rice with a sal-ad (a meal that Joe had mostly prepared), but Chick raved about everything for weeks. He was basically a standard helpless male in the kitchen, totally accustomed to fast food, canned goods, Doritos, and frozen pizza.

"I know," said Joe. "Plus, she pays most of the bills. She is great. She's a great woman."

Chick shrugged again. "Fuck it. Go ahead and slug me. I'm still calling dibs on her."

Joe socked Chick in the arm. Joe was surprised when it kind of hurt his knuckles. Chick worked out a lot.

"That's all you got?" said Chick, half laughing. "I got a four-year-old niece who can hit harder than that."

Malcolm turned to Joe. "What's up? You want to talk about it?"

Chick looked pained. "What is this, sensitivity training? We're men. We should be bottling up our feelings."

"Shut up, Chick."

"Fine," he said, flaring his fingers in the air, an angry variant of jazz hands. "Let's all be pussies then and *talk*."

Joe wasn't sure he wanted to talk about it, yet he kind of

did. *Why can't I talk about this with my friends?* "Well, we'd been arguing anyway, then things kind of came to a head the other day." No one said anything. They were waiting for him to continue. "I really don't think this was the problem, per se. But maybe it was a symptom."

Another long pause.

"What the *fuck* are you talking about?" said Chick, finally.

Joe turned to him. "You remember that episode of *Seinfeld* where George gets caught by his mother?"

Chick's eyes lit up, he nodded excitedly. "Yeah! That's a great one."

"Oh jeez," said Todd, the first to understand. "Hoo boy."

Then the table let out a collective pained groan, a labored *oof*, as if they had all been simultaneously punched in the solar plexus.

"O monstrous folly," said Todd.

"Yeah," said Joe, grimacing.

"Not good," said Malcolm.

"Yeah, let's just say it hasn't helped things much." Joe turned to Chick again. "You were right. This was a bad idea."

Chick pointed his index finger at him accusingly. "I told you. *Feelings*. They're nothing but trouble." He leaned back in his chair, crossing his arms.

Malcolm set his beer down and turned back to Joe. "Is that the only reason Ana's pissed at you?"

"Um, I don't know, I think maybe she's getting tired of supporting me. Or maybe I'm just getting tired of being supported. Of her being my safety net."

"And you're taking it out on her?"

"Sounds like you're more taking it out on Lil' Joe," said Chick.

Everyone turned to him, as if to say: *We're trying to be serious here.*

Chick lifted his hands from the table, palms up in exasperation. "What? It's always the penis that suffers in these domestic squabbles. Unfair if you ask me."

There were a few reluctant chuckles around the table, but mostly they just stared at Chick.

"Fine. Everyone wants to talk seriously?" he said. "Let's talk serious." Chick turned to Joe, pointing his index finger at him again. "Of course she's tired of supporting you. Why wouldn't she be?" He paused for a second, as if deciding whether or not to say what he was going to say. "No offense, man, but you're a deadbeat. Women dig security. It's hot to them. Security to a woman is like big tits are to a man."

The table laughed. Chick frowned and held his hands up as if to quell the noise.

"So how about this: why don't you get a real fucking job? Maybe you'd both feel better about you. I know you're pursuing your literary dreams and shit, but it isn't working. Writing about all your cool obscure bullshit. Maybe you should try something that actually *pays* for a living. Get an effing job."

This was a surprise from Chick, who didn't usually say things like this. Joe wasn't sure if it was the persona or not who was talking, but whoever it was, he didn't like it so much.

"Easy for you to say," Joe countered timidly. "You're successful."

Chick tapped his chest with his fingertips. "Don't make this about me, fucko. I never once said I was successful. I write about talking lemurs and robot rebellions and buddy movies with high-octane action. They don't even get made."

He shook his fist at some unknown nemesis. "I don't consider myself successful. But at least I make some bank being unsuccessful. Dude, you need to step up. Pull your weight. Be a fucking man."

Joe stared down at his beer, face burning. Everyone was looking at Chick, slightly stunned.

Chick shrugged, elbows pinned to his sides, palms up. "What? You all wanted to talk. We talked."

The rest of the table remained silent. Joe didn't hear anyone disagreeing with Chick. He was glad for the jukebox, which was playing "Rag and Bone" by the White Stripes. (Another successful Detroiter mocking him.) Then the song ended and no new song followed. Everyone was just sitting there, taking long, quiet gulps of beer. The din of the bar only seemed to accentuate the fact that no one at their table was saying anything. All the fun had been somehow sucked out of the room, thanks to Joe. Shouldn't they all have been laughing, sharing in communal manly empathy? What happened?

"This round's on me," said Joe, standing up and gathering glasses. Even though he knew he couldn't really afford it and it probably wouldn't help.

10

Carpe Per Diem

In Los Angeles, Ana was having dinner with Adrienne and Bruce Kellner. They had finished their location scout early, had gone back to the hotel to change, then met back at the lobby. Joan the producer had begged off dinner, opting instead for room service and a Skype visit with her husband and kids.

The three of them were at Chaya Downtown. Normally when she and Adrienne went out of town, they had to be careful not to exceed their ever-shrinking per diems, lest their expense reports get bounced back to them by the bean counters. This led to a number of delicious but decidedly low-budget meals at Armenian chicken joints. This was not the case when dining with a creative director. Through rounds of slingchi martinis and saketinis and basil gimlets, Bruce proceeded to order enough for about six dinners—all of it pan-seared, free-range, dry-aged, line-caught, small-batch, locally sourced, and expensive as hell. At first, Ana couldn't stop herself from tabulating their bill in her head, but after the third round of cocktails and appetizers, she gave up. Bruce ordered Châteauneuf-du-Pape with dinner. It was insanely yummy and obscenely pricey, the kind of wine she'd never order or even buy at the store. Bruce was being his charming self and Adrienne was eyeing him with suspicious longing. It was fun, but there was something else going on that left Ana feeling vaguely uneasy. She knew that it wouldn't be long, especially after all the drinks, before Adrienne was saying exactly what was on her mind.

Sure enough, just after the first onslaught of entrées, Adrienne took a long sip of the blood-dark wine and fixed her eyes on Bruce. She put the glass down. "So what are you doing here, Bruce? Do people back at the agency think we need watching over or something? Ana and I have both been doing this for a long time, you know."

Ana nervously fidgeted with the strap on the one dress she had brought with her to LA, a candy-striped, retroish frock with a pleated waist that almost fit in at the restaurant, but not quite. "Not that we're not happy to have you," added Ana, as palliative to the edge in Adrienne's voice.

Bruce laughed self-consciously, and Ana watched the creases deepen around his eyes. Judging from the immaculately groomed salt-and-pepper hair, he was well into his forties, but he wore his age proudly and didn't try to hide it with hair plugs or fake tans or by dressing like a twentysomething creative. (She knew one CD who dyed his soul patch. So sad.) It also looked like Bruce worked out regularly.

"Come on, Bruce," said Adrienne, jabbing him with her index finger (a gesture that seemed aggressively male). "What's up? Are we getting shitcanned?" Adrienne was smiling, but Ana wished she hadn't brought that up.

Bruce took a breath and regarded them both. Ana was surprised at how the energy at the table changed so abruptly and how nervous she got. Bruce thoughtfully poked a piece of salmon sashimi on his plate with his chopsticks and let the tension build. Then he put down the chopsticks, looked up at Adrienne, and nodded somberly.

"Yes, Adrienne," he said, pushing the palms of his hands together. "This is how the agency lets people go. We fly them out to Los Angeles for a fabulous dinner with cocktails at an expensive restaurant." He shrugged. "It's just *nicer* this way. It's like a delicious severance package. Plus, you're three thousand miles from the office, so it really cuts down on the workplace violence."

Adrienne narrowed her eyes at him. "Ha ha."

Bruce frowned. "Come on, you two. Don't be ridiculous." He finished his saketini and set the glass on the table. There was a beat of silence before he smiled. "Although Adrienne is right. There is something going on."

Adrienne's eyebrows raised, then she shot a glance at Ana as if to say, *See? I know what I'm talking about.*

Bruce rubbed his palms together, then placed his hands on the table as if to get down to business. "Here's the deal: We're starting a new division at the agency that will be completely devoted to marketing to women. We thought you two would be perfect to head it up."

"Are you fucking kidding?" said Adrienne, glancing over at Ana.

"Nope. You guys were the obvious choice. You've been doing some great work that's strong and smart, but with a decidedly feminine point of view. Which is exactly what we want for this division. I don't need an answer right now, but—"

"We're in," blurted Adrienne.

Bruce looked a little surprised. "You don't have to answer now. It's going to be a lot of work, just so you know."

"We're in," repeated Adrienne.

Ana glared at her, half wanting her to shut up, half wanting to join in. *Do we have to decide this right now?*

Adrienne turned to Ana, eyes expectant. "Well, aren't we?"

Ana dropped her head and raised her hands in submission. "Of course we are."

"Excellent," said Bruce, beaming. "Who wants champagne?"

Two hours later, they were all up in Bruce's massive suite at the Standard. Both Adrienne and Bruce had been lobbying for a nightcap, ever since they'd left the restaurant. It seemed like a bad idea to Ana, considering she was already pretty drunk. All she wanted to do was go to her room and settle dizzily into bed, but she went along to be a good sport. Besides, she was worried about Adrienne, who seemed much drunker than her. Despite their promotion (and a big raise, they later found out), sleeping with the boss would still be inadvisable.

Ana poked around the suite while Bruce was in the other room raiding the minibar. She couldn't believe how these guys lived. Of course, it wasn't like her room was horrible, far from it, but it was a broom closet compared to this museum of modern design. Ana looked over at Adrienne, who seemed to be dozing briefly, legs just slightly akimbo. She was glad that her friend had opted for jeans and not one of her shorter skirts that evening.

She put her hand on Adrienne's knee. "Hey, are you okay? It would actually be all right if we didn't drink any more tonight."

"What's the difference?" said Adrienne, surprisingly articulate for someone who was unconscious a moment earlier. "We're already going to feel like shit tomorrow."

"We could cut our losses. We do have a prepro meeting tomorrow."

"Fuck it. I feel like celebrating," Adrienne slurred. Suddenly she was drunk again and smiling at Ana. "Hey, lady." Adrienne got this way sometimes when she was in her cups, all lovey-dovey and best-friendy.

"What, Ade?"

Adrienne held out her hand for Ana to shake. "I'm proud of us."

"Me too."

Ana leaned forward to shake her hand, at which point Adrienne fell toward her to give her a big hug. "*Sooo* proud."

Just then, Bruce walked in with two fistfuls of tiny bottles to find Adrienne lurched forward in Ana's arms.

His eyes widened in an exaggerated way. "Okay, am I missing something here? Are you guys more of a team than we all figured?"

Ana chuckled uncomfortably as Adrienne became a dead weight. Time to be a good sport. "Yeah, well, heh-heh. 'Women-to-Women' is more than just a marketing phrase to us."

Bruce looked like he was trying not to laugh as he twisted the tops off of two tiny bottles of cognac. "Or is she just hammered?"

Adrienne now seemed to be sleeping in her arms. "Hammered," confirmed Ana. "I think this girl needs to get to bed."

Bruce poured a cognac into a thick-bottomed glass and held it up. "Aw, come on. Stay for one. Please. Then you can go. I know I'm never going to get to sleep. My sleep patterns are all messed up. I'm out here so much."

Ana nodded and a few of Adrienne's hairs stuck to her lips. "You must be perpetually jet-lagged."

"Yeah, I'm used to it though. Um, do you want some help there?"

"Yes please."

He got up and pulled off his suit coat. "Oh jeez, I can hear the voice of human resources in my head right now, telling me not to do this. *That's a verrry bad idea, Mr. Kellner,*" he intoned in a high-pitched matronly voice.

Ana smiled at the way Bruce made Sue Smithick, their human resources supervisor, sound like Julia Child.

Bruce reached toward her to place one arm around Adrienne's shoulders, the other behind her knees. Then he gently carried her back to her chair.

Ana, happy to be relieved of Adrienne, also raised her voice to a clucky soprano: "*Ms. Urbanek, could you please show me on the doll where Mr. Kellner touched Ms. Kaminski?*"

Bruce leaned back in his chair and laughed. Ana felt pleased having amused him. Just then she understood what all those women liked about him. In addition to being good-looking and powerful, he was nice. Then just as quickly, she thought better of it. Most creative directors certainly knew how to be nice, but they also knew how to use people. Bruce was no different.

"Well, it'll be our secret," she said.

"Thanks."

"Unless you don't automatically approve our work, then things could get messy."

Bruce scooted his chair closer to her and put his hand on her wrist. "I think you're great, Ana. I just want to tell you that."

"Excuse me?"

"I just think you're great. That's all."

Ana felt a kind of atmospheric shift in the room. "You mean my work?"

"Well, sure, yes. I think your work is excellent. That's

why you and Adrienne are getting this opportunity. You're both super-hard workers and you both continue to have consistently good ideas. You two have really been an asset to the agency." He paused. "But I also mean, I just think *you're* great."

"Oh." She had no idea of what to say.

"I like the way you carry yourself, the way you don't take any shit from the guys at work."

"You do? I think you're confusing me with Adrienne. She's the muscle. I'm the one that cowers in the background."

Bruce watched her ardently. She could see flecks of amber in his pupils.

"I like how in meetings you'll say something really funny and everyone in the room will laugh except you. You'll just sit there, looking almost uncomfortable at being funny. It's very fetching."

Ana exhaled loudly through her nose. She wondered if she was blushing. "Are you sure we're talking about *me*?"

"I'm sure."

He patted her wrist once and smiled. She could smell him, a combination of something spicy and expensive, but with an edge of something else more human, a delicate muskiness. She wanted him to move away, but not quite yet.

"Bruce?"

"Yeah?"

She wasn't sure what she was going to say, then she said, "I think I'm going to get Adrienne to her room."

He bit the edge of his lip, let go of her wrist, then turned and grabbed one of the glasses and held it out to her. "You didn't even have any of your drink."

"I really don't need any more. You take it. It'll help you to sleep."

She stood up, veering a little too close to his face. Then Bruce stood as well, still holding the drink. Ana couldn't tell if he looked mad or disappointed.

Finally, he smiled. "Okay. If you have to go." He took a sip of the cognac. She could smell the liquor mingling with his scent.

"I do."

"Then you should go. I'll see you two tomorrow." He nodded toward Adrienne. "Think she can get to her room okay?"

Ana approached the chair. "Time to go, drunk girl." She gave Adrienne's leg a kick and not a gentle one.

Adrienne jumped in her seat, opened her eyes, and scowled at Ana. "Ow. Jesus Christ! Why did you do that?"

Ana gave a fake smile as if she hadn't meant to hurt her. "Come on, Ade. You don't want to be late for your hangover tomorrow."

"Don't want to go." Then Adrienne noticed Bruce standing there smiling at her. "Hey, Bruce. You fucker. You fucking fucker. You're hot."

He pushed his lips together and nodded, stifling a laugh. "Adrienne, listen to Ana. You should go."

Ana kicked her again, less hard this time. "That's your boss talking. Get up. Come on. We've got a prepro meeting tomorrow at nine with the client."

"Fine." Adrienne pulled herself up from the chair with a slight weave. Ana took her hand to steady her. "Bye, hot Bruce," slurred Adrienne as they headed toward the door.

"See you, Bruce," Ana said, opening the door and leading Adrienne out first. Ana didn't mean to look back, but she found herself doing it anyway.

Bruce was looking right back at her as if he had known all along that she would turn around.

11

Is Selling Out Even a Thing Anymore?

Normally Joe would be up by eight and probably working by then, but this morning, after last night's many pints, sleeping in sounded like a better idea. Around nine thirty, he finally dragged himself out of bed, heavy-lidded and muzzy-headed. Not unusual these days. Ten years ago, the morning after a night of drinking was not a problem. Bright eyes? *Yep*. Bushy tail? *Check*. Not now though. Not today. Today, coffee was imperative.

When he sat down at his desk with his second cup (first one slammed in the kitchen, standing next to the sink), he remembered why there had been too many pints. Even now, face burning, he still felt the sting of Chick's words and the shame he had experienced upon hearing them. It wasn't that he was angry at Chick. He certainly wasn't thrilled with him right now, but saying what was on his mind, whether it was part of the persona or not, was what Chick did. It just didn't seem so funny when he told the truth about you.

In this case, Joe was pretty sure that Chick was correct. His literary dreams were a joke. He didn't even know what his literary dreams were anymore. So why not at least pull his own weight until he figured it out? Maybe it *was* time to be a man for a change. Step up.

Joe touched the space bar on the computer to make it come alive. Instead of checking his usual music, book, pop culture, and film blogs, or even *The Paris of the Midwest Is Crumbling*, he found himself going to the Association of Alternative Newsweeklies website. On the left side, there were top stories from weekly, mostly free newspapers from all over the country. They had "alternative" names like *Creative Loafing* or *City Pulse* or *Weekly Alibi*. Joe told himself that he was there to see what the other papers were writing about, maybe get some ideas. He hadn't planned to check out the job listings on the opposite side of the page, but there they were.

And lo and behold, right there was a listing for the Detroit area. It was for a paper called the *D Daily*. He had never heard of this paper, but they just happened to be looking for a staff writer. Joe clicked through to the listing. It was encouraging: *Immediate opening; full-time staff writer; looking for well-crafted magazine-style articles; culture and lifestyle background preferred.* Why hadn't he ever heard of this place? It sounded perfect for him. A quick Google search for *D Daily alt newspaper* produced confusing results, pulling up mostly hits for the two city dailies. Not much help.

Fuck it, he decided. This was too exciting. Joe cobbled together an e-mail with a résumé and four of his best clips and sent it off to a tblanken@ddaily.net. *What the hell,* thought Joe. *Why not?*

Less than five minutes later his cell phone rang. Joe didn't recognize the number. He wasn't sure what to do. *It couldn't be this place, could it? No way.* He decided to let voice mail get it. But on the last ring before VM clicked in, he quickly picked up his phone and hit the talk button.

"Hello?" Joe said, trying not to sound like he had just

crawled out of bed hungover half an hour ago. He was conscious of how scratchy his voice sounded. Booze and yelling
over the din of the bar, no doubt.

"I'd like to speak to Joseph Keen."

"Speaking."

"Hello, Joe. My name is Terrance Blankenship. I'm the
editor of the *Daily*. I just received your résumé and clips."

"Oh, great. Wow. Well, that was . . . *fast*. I didn't think
I'd be hearing from you so soon."

"I normally wouldn't contact someone so quickly, but
I'm actually quite familiar with your writing. I've read your
stuff in the *Independent* and was very impressed. I'm a fan of
your work."

"You are? Wow. Thanks."

"Are you familiar with our publication?"

"Um. Not terribly familiar." It was not a good answer,
but he didn't know what else to say.

"I'm surprised. We're distributed throughout the metro
area. The *Dollar Daily*?"

Finally, it made sense. *Dollar*. That was what the D stood
for. Not *Detroit*. Joe knew all about the *Dollar Daily*. It was a
crummy little rag that appeared with their mail every week.
It was filled with silly articles about the new ice cream par-
lor opening up in town, the local old woman who finds a
rutabaga in the shape of President Obama's head in her garden, updates about the high school marching band, and lots
of advertising. Page after page of it.

"Ohhhh," said Joe, experiencing a surge of disappointment that actually surprised him. "I guess I am familiar with
your, uh, newspaper. We get it at our house." *And immediately
pitch it in the recycling bin*, he kindly neglected to say.

"Ah, good. Then you know what we're about."

"Yes, I guess I do." He wasn't sure if he sounded snotty or just bummed, but he didn't really care since he'd be getting off the phone momentarily. He had no intention of doing anything for this rag. This was no newspaper, alternative or otherwise. It was a shopping tabloid with local interest.

It was then that the voice over the phone changed, as if the guy knew where this all was headed. "Look, Joe. I know we don't exactly seem like your kind of paper, but we desperately need a good staff writer. I think you'd be great working for us."

Whoa, daddy. "Uh, thanks so much for thinking of me, Mr. Blankenship." (He was amazed that he could remember this guy's name.) "But I'm not really looking for anything like what you guys do."

"I figured you weren't, but before you turn me down, let me just tell you about it. You know what the job would entail if you've seen the paper. It's not exactly fancy, but the *Dollar Daily* is doing very, very well. I can offer you a full-time position with benefits."

Then Mr. Terrance Blankenship mentioned a salary. A salary like the kind that Joe had never before been offered. A real salary that would allow him to not be constantly poor, that would allow him to pick up a dinner bill once in a while (actually, more than once in a while), that would take the financial pressure off of Ana, that might let the two of them buy a house instead of renting until they were both too old to work and then cohabitating in that cardboard box under the 8 Mile overpass. Perhaps it would even take the financial pressure off of him enough so he could finally figure out what it was that he really wanted to write.

"Really?" said Joe, still reeling. "That much?"

"Plus three weeks of paid vacation. And a profit-sharing

bonus after the first year. I need someone good, Joe. And I'm willing to pay for it."

"Uh, wow. I don't know."

"Look, I know you're probably pretty leery of our type of newspaper and I completely understand, but I'm very open to changes. I'd really like to give the paper more of an alternative press feel, which was why I joined the AAN. I want to make the paper more interesting, quirky, more of an arts flavor, and I know you're great at that sort of thing. So please keep that in mind. You could be the person at the helm, taking us in those new editorial directions. It could be an exciting opportunity for you."

"Really?" Joe wasn't sure if he completely believed this guy, but it was exactly what he wanted to hear.

"Yes, really. Look, Joe. I want you to think it over, talk to your wife, whatever. I can give you twenty-four hours to decide, but that's it. I'll need an answer by this time tomorrow."

"You're offering me the job over the phone?" said Joe.

"Yes, I am offering you this job over the phone. I know all I need to know about you." The man's voice was steeled with conviction, and Joe was finding it all rather heady. He kept telling himself to say no, but couldn't seem to spit it out. A few beats of silence. "Shall I talk to you tomorrow then?" said Mr. Blankenship, his voice now lowered, as if he didn't want to disturb the delicate trip wire of his offer.

"Um. All right," said Joe, unable to believe that he was considering this.

"You can let me know earlier too, if you decide to accept it. And I really think you should, Joe." A timid laugh on the other end.

"All right. Uh, well, thanks for thinking of me."

"Thank *you* for getting in touch with us. I am so thrilled that you did. Believe me, I wouldn't be doing this if I didn't think you were exactly right for us. I'll talk to you soon."

Joe hung up and just sat there at his desk for a long time, phone still warm in his hand. He felt like he had just been in a minor automobile accident. Physically fine, but disoriented and hyperadrenalized. There was something oddly exciting about this happening so quickly. It was like Chick had made everything happen, simply by shaming Joe. So instead of a prompt but polite blow-off, which is what Mr. Blankenship would have probably gotten two days ago, Joe was now actually considering this job offer.

A real job offer. A good job offer. Or rather, a real good offer for a crappy job. His first instinct was to call Ana, but he then realized that would be a bad idea. If he did take this job, it needed to be *his* decision. He had to figure out what he wanted himself. Right now, he had no idea of how he felt about the whole thing. Okay, that was not entirely true. No matter how confused he might feel about something, if he really thought about it, there was usually some notion, a vague clue, a whisper of a voice inside his head gently murmuring what it was that he actually wanted.

That whisper was currently screaming at Joe: *Take the fucking job, idiot! It just fell into your lap! Take it!* What was so alarming was that no deliberation was required. He thought there would be much gnashing of teeth and wringing of hands. *What about my principles? What about my artistic integrity?* Fuck all that.

Chick was right. Joe needed to pull his weight, to not have to worry constantly about where his next assignment was coming from. He was tired of cobbling together enough income to pay his tiny, disproportionate slice of the rent.

Even though he had always prided himself on his utter lack of concern about manly demeanor, at this moment, he wanted to feel like a man. He wanted to be a man for Ana, instead of the worst roommate in the world, who not only leaves the toilet seat up but gets caught masturbating too.

The strange thing was, if he had gotten a job offer like this ten years ago, or even five years ago, he would have turned it down flat, and then been kind of a dick to the guy to boot. But today, he was so happy about the whole thing that he wanted to cry. He didn't even care that he'd probably be doing the worst kind of crap writing possible.

Joe hadn't realized that he had been this eager to sell out. Turned out he hadn't even been waiting for the right price. He had simply been waiting for someone, anyone, to just make him an offer.

12

Getting into Cars with Strangers

Everyone acted like nothing at all had happened the night before. So maybe none of it did happen, Ana couldn't help but think. But if it didn't, why was she still experiencing this sense of uneasiness about the entire evening? She had done nothing wrong, but still.

At least there was the preproduction meeting to distract them all from the fact that nothing had happened the night before. Though this was a fairly standard prepro meeting, with the requisite endless discussion, dissemination, and reiteration of details regarding actors, wardrobe, locations, reads, looks, feels, tonality, and other minutiae that were essential in the production of a television commercial, it certainly kept everyone occupied.

Adrienne, who generally had something to say about everything, was uncharacteristically quiet. She spoke only to excuse herself when she had to abruptly leave the meeting. Everyone watched as the poor thing returned ashen-faced, with a hint of acrid stink clinging to her clothes. (It was difficult for a 6'1" woman to unobtrusively slink back into a room.) The second time she got up to leave, the director, a fairly good guy (as directors went) with a thin-on-top, straggly, graying mullet and a barbed-wire tattoo that looked like a bad EKG (his eighties filmic heyday thus divulged: music videos for metal bands—teased-out power ballads, spandex-clad Tawnys and Kymberlys straddling muscle cars and stripper poles, and mountains of cocaine), asked if she was okay. Adrienne nodded frantically and hurried out of the room.

Not a great look in front of the client, a woman who managed to be both mousey and opinionated, who needed constant reassurance that she was doing the right thing by allowing an advertising agency to produce a television commercial.

"She's got a twenty-four-hour bug," Ana said to the client. "Picked it up on the plane, we think."

The director went back to talking about a tracking shot that he was obviously looking forward to pulling off for the spot.

After the third time Adrienne got up, Bruce had to actively suppress a laugh, then he slyly glanced over at Ana and smiled. She smiled back, then made herself turn away. There was something alluring about that smile, like the desire to stare directly at the sun. It was a smile that assured you that you were worthy of basking in its brilliance. Until later, when you weren't so sure anymore.

Ana tried not to think about any of it. She did not feel wonderful this morning, but had certainly felt worse. Bruce, for all appearances, was fine, his usual hearty, together self. When lunch was served, Adrienne excused herself for a quick nap. Ana filled a plate with salad, fruit, and a few pieces of tarragon chicken breast and tried to find a place where she could sit by herself. She ended up outside, in front of the production company, on a bench by the window. As she ate, she looked out onto 10th Street, a very unexciting, unpretentious street for Santa Monica, in the middle of an industrial district, filled with movers and warehouses as well as sound studios and film production companies. The blandness of the environs reminded her of certain areas in Ferndale, where there was nothing but machine shops and mold-making companies and places that produced mystifying products like spline gauges. Of course, that was back when the auto industry was booming. These days, a lot of those places were empty.

On the way into Santa Monica that morning, they had passed men lined along the street—day laborers for hire. They had reminded Ana of the crowds of prostitutes she had passed in cabs very late at night in New York City, back in the midnineties, on her second or third TV shoot as a still-green junior art director. She remembered them trying to look desirable from the side of the street, while hiding their desperation. Ana felt bad for all of them, men and women who had to make a living along the side of a busy avenue, scared for those who had to climb into strangers' cars to perform tasks of manual or sexual labor. Ana felt lucky to have a good job, one that was going to get even better. She still hadn't even called Joe with the news. It was all she could do to just get herself out of bed and ready for this meeting.

Next to her, the front door squeaked open and she watched as Bruce stepped outside with his cell, caught up in a conversation. He walked out toward the street, his back to her. She wondered if she could slip back into the office without him noticing her, but he turned right around and looked at her with no acknowledgment. He sounded a little gruffer than usual.

"Just PDF the layouts to me, okay? I've got my laptop. I've got a team here who can look at them too, all right?

Okay, bye." He pushed a button on his cell, shook his head, and rolled his eyes.

Ana forgot about trying to escape. "Things falling apart at the agency?"

"No worse than usual. I may need you guys to look at idea boards for some new business."

"I didn't hear about any new business. Who are we pitching?"

"Parnoc Industries."

"Who's that?"

"They manufacture things for the government, a lot of it for the military."

"Really? Like what?"

"Things for defense, homing devices, stuff like that."

"Jesus Christ," said Ana, not at all disguising her displeasure. "You mean they make stuff for killing people?"

"I think they'd prefer to say that it's for protecting our country."

Ana couldn't help but look distressed. "What the hell, Bruce? Could we find a more evil account? What's next? Are we going to pitch NAMBLA?"

Bruce feigned excitement. "Is it up for grabs? I'd heard it was in review. I know man-boy love is huge with the millennials."

Ana exhaled, trying not to be amused. "Come on, you know it's creepy."

"Yes, I know, but the agency is very excited. This account would mean a lot of money and a lot of new jobs. Which we desperately need. Especially since the Big Three are fleeing Detroit like rats leaving the *Titanic.*"

Ana frowned, having heard this story many times. "Yeah, but we don't even have a car account."

"We're all hurting. Look, I know what you mean. I feel pretty much the same way. Still, if I were you, I wouldn't express those opinions back at the agency. They won't go over well, especially after you've just been promoted. Know what I'm saying?"

Ana nodded wearily. She would keep her yap shut. She knew the score: Satan didn't like to be scolded.

"How's our friend doing?" he said, motioning inside, cell still in his hand.

"I think she's napping."

"She shouldn't drink so much."

"Well, you weren't exactly preaching temperance last night, Reverend."

"You seem fine."

"For one thing, I didn't have that nightcap you were promoting." She thought about being in Bruce's hotel room, Adrienne asleep and Bruce possibly coming on to her (or maybe it wasn't that at all), and it all felt a bit unseemly. It wasn't really, she knew. On shoots, sometimes you wound up spending time in hotel rooms with people you didn't know that well. There was work to be done on scripts, conference calls, or just random client-driven circumstances. Still, it felt odd having it happen with Bruce, someone with whom she hadn't even shared much in the way of personal conversation until yesterday.

"You should have hung around."

Ana peered at those hazel eyes and said with complete conviction: "I couldn't—I had a meeting to get to. In fact, it's still going on right now. I should get back in there." She headed for the front door. She didn't wait for Bruce to go first. And she didn't look behind her this time.

* * *

Ana called Joe early that evening to share her news with him. When he answered, he sounded really happy to hear from her. Which made her happy. "Hey, I've got something to tell you," he said.

Joe's voice was so animated that Ana was a little worried. "What's going on? Everything okay?"

"Everything's fine, Ana. Guess what? I got a job offer."

This she did not expect. "A job offer? Really? Wait, like a freelance job?"

"No. Like a *job*-job."

"Oh my god. Is the *Independent* hiring you full-time? Did they get some funding somewhere?" She could hear her own voice accelerate and rise in pitch.

"No, it came out of nowhere. There was an ad, so I sent my résumé and clips and the guy called me back right away and offered me a job with a great salary, full bennies, profit sharing, the whole shebang."

She had never heard Joe use the word *bennies* before, unless he was making some reference to beatnik amphetamine use. Corporate officespeak (especially obsolete corporate officespeak) was a bit chilling coming out of his mouth. "So I guess it's not at the *Independent* then. They wouldn't give bennies if they were the last alternative paper on earth."

"It's not the *Independent*, Ana. It's the *Dollar Daily*."

Ana had to think for a moment. "You mean that little free thing that we get on our porch on Thursday and immediately throw away?" She could hear him sigh, even over the phone and across the country.

"Yeah. That's the one. But I guess they want to change their image, get a little hipper, more arts-oriented."

"A *little* hipper? *More* arts-oriented?"

"I know, I know."

"But there's nothing the least bit hip or arts-oriented about it."

"I know, Ana. It's a horrible little newspaper."

She knew she was not being appropriately supportive, but she just couldn't stop herself. "Joe, if you know that it's a horrible paper, why would you want to work there?"

Loud, shallow breath. "Because they're offering me a job, that's why." His tone was hard to read. Was it aggravated or piteous?

"I don't get it. Other places have offered you a job and you didn't take those."

"Those were like ten, thirteen years ago. No one's offered me a job in a long time."

"Aren't you going to be miserable?"

"I don't know. Maybe I will be, but I want to find out. I'm tired of freelance. I'm tired of constantly begging for jobs. I'm tired of self-starting. I'm tired of pitching stories. I'm tired of not getting paid shit for all the time I spend working on things. Fucking fifteen cents a word. It's horrible being poor all the time. I can't keep letting you pay for everything."

"Honey, I don't care about that."

"Thank you. I appreciate that, Ana—but yes, you do. You're just too nice to say anything about it. Usually. Unless you're mad at me. But I can tell it bugs you. Besides, I care. It bugs me. I hate always being reliant on you for everything."

This was not like her Joe. She couldn't believe what was coming out of his mouth. "Are you sure you want to do this? It really does sound like something that will make you unhappy."

"I'm unhappy now."

"You are?" She could hear him breathing.

"I'm sorry, but yeah, I am."

"Are you unhappy with me?" The words caught in her throat.

"Baby, I'm unhappy with everything."

"Me included?"

"I don't know, sometimes. But I'm mostly unhappy with *me*. I hate this. Maybe a change will help."

Ana let it sit there for a moment. "Okay then. You should take the job if that's what you want."

"I already have."

"Oh," she said. "Okay. Well then . . . great. Congratulations."

"Thanks."

Ana didn't tell him her news.

3

13

Full-Time Jobs and Other Petty Crimes

Who would have thought that a column called, "Rap Sheet" would turn out to be the favorite part of his job? As far as Joe was concerned, it was the one page of the paper actually devoted to something interesting. It wasn't a rundown of the new hip-hop releases, but a tally of the area's petty crimes for the week. Not that there were only petty crimes being committed—Ferndale did have the occasional drug bust or murder or knifing or robbery or carjacking, even some guy performing voluntary castrations on the kitchen table of his house. (After the procedure, at the very same table, the "surgeon" served pie to the new *castrato*. Amazing.)

"Rap Sheet," despite its tough-sounding name, was solely devoted to crimes of a small-time nature, committed mostly, it appeared, by extremely stupid citizens, which Joe surmised was why it was so much fun to write and read. An excellent example: Stupid citizen gets pulled over for suspicion of driving while intoxicated. Police officer asks for license and registration. Stupid citizen freaks out, tells officer, "Please don't look in my trunk!" thus giving said officer just cause to look in stupid citizen's trunk, thereby revealing a garbage bag full of hydroponic marijuana.

That was some good readin' right there.

Expanding the column and giving it a humorous edge that accentuated the stupidity of the criminals had so far been the only change Joe had been allowed to put into action for the past two months. And he hadn't really told Terrance that he'd done it. The rest of the paper was exactly as it had been when Joe started. "I just don't want to scare away our core audience" was what Terrance kept saying to Joe. "We'll implement changes a little at a time, and before they know it they'll be reading an alternative newspaper with real features about real issues." The "core audience" that Terrance kept talking about was, much to Joe's dismay, older, more conservative people who lived in the metropolitan Detroit area. (Shortly after starting, Joe discovered that the *Dollar Daily*, while headquartered in Ferndale, was distributed in various editions to most of the suburbs surrounding Detroit. This was also one of the reasons for the sizable income generated by the paper.) According to Terrance, these masses frowned upon (in roughly this order): minorities, homosexuals, liberals, artists, musicians, peaceniks, hipsters, tree huggers, pinkos, and younger people in general. In Ferndale, the core audience was a small but vocal group of holdovers who had lived there when the storefronts were deserted and the area was a trashy DMZ between Detroit and its suburbs, but at least all the faces were pale. That, in Joe's opinion, was their precious "core audience."

Meanwhile, Joe was writing articles like: "Good Neighbor Awards!" or "Senior Citizen Update!" or "Kickball Comes to Town!" All of the headlines reflected Terrance's undying devotion to the exclamation point, which he lovingly referred to as "a slam." Every time Joe mentioned an idea of his for the paper—say, a short piece on the new

LGBT community center, or even the upcoming Chin Tiki night at the Midlands—Terrance would say something like, "That's great. Hang onto that for the idea file," or, "Let's put a pin in that one." Joe's idea file was rapidly growing, but not as fast as his overall sense of dissatisfaction. Tack that onto the fact that he hardly ever saw Ana anymore, since she was so busy with her new position—always working nights, weekends, holidays. When they talked, it was either on the phone or just before bed. Ana would be completely wired at eleven p.m., full of chatter about some exciting project she was working on; meanwhile, he was dozing off, aching for the sweet escape of slumber. Joe wasn't working as many hours as her, but after years of freelance, he was completely unaccustomed to standard workdays and the relentless tedium of nine-to-five. Or nine-to-nine, depending on how close they were to press time. He only complained about the hours once, but there was no sympathy forthcoming from Ana.

"Welcome to the working world, Joseph," she said, a gleeful edge of derision in her voice. "Try to remember that most people work way harder than either of us for far less money. We're lucky."

"You're right," he said, thinking of his grandfather working for Cadillac in the thirties, his father on the line at the Chrysler Jefferson Assembly Plant, grabbing every hour of overtime he could to help pay for Joe's college. "Duly noted."

Then she started laughing at him. "Look at you. You're like a delicate hothouse orchid suddenly exposed to the elements. Your little petals are shivering."

"All right," he said. "Now you're just being mean."

Unfortunately, that was probably closer to the truth than he cared to admit.

In some ways, Ana seemed happier than he had seen her in years. He knew that she and Adrienne had always wanted something like this, to have a little more control over their work and their destinies. It meant a lot to her that they were doing work that was directed toward women.

"Bruce says that we just need to win two new business pitches this year and the company will feel like this whole idea of marketing to women is justified." She had probably told him this four or five times already. Joe would just nod and smile supportively. After living together for this long, he had learned that Ana didn't want to hear his opinions or his advice when she was venting about work. She just wanted him to listen. So he listened. He was, however, getting a little tired of hearing about Bruce. Years back, Ana had filled him in about Bruce Kellner, telling him about how all the women at the agency adore him, how clients love him and all that. Joe had met him once at an agency holiday party where spouses were invited, and another time at the Midlands. As much as Joe had wanted to hate the guy, he actually couldn't. (He may have done shots with Bruce, now that he thought about it.)

But what had changed the most was their financial situation. They were abruptly and quite amazingly flush. It was *sooo* nice to have some money for a change, to pay for his full half of the bills, go to whatever shows he wanted (he was still getting free review copies of CDs and DVDs too, which he happily hocked), lunches or dinners on those rare occasions when he did see Ana, even pick up some brand-new clothes (he hadn't shopped at a thrift store for months) or whatever else he needed without worrying about it.

For the first time in his adult life, Joe was stable financially. It was a peculiar sensation. Still, after a couple of months of giving his job a chance, he was officially starting to hate it. Not working itself, but The Job. Yet until another job appeared, he wasn't going to give up on this one. And with the way things were going around town, it didn't look like another one was coming along anytime in the near future.

The day that the *Dollar Daily* called Joe and he realized that he did indeed want a real full-time job, he had gone down to the offices of the *Detroit Independent* and officially lobbied the managing editor, Tim Shudlich, for one. Just to see if there was any chance he could go full-time there.

Once Tim stopped laughing, he filled Joe in on the realities of the situation. "I don't know what to tell you, man," he had said, taking a long pull on an American Spirit menthol and blowing the smoke in the general direction of the closed window. "We love your work, but I can't offer you shit. There's only one person in editorial with a full-time position and that's amazing in itself. I fear they're trying to figure out how they can get freelancers to do *my* job."

"So there's nothing?"

Another deep drag on the cig. "Joe, this is an alternative newspaper. Part of 'alternative' refers to finding alternatives to actually paying people money."

Joe sighed. "Really? I thought it referred to an alternative to the giant corporate newspapers that were the propaganda tools for the military-industrial complex and the evil establishment conglomerates."

Tim leaned back in his chair, hand splayed across his chest as if to somehow contain his silent laughter. "Oh, Joe, Joe, Joe. How quaintly amusing of you. That is just adorable. What do you think this is? The nineties?" He then gazed up at the ceiling and smiled wistfully. "Ah, the nineties. *La belle époque.*" He sighed, then crushed out his smoke in an overflowing Reddy Kilowatt vintage ashtray. "Perhaps you'd like to broach this distressing theory of yours with the giant conglomerate that now owns the *Independent*. Of course, *they're* not evil." Tim held up a blue plastic bucket next to his desk that looked like something Joe once used to bus tables at Big Boy. It was filled with wadded fast-food wrappers and pop bottles. "Look at this. See? Recycling. They're *green*."

"If by green you mean profitable, I see what you're saying."

Tim shrugged. "Hey, conserving the environment, conserving profits, what's the difference?"

Joe stood up. "So the only tools around here are us? For putting up with this shit?"

Tim touched the tip of his nose. "*Ding, ding, ding.* We have a winner."

On the drive home, Joe had called Terrance Blankenship and signed on with the *Dollar Daily*.

Joe had long since finished up his assignments for the *Independent*, though he continued to think about writing a piece for *The Paris of the Midwest Is Crumbling* when he had a chance. At first, it seemed like the kind of thing that would have been perfect for the new and improved *Dollar Daily*. When he pitched the story, it was enthusiastically considered until Terrance realized that it involved an illegal activity, and then it was immediately relegated to the black hole of the idea file.

Joe wasn't giving up so easily though. There was something about it that fascinated him, enough to make him think that there was there was a big story there. He'd e-mailed Brendan Sanderson, the blogger-in-charge, a couple of times, to see if he could call to ask him some questions about urban exploration. Even though Joe wasn't sure if he'd ever get around to writing the piece, he still wanted to talk to the guy.

When they finally spoke on the phone, Brendan actually turned out to be pretty cool. Though Joe couldn't quite get a bead on him. He was like some curious hybrid—archaeologist/anthropologist/profane philosopher/hip-hop beatnik. Still, he was willing to be interviewed.

"What are you most likely to find while urban exploring?" Joe asked.

He could hear Brendan on the other end of the line tapping a pencil. The tapping stopped, replaced by a plosive throat sound that led him to believe that Brendan did not approve of his question.

"Motherfucker, don't even call it that," the guy said bitterly. "These days, every twenty-year-old art student going into an abandoned building with a digital camera is an 'urban explorer.' Putting it on the Internet, creating more ruin porn, perpetuating the media hatefest on Detroit. Fuck that shit." Pause. "Sorry. What was your question?"

Joe was taken aback, but he trudged onward. "What are you likely to find?"

"Does rubble count?" said Brendan, calm now after considering the question. "Because if it does, it would be rubble. Or dust. Or debris. Or broken glass or crumbled plaster, all of which I suppose are forms of rubble."

Joe laughed because he thought Brendan meant it as a joke.

"Why are you laughing?" Pencil tap.

"I just . . . I thought you meant that to be funny."

"Tramping around in abandoned buildings is a lot of things, but funny ain't one of them."

"I'm sorry."

"Unless, of course, one of the people you're with slips on a big steaming pile of hobo poop."

Joe again thought that Brendan might be kidding. "Can I laugh at that?"

"How can you not? I'm just messing with you, dude. There's not that much hobo poop anyway, and most of it is like coprolited Tootsie Roll."

Joe was glad that Brendan felt comfortable enough to mess with him, but he wanted to find out more. "What are you trying to do with your photography?"

"I'm trying to give these buildings back some of their fucking dignity, son. When you step into these places, you can feel their sickness. It's like walking into the first circle of hell. They are dying, yo. These were important places for Detroiters in their time, and now we have turned our backs on them. This shit needs to be seen. And if it takes a little illegal trespassing, so fucking be it."

Joe liked the fact that Brendan took his website so seriously, like it was a mission. When he asked Brendan about the interior graffiti art, he wound up listening to the man wax enthusiastic for three minutes straight.

"You'd be surprised at how incredible some of it is. I mean, there's endless gang tags—most of them boring—but the old buildings do seem to attract the real artists. The United Artists Theatre? A few years ago, every window was covered with art. You remember that place?"

"I think I do," said Joe. He wasn't sure.

"Come on. Fuckin' *suburbanite*."

Joe hadn't heard that word spoken with such ire in a long time. And how did he know?

"It's a C. Howard Crane theater. Twenties? With a big out-of-character fifties streamline marquee?"

Then Joe did remember. "Yeah! I do know that place. Was there like a crazy Googie ripple canopy right by where the ticket booth used to be?"

"That's the one. Shit was awesome. Artists had taken it over, bombing the fuck out of the place. Throwing up pieces everywhere. Not tags either, but art. Some of it like Botero or Miró. Mayan hieroglyphics. When you stood about a half a block away and looked at the whole thing with the windows all full of color, it was like a skyscraper of stained glass. Shit was *sick*."

"That sounds incredible."

"That ain't the whole story." Joe heard the pencil start tapping again. "You really interested in this?" Brendan said, suddenly agitated. "'Cause if you aren't, you shouldn't be wasting my time. If you are, you need to come with me and experience it."

Huh? "I do?"

"Yup. I think maybe you'd get it. There's a horrible beauty to it all that not everyone understands. A kind of freaky elegant crumbling quietude. A friend of mine, a prof over at Wayne State, calls it the 'verity of decay.'"

"What does that mean?"

"I can tell you, but I'm not going to. If you want to understand, you've got to see it. Believe me, I don't ask too many people to do a ride-along."

"I'm flattered."

"So you in?"

"Okay." Although Joe was perversely fascinated by the whole idea of exploring an abandoned building, he wasn't so sure he actually wanted to do it. There was something about it that sounded too real, too scary. This might have been a little more Detroit than even he was willing to experience. Maybe he was turning into a scared suburbanite. Anyway, it's not like he had the time to devote to a bizarre and dangerous-sounding new hobby. He was too busy writing articles about the new Coffee Beanery that had moved into town, working very hard to put Café Limbus out of business. Score one more for The Man.

Oh, wait. Right. That was him now.

14

The Mythos of the Broken Hipster

It had been different being around Joe during his first few months of gainful employment. It was certainly different in the mornings, with both of them rushing around trying to get ready for work at roughly the same time. If they were lucky, they just had enough time to sit down and have breakfast together. That part was nice. They had even started experimenting with healthy cereals from Trader Joe's, which tended to get new names after a couple of days.

"You want a bowl of Honey Clusterfucks?" Joe would call up to Ana while she was getting dressed. Their other favorites included Frosted Hemp Wads and Count Carobula.

Though lately she'd also been seeing more of Joe's curmudgeon-y side. He'd definitely become grouchier, prone to go off on a rant at any given moment. She'd noticed that his rants often had to do with some form of punctuation. The first one came after seeing a sign behind Rite Aid that said: *It is illegal to dump "trash" in this dumpster.*

"What the hell does that mean?" Joe said, shaking his head. "Why would anyone put quotes around *trash*? It makes no sense. Are they being ironic?" He curled his index and middle fingers into air quotes. "No 'trash,' please. I mean, who does this? It's the work of crazy people."

Yet it was nothing compared to his latest rant, which he referred to as "the overapostrophization of America." It had obviously been brewing for a while.

"Did you see that?" he said to her one night in the car, after they passed a billboard for some local slip-and-fall ambulance chaser. "There were like fifteen apostrophes on that billboard, not one of them used correctly. What is the fucking deal? Why is everyone apostrophizing so much now? Any time a word is plural, someone adds an apostrophe to it!" His voice got all stammery and sputtery, and both his hands left the steering wheel so he could beseech the syntax gods. "What the fuck! They're on signs, menus, newspapers, store windows—everyone's apostrophe crazy! It's like, *I better put an apostrophe here just to be on the safe side.* Unless it's a contraction—where you *need* an apostrophe—then there's nothing! Christ on a bike, what the fuck is wrong with everyone?" Then he turned to Ana. She was trying very hard not to laugh, so she didn't say anything. "What?"

"Nothing."

"Glad you find me so amusing," he said, glaring at her as if she were gratuitous punctuation.

Yes, it was different.

Then there was the matter of Bruce. She and Adrienne had been working even closer with him since LA. This was also different. She had known that creative directors were, well, *special.* She had figured that one out early in her advertising career. They were equal parts confidence, intelligence, imperial comportment, good looks, wit, perspicacity, attention deficit disorder, and neediness, mixed with an authoritatively low-pitched voice and a healthy dollop of bullshit. (And despite the awesome Mary Wells Lawrences, Jane Maases, and Caroline Joneses of the world, it was almost always a man, more proof of advertising's silent and subtle sexism promulgated by the patriarchy and executives too shrewd to expose their true selves to the world, and most certainly to human resources.)

What was a surprise to Ana was that one of these questionable creatures was, for the first time, interesting to her. Since she and Adrienne got promoted, she had noticed small things—glances, lean-ins with inhalations when he needed to look at Ana's work, laughing a bit too heartily at her jokes, even the occasional hand on the shoulder.

Ana attributed this minor fascination to the fact that she and Adrienne spent so much time at work. They were there every night, at least until eight, sometimes later, and usually one day of every weekend, often both. They had known it would be like this at the beginning while they were trying to establish the department and, most importantly, trying to win new business for it. So far, they'd participated in three new business pitches: one for a midsize shoe warehouse chain, the second for a P&G fabric softener, the last for a women's energy drink, a disgusting concoction called Grrlpowrr! (The label: *Suppresses Appetite! Inhibits Fat!* After chugging a can, Adrienne had shivered and said, "I feel so stabby.") They had ended up in the final two twice, but had won neither of them. The energy drink folks had loved their presentation, told them they were a shoo-in, but at the eleventh hour, the company president gave the advertising manager the mandate that they were going with the other shop. They had heard later that he didn't want to have to come to "that shit stain of a city" to meet with his ad agency. Lovely.

At least she and Adrienne were overseeing one account that the agency already had, a Michigan-based manufacturer of vacuums, spot cleaners, and deep-cleansing systems. (Client-suggested headline: *Get Mom what she really wants for the holidays!* Cut to Ana and Adrienne sighing deeply.) Despite the utter obviousness of it, they were still happy to have the account. Both Ana and Adrienne were starting to get the feeling that if they didn't acquire some new clients for W2W, they probably wouldn't be going back to work as a regular art director and copywriter team. They would instead just be canned, for they were now senior vice president associate creative directors (SVP ACDs) with accordingly inflated salaries. As Adrienne put it: "Our firm, shapely asses are now officially on the line."

Ana also couldn't help but think that perhaps her little infatuation with Bruce had something to do with her now being officially in her forties. Happily, her actual birthday had come and gone with zero fanfare—she had made sure of that. She and Joe had stayed in and made coq au vin and opened a really good bottle of wine. After that, they had sex for the first time in about three and a half months. It was semisuccessful. She didn't officially have an orgasm, but she was so happy to have broken the curse of no sex that she didn't actually care. Still, just the fact that they had gotten as far as they did meant it was one less thing she had to worry about. In the middle of it, feeling so good and feeling so close to each other, they said what they always said to each other these days:

Ana: Oh my god, we're actually having sex.

Joe: I know. It's like a Christmas miracle.

Ana: Why don't we do this more often?

Joe: I don't know. Why don't we? What's wrong with us?

Ana: We're too tightly wound. It's so much work for us to just get to this point.

Joe: Why is this so difficult? Why do we think so much?

Why can't we just be like everyone else and just fuck? Would that be so wrong?

Ana: No it would not. I love you.

Joe: I love you too.

And they fucked until Joe came and she didn't. Normally, she would have asked for some manual assistance in that department, but it just didn't seem to matter to her that night. She was just happy to have had sex and to have the much-dreaded birthday behind her. Afterward, she tried to forget that the closest she came to coming was when an image of Bruce popped into her head. She let it stay for a moment or two, then banished it after deciding that it was a bad idea. After that, though, there wasn't much hope for an orgasm.

After eight and a half weeks of intense work for her and Joe (and, of course, no sex), he had his birthday as well. They were born roughly two months apart, both delivered at the same hospital. This fact had always made Ana strangely happy. On his birthday, they had a quiet evening of beers and burgers over at the Midlands, where they ran into Chick, who knew it was Joe's birthday.

"Well, well, well," said Chick, nodding and smirking, "if it isn't my favorite two forty-year-olds."

Joe sighed. "I really should never tell you anything."

Chick grinned at this. "No, you really shouldn't. Thankfully, you never seem to learn." He raised his hand. "Hi, Ana. How are you?"

"Hi, Chick. You just stop by to harass Joe on his birthday?" She quietly placed her hand on Joe's thigh and gave it a squeeze under the table.

"Actually, I'm supposed to meet a young woman at the bar."

Joe brightened at the mention of this. "Another one of your Match.com hussies?" He leaned back in his seat, placed his hand over Ana's on his leg. "Sure she's old enough to enter a bar? Probably good that you're meeting in public—wouldn't want to get caught up in some child-predator sting operation."

Ana chimed in: "We just saw a drag queen head into the men's room. Maybe that was her."

Chick suppressed a smile and lowered his head as if saddened by this exchange. "Oh, okay. That's the way it's going to be, huh? I come over to offer a friendly greeting and you both viciously attack me."

Joe shrugged. "You attacked first. Called us your forty-year-old friends."

"You *are* my forty-year-old friends. What am I supposed to say?"

"A simple hello would suffice."

"Ah, of course. A return to civility. Isn't that what all you oldsters want? Fine then," he said, doffing an imaginary chapeau. "I bid you both good day. You two enjoy your early-bird special." Chick started to head back toward the bar. "I'll see you broken hipsters later."

Broken hipsters. That was the part that got to Ana. She was used to Chick and Joe giving each other shit, but that expression caught her off guard. Was it the subtle reference to osteoporosis, which she was now officially starting to fret about? It certainly wasn't because she thought of herself as a hipster. She wasn't even sure what a hipster was these days, other than the poseurs who swanned around various neighborhoods of Brooklyn, with their tribal body modifications and trust funds, their oversize eyewear and undersize pantwear, who had turned the term into an insult. Even when she had been clearer on the concept, she'd rarely been called one. The last time was at her twenty-year high school reunion. Sarah Kettering, a former fellow band nerd turned roundish smug hockey mom, living far, far away from scary Detroit, with four kids and a sensible midsize husband. When Sarah called Ana a hipster, it too was used as an insult. ("How dare you not live a life exactly like mine?" was what Ana heard.) Compared to Sarah, Ana actually did feel like a hipster.

Then there were people who thought everyone who worked in the creative department was a hipster of some sort. Yes, sometimes it seemed as though Ana was constantly surrounded by good-looking young'uns with art-directed tattoos and ironic facial hair, who spent a lot of money on hair product and the aforementioned vintage hair metal T-shirts and meticulously shrunk, artfully wrinkled clothes from Urban Outfitters, designed to make the wearers look like they'd just crawled out of a multipartnered bed. (But was she any different, with her retro-yet-expensive versions of the thrift store frocks that she used to wear? Why did everyone want to look like a worn and rumpled version of themselves?) Of course, they weren't the only people in a Detroit creative department. There were also smelly record store loners who name-checked insanely obscure bands, former high school jocks who'd fervidly hid their artistic tendencies, compulsively complimenting bipolar tantrum queens, hallway-roving rumormongers, mechanic gays who loved cars as much as any GM retiree, Mensa-level cubicle hoarders, bookish roller derby girls, deer hunters whose fathers questioned their sissy profession, earth/soccer hybrid moms, as well as people who look so normal you're sure that they'll be the ones to come in and shoot up the place on the day they get laid off. There were all these and much, much more.

Because it's difficult to peg oneself as a workplace cultural stereotype, Ana had never really figured out her own category. (Passively competitive childfree quasi feminist?) At her advanced (for advertising) age, did it really even matter? Yet "broken hipster" sort of fit, at least for her and Joe. And maybe for a lot of the people they knew, who were getting older and still figuring out what to do with that information.

The people she worked with were now almost all younger than her. When she spoke to people in their twenties, they were always up on the latest music, games, videos, websites, social networking, etc. Ana kept up fairly well, but it was starting to feel like a lot of work. Everything changed so quickly and so often. And now the kids were suddenly antitechnology—cameras with film, monaural record players, gearless bicycles, typewriter parties. What was next? Return of the telegraph? Were the handlebar mustaches going to be tapping out Morse code while they waited the half hour for their pour-over coffees? And, damn it, why did it look like they were having so much fun doing it all?

Yes, these were exactly the sorts of things that a broken hipster would say.

Later, when she mentioned the expression to Adrienne over lunch in her office, her friend had just smiled. "It is kind of funny, but you're not that old. No one here thinks you're forty, so you're not."

Ana was leaning against the front of Adrienne's desk. She dipped a small chunk of romaine lettuce into low-fat ranch dressing and squinted quizzically at Adrienne, before shoving the piece into her mouth.

"Yeah, but . . . I *am* forty," she said after she finished chewing.

Adrienne stared at her like she was out of her mind. "Might I remind you that we are employed in advertising, where perception is reality? You don't look forty, thus you aren't forty."

"Except for the fact that I am actually forty years of age."

Adrienne set the turkey sandwich she was eating on top of the latest *Lürzer's Archive*. "Please stop saying that so loud. I don't want to have a forty-year-old partner. It doesn't reflect well on me."

Ana leveled her spork at Adrienne, a carrot shred on one of the tines. "Look, I'm not going to go around advertising my age, but I hope you're not suggesting that I lie about it. That is not cool."

Adrienne sighed. "Pushkin said that the illusion that exalts us is dearer to us than ten thousand truths."

"Pushkin? Really? You're quoting Pushkin to me now?"

"What? I was an English major, you know. I've read books. I still occasionally read them when I'm not here exalting the grandeur of carpet steamers. And stop pointing that fucking spork like you're planning to shiv me in the yard."

Ana lowered the offending implement. "You really think youth matters that much around here?"

"Of course it does. You know this business—it's all about youth. The newest. The latest. It's always been that way."

"We're not the newest and the latest anymore, Adrienne."

"I'm aware of that, lady. We haven't been for quite some time. Still, you needn't go around reminding everyone of it. Truth, like light, blinds. Falsehood, on the contrary, is a beautiful twilight that enhances every object."

"Stop making things up."

"Tell that to Camus. He's the one who believes that lying is glorious, like a magic-hour sunset where you get all the best footage. Or tell Bruce, who just walked in and is currently standing right over your shoulder."

Ana rolled her eyes. "Fuck you."

"No, really. Hi, Bruce."

Ana turned around. Bruce was indeed standing there right behind her. He had on a fairly tight (but not *too* tight) black T-shirt, with jeans and laceless black Chuck Taylors, the expensive designer version of what the Ramones wore.

"What is it you need to tell me?"

Ana couldn't think of anything to say.

"Ana is late with layouts for Fanning," said Adrienne, rescuing her.

Bruce looked disappointed. "Oh. Is that due? No one's talked to me about it. I think we got an extension anyway." He brushed behind Ana. She could smell that expensive spicy scent again. "Can I talk to you two about something?"

"Sure, Bruce. Of course," said Adrienne. "What's up?"

Bruce settled into the chair next to Ana. His knee touched hers at first, so she pulled back ever so slowly. It was one of the rare days that she was wearing a skirt and it wasn't a long one. She had noticed her tastes in clothes seemed to be running more along the shorter, tighter, sluttier lines of what the kids were wearing currently. *The birthday, you know.*

Bruce glanced briefly at Ana's legs. "We've got a new business pitch coming up."

Ana felt a tautness in her chest. This was never going to end. They were just going to be working nonstop for the rest of their lives. She would die one of those sad, cautionary deaths that teach others to live each day to the fullest, and that on your deathbed, you're not going to wish you had worked more.

"It's for an company that's got a lot of money and that wants to market to women. Only to women, actually."

Adrienne leaned forward, obviously much more interested in the possibility of yet another new business pitch than Ana. "What is it? Packaged goods? Health? Beauty? Come on, spill."

Bruce placed his hand on his chin, a couple of fingers twisting his lips. "It's actually more of an organization. It's called WomanLyfe."

Ana watched Adrienne bite her lip, then frown. "Sounds crunchy. Is it some sort of hairy-armpit, woman-spelled-with-a-*y* company?"

"Those people don't have any money," said Bruce. "No, *woman* is definitely spelled with an *a*. Actually, it's *life* that's spelled with a *y*."

"Weird."

"You know, copyright. They can own it better if it's misspelled."

The name WomanLyfe ticked some subtle recognition in Ana's head. She couldn't help a slight sneer. "Why do I think it's like an Avon or Mary Kay thing, where women pimp each other out to sell stuff to other women?"

"You mean like what *we're* doing?" said Adrienne.

Ana squinted at her. "But different."

Bruce shook his head. "It's actually more of a wellness center, like a fitness club."

"That sounds cool," said Adrienne, turning to Ana, her brows raised. "That sounds perfect for us."

"It's also kind of a resource center for women," continued Bruce. "A place for them to go for information, for counseling, for guidance."

Ana felt the tightness in her chest increase fivefold. "Oh no. WomanLyfe? It's not that crazy Christian health club, the ones that are all antiabortion? It's not that one, is it?"

Bruce took a long breath through clenched teeth. "Actually, I believe they prefer to think of themselves as pro-child."

"Why is the agency getting involved with something like this? It's crazy."

Another breath, then Bruce's shoulders dropped slightly. "It appears that our esteemed chairman is married to someone adamantly committed to the company as well as the cause."

"What cause?" said Ana, her voice rising. "Bombing abortion clinics?"

"The biggest political hot potato in America," said Adrienne, putting both elbows on her desk, then nesting her face in her hands. "What are we supposed to show? Happy, smiling nonaborted children working out?"

Ana joined in: "And the joy they bring to poor, unemployed women who can't even feed themselves?"

Adrienne put on her best schmaltzy announcer voice. "*WomanLyfe. It's spelled with a y because there's no room for I in your life.*"

"There's our tagline," said Ana.

Bruce held up a hand. "Okay, enough, my little bleeding hearts." He looked as stern as Ana had ever seen him. "First, no more of that kind of talk. It will get you fired. Not by me, but by other folks who are close to those in charge around here and whom you don't know are listening. Second, we're going to work on it whether we like it or not. And thirdly, it's not really a new business pitch at all. We've got the business. I just thought it would go down easier if I couched it in that manner. A new business pitch that we don't have to pitch."

"Well, fuck me," said Ana.

"Ack," said Adrienne.

Bruce peered at her, then continued: "There's nothing we can do about it, you guys. It just happened."

Ana tipped her head to one side, her spirit collapsed. "Bruce, we're an ad agency," she said. She didn't even care that she was whining. "Ad agencies are notoriously liberal. How can this be?"

Bruce regarded her as if she were a child. "No, Ana. The people who *work* in creative departments are notoriously liberal. Ad agencies themselves are notoriously self-serving. And the people who run them are notoriously greedy."

Adrienne slumped forward till her face was resting on her desk, then started singing in a snarky falsetto, "*I believe the children are our future. Teach them well and let them lead the way—*" She stopped. "It's always about the children."

"Adrienne, hush." As soon as Ana said it, she regretted it.

Adrienne gave her a piercing *what the fuck?* glare. "Hey, lady, need I remind you that I picked up all that shit from you? You're the one who's always ranting about how any time these bullshit organizations want something, they just say, *It's for the children.*"

Bruce stood up. "All right. Both of you, knock it off. There's nothing to talk about. It's done. Fait accompli."

Ana, not wanting him to brush by her again, stood up as well. Together, they moved toward the doorway of Adrienne's office.

"Look, I know you're upset, but I wish you could see this for what it is: a chance to work and get some much-needed money for the division. Okay?"

Ana stared at Bruce, half pouting, half pissed. "I'm sorry, Bruce," she said. "You can make us do this, but you can't make us happy about it."

He did not look pleased.

15

Cool in Europe and the Tao of Funny

Joe's parents were so very proud of his new job writing for a real newspaper. *Joe's got a real full-time job! It's about time!* He knew too that Ana's folks were beaming as well over her new senior vice president associate creative director position and its accompanying raise in pay and status. (He had a sneaking suspicion that both were also saying: *Now if they would only get married, buy a house, and start a family, everything would be fine.*)

Despite their successes, they were both miserable. He knew Ana was discreetly looking for another job, but there were none to be had. It seemed to Joe that every decade Detroit went through another of its economic slumps as dictated by the vicissitudes of the auto industry. This was the worst one ever, and they both knew a lot of people who had just been laid off. All anyone said to either of them was, "You should be happy you even have a job."

The thing was, Ana and he *were* both happy to have jobs. There it was again: that old Detroit factory worker ethic, the one that pervaded every aspect of life in the area. You didn't just quit your job because it was making you unhappy; you sucked it up and ground it out. After all, you had responsibilities—families, mortgages, car notes. (The latest model of whatever you built was parked in the driveway.) Certainly there were casualties: people drank, beat their spouses, ignored their children, or just silently suppressed all their rage at the systems (both corporate and societal) that voluntarily indentured them to a physically fatiguing, mind-numbing, spirit-crushing but well-paying union job. They shoved it deep down into a tiny dark cubbyhole inside of their hearts, until those organs eventually ruptured, often shortly (and ironically) after retirement. There were generations of stories like this. It was what people did in a low-self-esteem city like Detroit.

Now even Joe felt it, perhaps more strongly because of his years of low-paying freelance work and his surprising reluctance to go back to it. Joe, the so-called sensitive boy of his family, whose father had told him that he was going to college no matter what, that "no son of mine is going to work in a factory." When a Detroit factory worker father said that to a son, it meant something. Joe had listened to his father. Apparently, he had listened too well, for he never bothered to get a full-time job anywhere until now. (Was it a coincidence that he had never bothered to get the wife, kids, or mortgage either?)

Despite how much Joe hated working for the *Dollar Daily*, now that he had this full-time job, like Ana, he didn't want to lose it. (Even though Terrance still wouldn't change the name, not to a typical alternative newspaper moniker, or even to the eminently more appropriate *Dollar Weekly*.) It was like his long-dead maternal grandfather who worked in chrome plating at the old Cadillac plant on Clark Street all his life was somehow telepathically communicating (complete with thick Armenian accent) with Joe from the grave. *Joey, don't you quit that job. You got a good job, you stick at it, you hear me? And don't take drugs.* Hell, he could barely remember what his grandfather sounded like. The guy died when Joe was twelve, so why was he hounding him from the grave? The funny thing was, Joe's grandpa used to tell him stories about how when they wanted to take a break, they would throw the wrong part in the chroming machine. The machine would break down and they could take a breather until it got fixed. (Thus revealing a lesser-known codicil in the Detroit Worker Ethic: just because you should never quit your job didn't mean you had to work all that hard at it. At one point, even GM, Ford, and Chrysler decided that it wasn't mandatory to work that hard to build something of quality, e.g., the rustifying, self-deconstructing, planned-obsolescence cars of his seventies childhood—the Vegas, the Pintos, the Gremlins, with their tinfoil-like sheet metal, built to dissolve. Those cars would be physical proof of this codicil if any of them were still in one piece. They certainly weren't in Michigan, not with its five-month-long, salt-strewn winters.)

And it wasn't just the Detroit economy, since even Chick, who'd had a long, lucrative streak of optioned and unproduced scripts, had not sold anything in quite some time.

"They're killing me out there, Keen," said Chick, one night at the Midlands. "Those LA motherfuckers. I keep getting pulled in to pitch jobs. I work on them for a month, like an idiot, because I can't help myself. Then they just choose some local hack to do it."

Joe was accustomed to this from Chick because he much preferred to talk about his failures rather than his many successes (more local modesty), but he had never heard the guy so down.

"I'm doing treatments for animated features and they

keep telling me that my ideas are too adult, too smart." Chick shook his head. "No they're not. You've heard my ideas—they're infantile."

"Quit it. They're not infantile at all. They're just populist." Joe had said this to cheer Chick up. Since Chick liked to regard Joe as some sort of nose-in-a-book egghead, he occasionally liked to actually play the role. "You have your finger on the pulse of popular culture. You're tapped into the trailer-park zeitgeist, Chick. You're Joe Six-Pack."

Chick held up a hand. "Stop it. You're just being nice."

"Seriously, though. You think it's because you live here, instead of LA?"

"Maybe. I don't know. It used to not be a problem that I was here. In fact, I think it kind of gave me, uh—"

"What? Like a kind of cachet?"

Chick shook his head. "No, not quite. Almost like street cred."

Joe leaned back and nodded knowingly. "Okay, right. You were the badass guy from Detroit."

"Exactly. It was cool that I was from this place that the rest of the world didn't give a shit about. Detroit was so far off the radar, it was kind of cool."

"I hear you. So bad that it was good."

"Yes!" said Chick, poking a finger into Joe's arm.

"We're cool in Europe for some of the same reasons. We're like a different universe to them. Despite being messed up, they think it's beautiful in some inexplicable dadaist way. It's like they believe that Detroit possesses some majestic authenticity."

Creases formed in Chick's forehead as he waited for Joe to stop talking. "You done theorizing, professor? 'Cause I'm spilling my guts here."

"Sorry. So what happened?"

"I don't know." Chick exhaled, let his hands drop onto the bar. "Yes, I do. They just got bored. They just moved on to the next guy that's got a little heat."

"So now the badass from Detroit is just the dope who should be in LA?"

"Exactly." Chick drained his pint glass and focused on the polished concrete of the bar. "I don't know. I just want to write something really funny and get it out there, get it made. Then be done with the whole business."

"Really?"

"Yeah—" Chick stopped speaking as the guitar intro of a Detroit Cobras tune blasted way too loudly through the jukebox. Someone behind the bar turned down the volume a few notches and Chick continued talking. "I don't care if it's animated or whatever. I wouldn't even care if it were dumb humor. Actually, I'd love something that parents could laugh at with their kids. That would be great. I just want it to be *funny*."

Joe could tell that his friend was being serious. He was not usually this forthright. "Why does it matter so much to be funny?"

Chick shrugged slightly. "I don't know. I just think something that's really, truly funny is pure. Laughing is an involuntary response. It takes you out of yourself. You stop thinking. You can try to write something for the ages, but funny *is* for the ages. I mean, you can acquire all this wisdom about life, yet ultimately what else is there to do but laugh about it? Funny means something."

"I think I understand."

"God is in the punch lines, my friend."

"The Tao of Funny," said Joe. "Wow, listen to you— Earnest Chick."

"Ugh, now you've ruined it."

"How? What's wrong? It's good. I like Earnest Chick."

"Don't call me that." Chick shivered for a moment, as if a demon spirit had just entered his body. "And stop being all touchy-feely."

Joe had to laugh at the abrupt reappearance of Chick Classic.

"Forget everything I said," said Chick. He rubbed his hands together. "New subject: how's Ana and the pro-life Nazis?"

"Dude, I don't even think *she* refers to them that way."

Chick made a face. "You're forty years old, man. Don't say *dude*. What are you, trying to seem 'hep'?"

Joe sighed. "She's not really happy at her job, as far as I can tell, but I really don't know because I never see her. She's always working."

Malcolm walked up to the bar just then. He was wearing a green leather motorcycle-style jacket over a T-shirt with a raven on it. "Hey, you guys."

"I don't know about that jacket," said Chick.

Malcolm's expression grew serious. "I guess I better get rid of it then, if you're not sure about it." He caught the bartender's eye, held up three fingers to indicate a round of Two Hearteds for all of them.

"I'm going to hit the head," said Chick, starting to walk away. "I don't want to see that jacket when I get back!" he yelled over his shoulder.

Malcolm turned to Joe and moved slightly closer to him. "Hey, I wanted to talk to you about something. I'm sure it's nothing, but there's a strange vibe around work lately."

"What do you mean?"

"About Ana and Adrienne."

"Really? What's up?"

"I've just been hearing . . . things. People think they're getting preferential treatment from Bruce. A couple people have mentioned it. I'm not sure everyone knows that we're all friends. Anyway, I kind of get the feeling they think Adrienne is hooking up with Bruce."

"Shit. Really?"

"Yeah, it's totally fucked up." Malcolm took a breath. He looked genuinely distressed. "I feel funny about it. I'm not sure what to do."

Joe nodded. "Yeah, I see what you mean."

Chick returned to his stool and said: "Man, is there anything in the world more satisfying than peeing on ice cubes? I don't think so." He looked at the two of them suspiciously. "What's up? What are you hens talking about?"

Malcolm spoke up: "It's me. I just really like this jacket. Joe suggested that I ask you for a reprieve."

Chick made a show of deliberating. "Fine, but you have to call me before you wear it again." He glanced up at the sole TV screen in the bar. "Anyone catch the Tigers score? I think there was a day game today." He was met with empty stares from Joe and Malcolm. Chick exhaled loudly. "Oh, right. I forgot who I was with."

"Sorry," said Joe. "We'll try to be more manly in the future."

"Maybe we should get testosterone injections," said Malcolm.

Chick shook his head. "I'm hanging with eunuchs when I should be out chasing tail. Christ, would you look at *that* down at the end of the bar? She's killing me."

"You should talk to her. I'm sure she'd love being referred to as *tail*," said Malcolm.

Todd walked up and nodded to everyone. "Lads," he said. The bartender with the lower-back tattoo sauntered over. "Could I get a Guinness, please?"

Chick stared as she left to pour the stout. "Todd, did *you* see the game?"

Turning back to the group, Todd simultaneously scratched and smoothed the patch of long hair under his lip. "If you mean European football, I did indeed."

"Oh, for fuck's sake."

"Todd loves his Man U," said Joe, smiling at Todd, who was obviously torturing Chick. He wasn't done.

"Little Bang Theory is playing over at the Majestic Café tonight," said Todd. "Who's in the mood for whimsical silent film music played on antique toy instruments?"

"Sounds interesting," said Malcolm, looking directly at Chick. "Let's do it."

"I'm in," said Joe, also looking at Chick. "Those guys are really good."

"I am so fucking out," said Chick. "I couldn't be any more out."

"Come on," said Joe, joyously poking Chick in the shoulder. "It'll be great."

Todd stood there, looking innocent.

Chick turned to him. "You son of a bitch."

The next morning, Joe managed to drag himself out of bed mildly hungover, but in time to get ready for work. Ana was just about to leave as he slammed down a cup of coffee in the kitchen. That was when he decided that he should probably mention what Malcolm had told him.

"Are you fucking kidding me?" was Ana's enraged response. He had known that she probably wouldn't be pleased, but he didn't expect this wrath. She also had three cups of French roast in her and was pretty wound up. These days, she was stressed before she even walked out of the door. "I can't believe this. People at work think Adrienne and I are getting preferential treatment? We're fucking killing ourselves there. We're working on a horrible account run by idiots. Did he say who was saying it?"

Joe shook his head, wishing he'd poured himself a second cup before he started all this. He'd hoped that Ana would just shrug it off. It seemed to him that ad agencies were full of petty jealousies and competitive bullshit. "He didn't say. He just said that he had heard it from a couple of people."

"Goddamnit. Did he say anything else?"

Joe stared at the bulging tendon in Ana's neck. He did not want to say what he was going to say, but he knew that he had to. "Yeah."

"What, Joe?"

"He said some people think that Adrienne and Bruce have hooked up."

Ana raised her right hand to her forehead, then pinched her thumb and middle finger between her eyebrows just above her glasses, as if trying to staunch the neuralgia. She closed her eyes. "Are you fucking *joking*?"

Already exhausted from this conversation, Joe just shook his head. "Still not kidding or joking. Too early."

"I've got to track down Malcolm today and find out who's behind this."

"Maybe you should try to calm down first before you do anything."

Ana sat on the step just off the vestibule. Her face was blank for a moment, then she let out a solitary sob.

Joe walked over to her. He now wished he'd waited for tonight to do this, but most likely no time would have been right for it. He squeezed down next to her as she held her face in her hands. "Baby, it's okay. Who cares what these cretins say? They're just envious because you guys are doing so well." He caressed her arm. "Ana. It's not worth it. Come on."

She put her hands down and gazed up at him. "It's not only this. It's everything. I'm just getting tired of it."

"I know you are. Look, if it gets too bad, you can just quit. Isn't that why we live the way we do? We don't have a mortgage, we don't have kids. Why stay in jobs that we hate? I have a full-time gig now. I can support us." It had sounded wrong in his head and even more so coming out of his mouth. He looked at Ana and got the feeling that she just didn't believe him.

"No, I'm not going to quit," she said. "I'm going to make this work."

"I'm not trying to make you feel bad, but this is hurting us."

She snuffled. "I know."

Joe put his hand on her knee, which wasn't hard to find below her short skirt. "So, is Adrienne sleeping with Bruce?"

Ana looked mildly annoyed at him for asking the question. "No. I think she'd like to, but even she knows that would be trouble. For both of us."

"Okay, good. Because you're right: it would be trouble for everyone."

Ana stood up. "I have to go."

16

What Would Jesus Drive?

drienne's response was the same as Ana's: "Are you fucking kidding me? I can't believe people are saying that."

Adrienne was sitting on Ana's lime-green seventies Knoll love seat, her computer open on her lap. Ana was across from her at her desk, glowering. She took a sip from her travel mug and emitted a low-pitched growl as she stared at her computer screen. (Dozens of job folders against a background of cool, striated Macintosh blue.) She had stewed over the whole thing in the car for a good twenty minutes on the way in and it just kept making her more and more angry.

"I think we should get Malcolm in here," said Adrienne, trying to take charge of the situation.

Ana sat back in her chair and nodded at her partner. "Good idea. Before we do that, are you sure there's nothing that you'd like to tell me?"

Adrienne looked hurt. "You shouldn't be asking me that."

Ana immediately regretted the implicit accusation and held her palms up, trying to quell the situation. "Okay, I just—I'm sorry."

Adrienne stared down at her laptop as she spoke. "I may do it now just to spite you," she muttered.

Ana smiled, but Adrienne didn't look up from her computer.

After a quick call, Malcolm was in Ana's office, looking a little spooked. Adrienne closed the door behind him after he sat down.

"So what's going on, you guys?"

Ana peered at him over her glasses. "Malcolm."

"Yeah?" he said hesitantly.

"What the fuck did you hear, dude?" snapped Adrienne.

Ana quickly turned to her. "I'll handle this, Ade."

Adrienne crossed her arms. "Fine."

"Soooo," said Malcolm, "I have a feeling Joe might have mentioned to you what I heard."

Ana cocked her head. "You had to know he would, Mal."

"Of course—I wanted him to. I'm sorry, I guess I just didn't want to be the messenger." Malcolm turned from Ana to Adrienne and back again. "But I hadn't been expecting this good cop, bad cop routine either."

Ana wanted to smile but just couldn't. "Who's saying this stuff?"

He sighed loudly and lowered his shoulders. "You know, all the usual suspects . . . You guys, it doesn't matter *who's* saying it. It's just that a few people are saying it, that's all."

"No idea why this is happening?"

Malcolm raised his foot and placed the heel of his burnished square-toed shoe on his knee. "I don't know what to tell you. They're probably just jealous."

Ana took a strained breath. "You're right. It just pisses me off that we have to be subjected to this. Are people so surprised when two women get a promotion that they have to stoop to this? Is this the only way anyone can believe that we'd get ahead?"

"People don't know how to behave," said Malcolm, shaking his head. "That's the problem." He turned to the closed door. "You guys, I have to go. I've got a ten o'clock and I still have stuff to prepare."

"Thanks, Mal," said Ana. "Appreciate it."

"Yeah, thanks." said Adrienne, closing the door behind him. "Well, that was useless," she said to Ana. "He obviously doesn't want to give anyone up."

"Malcolm's smart that way. I don't blame him."

"I don't know why he couldn't at least give us a name."

"Come on, Adrienne, you know why—because you'd march over there and bite the person's head off."

"No, I wouldn't." Ana stared at her skeptically. "All right, so maybe I would. Motherfucker would have it coming."

Ana tipped her travel mug up to her lips and drained her remaining coffee. Then she put down the cup, opened up her purse, pulled out a MAC lipstick and a compact. Flipping open the mirror, she applied a coat of Russian red. "I did not need this before our meet and greet with the WomanLyfe client."

Adrienne slumped farther down in her chair. "Oh shit. Is that today?"

"You forgot?"

"Yes I did."

"Wish I could have forgotten. Woke me up at four o'clock this morning. I kept imagining myself in the meeting telling them all to fuck off and die. Then I started to fret about having no ideas for Fanning TV, then it was pretty much time to get up."

"Very efficient of you."

Ana looked at her wistfully. "It's all about time management."

"When is that thing, anyway?" Adrienne said, getting up to leave.

"One thirty."

"Guess I'll go."

Ana raised her brows and laughed harshly. "Guess you fucking *will*, bitch."

Adrienne opened the door. "You are such a cunt, you know that?"

Ana leaned back and stared at her partner in astonishment. "I can't believe you just called me a cunt."

"Yeah, I just decided I'm reclaiming it. Like nigger and queer."

Ana checked to see if anyone was outside her office. "*Shhh.* Don't say those words so loud."

"What?" said Adrienne, raising her voice as she turned to leave. "You mean *cunt*?" Then she laughed and walked out.

Ana sighed and laid her head on the desk. The cool laminate soothed her forehead. This was one of those moments where she honestly questioned what she did for a living. Sure, she knew that advertising paid well because it really brought nothing to humanity's table. It seemed to Ana that the more karmic good you performed in a job, the less you got paid to do it—teachers, social workers, and public defenders came to mind. Then again, it certainly wasn't like all low-paying jobs were soul-enriching and helpful to humankind. Ana had worked her way through the Center for Creative Studies (along with her scholarship) as a wage slave at the Gap helping only those seeking cheap clothing threaded together by poor brown and beige people from third world nations. She had also done double shifts schlepping food to rude and ungrateful diners, all of it for minimum wage and often skimpy tips, so maybe this meant her theory was flawed. Either way, she hated those jobs just enough to make her not want to be poor.

It had always seemed sadly true to Ana that bad people survived better in America. And to her, advertising was just bad enough to help her survive. Aside from the money and the comfortable life it gave her and Joe, it was, for the most part, a pleasant way to make a living, filled with creative challenges as well as smart and interesting and funny people. Still, she had never managed to delude herself into thinking she was doing something important. She solved problems with creativity and, when she did her job well, it made her feel good. Yet she didn't do much more than create demand for things that people probably didn't need in the first place. Ana had always been comforted by the fact that there were much greedier, eviler jobs than hers out there, like narcotics kingpin or investment banker. But now, for the first time, she wasn't so sure.

"What we'd really love to show is a friendly environment where women can go to work out, to strengthen their bodies but also enrich their souls and spirits. Through our research, we've found that way too many women continually give of themselves without any consideration *of* themselves. Consequently, WomanLyfe would like to be perceived not so much as a corporate entity, but almost as a . . . I don't know, a doctrine. But then that's such a dry word. I suppose *lifestyle* would fit better, but that seems so outmoded these days. Anyway, I leave the terminology up to you advertising people."

This client, Karin Masters, was surprising Ana. She was articulate, she was friendly, even stylish, and she certainly was not at all the shriveled, malevolent, pro-life crone that Ana had been expecting. She was actually pretty, a slight, chestnut-haired woman dressed in what looked like Jil Sander. Still, weren't those the most dangerous kinds of enemies—the appealing ones? Maybe she was just some New York slickster hired by the clinic bombers to put a Cinderella mask on their Godzilla.

Ana watched as Bruce and Tara Exley, the account supervisor (young, smart as a whip, pretty cool for an AE, definitely not your standard-issue Michigan State MBA yes-bot), nodded in agreement at what was being said. Ana wondered if she was going to be expected to say anything. She probably was, though she had given it no thought at all. It was the one part of this new job to which she had found herself resistant, the whole client-agency interaction thing.

Ana had always had dealings with clients, but it was mostly just during presentations, when she was simply there in the capacity of art director. It was all different now; her place in the food chain had shifted. One of the lessons she was learning with every new day was that the creatives were people who were tolerated and, as often as possible, marginalized by corporate machinations.

She had known that despite advertising agencies' desire to be known as "cutting edge" or "leading edge" or "bleeding edge" or whatever fucking ludicrous edge they wished to be teetering upon these days, most of the clients were corporations that tacitly resented the fact that they had to go to so-called creative people for ideas of what to do for their brands. Creatives were the black sheep of the corporate world, the bad seed, the deranged and deformed offspring kept in the attic. Here was one of the few facets of corporate work that couldn't be quantified by the business wizards or overanalyzed by the research team or off-loaded to a foreign country to be done cheaper and faster. Ana long ago realized that most company representatives would be much happier not having to talk to some black-suited creative director (or worse: arty freak, gloomy bookworm, or young punk just out of ad school) to figure out what was a good idea.

It used to be that creatives could delude themselves into thinking that there was at least a certain artfulness and autonomy and perhaps even a jot of rebel spirit to what they did for a living. That particular delusion was getting harder for Ana to maintain these days. Especially since she was now one of the official faces of the agency. She had to talk to clients and had to act as if she cared what they thought. (This just in: *she didn't*.) So far there hadn't been many surprises—just a lot of myopic white men obsessed with their particular widget, thinking that the whole world was as widget-centric as them, more concerned about their own position within WidgetCo and making advertising that appealed more to their WidgetCo superiors than to the public, who didn't give a rat's ass about widgets unless their old one had worn out or broken down.

When Karin came to what felt like a natural pause, Ana finally spoke: "So you feel that a genuine concern for women is at the heart of everything you do?"

"Absolutely."

Ana nodded gravely. "So, if I understand this correctly, you want to encourage women to take better care of themselves. Which is a great thing."

"Right," said Karin, intensely meeting Ana's gaze. "I

mean, ultimately we want them to take better care of themselves so they can take better care of the people who really
matter: their husbands and children."

There was a beat of silence. Ana suddenly felt the blood
start to pound in her skull. "I'm sorry? Excuse me . . . did
you just say, the people who really *matter*?" Somewhere in
the room, Ana heard a pencil being snapped in half. She had
a feeling it was Adrienne. Ana smiled and nodded, her face
an unmoving rictus. She felt pinpricks along the tops of her
ears just before they went numb.

Bruce interjected: "Of course, you mean the people who
really matter *to them*."

Karin looked confused at first, then her face opened with
the realization of what she had said. "Certainly. Yes, I'm
sorry if I was unclear about that. You have to understand
that to the women who are our target audience, their families are everything to them. They tend to give them everything
they've got. But they don't understand that depleting all their
own resources—all their energy, all their time, all of their
selves—is not beneficial to anyone at the end of the day."

Okay. *Misunderstanding.* Ana felt the rigor-mortis grin slip
away. Was everyone looking at her? Was her face as red
as it felt? After that sudden blast of adrenaline, her brain
couldn't quite reengage.

Luckily, Adrienne jumped into the fray, bless her
heart. "What kind of tone do you think is appropriate for
the creative?"

Karin turned her laser gaze to Adrienne. "We think our
brand personality right now is friendly and approachable.
We'd like to continue in that vein, but with a more professional approach. I'm sure you've noticed that what we've
been doing so far is, well, kind of low-tech."

At this, everyone from the agency just smiled pleasantly and said nothing.

Karin started to laugh. "It's okay. I think what we've been doing is horrible too. It's awful."

The entire room broke out with relieved laughter. It was the kind of moment that didn't happen often in one of these meetings: someone speaking the truth. *Damn this woman*, thought Ana. *She's good.* What WomanLyfe had been doing were video testimonials that looked like they had been produced in the basement of a public-access television station in Pig's Knuckle, Iowa, in the mid-1980s.

"I've been trying to tell everyone that for ages, but they didn't want to mess with success. Yet one has to understand that part of what made WomanLyfe so friendly and approachable was that we didn't look so professional. Those crappy commercials made us look nonthreatening to the very people we wanted to reach. So, though it wasn't intentional, that approach worked in our favor."

Unintentional incompetence resulting in accidental success. If that wasn't advertising in a nutshell, Ana didn't know what was.

"So are you saying that you want to continue in a similar direction?" said Adrienne, pencil shard threaded through her fingers.

That was the big question. Ana was glad Adrienne had asked it and not her. Ana put her pen down next to her notebook, hoping that this woman wasn't going to say yes.

Karin paused for a moment, shifted her eyes to the corner of the conference room, then over to Bruce, before answering the question. *Not a good sign*, thought Ana.

"Well, it has been a very successful approach, and I'd be lying if I said it wouldn't be well received if you were to continue our current campaign with better production values, but we are open to other approaches."

Was it just Ana or could she feel a palpable sense of disappointment in the room? That answer, as far as Ana could interpret it, was a definite yes. Okay, maybe not a definite yes, but a yes that said, *We'll certainly look at another approach out of politeness, but we'll most likely be staying with the tried and true, thank you.*

Bruce's expression told her that this was indeed the correct interpretation. He was in full damage-control mode. "I'm glad to hear that you're open to other approaches, because if WomanLyfe wants to be perceived as something other than just—forgive me for saying this—a cut-rate, low-end, strip-mall operation, they will definitely have to raise the stakes somewhat. Across the board: creative, media, Internet presence, strategic thinking—everything."

Karin looked hard at Bruce and nodded. "Okay, I understand that. Thank you for your candor. I'll start to prepare everyone for the idea that they're not necessarily going to see just more of the same kind of advertising."

Bruce flashed his winning, market-tested smile at Karin. "That would be great. Thanks."

Ana wanted to go over and give Bruce a hug for saying what he did.

Karin started to reach for her bag, then stopped. She put both elbows on the conference table and clasped her hands. "There is one thing, though. I do think that they're going to expect a certain Christian sensibility to the work."

That was when Ana noticed the cross around Karin's neck. Why hadn't she noticed it before? Of course she was one of them. Was Ana that much of a liberal elitist to believe that a stylish, nice, funny Christian couldn't exist?

"Really," said Adrienne, her carefully styled eyebrows raised about as far as Ana had ever seen them. "What exactly is that?"

"One that reflects what we're all about at WomanLyfe: family, traditional values, Christian morals, Jesus." Her smile seemed to dare anyone in the room to defy her.

"We have to put Jesus in the advertising?" said Ana, before she had a chance to stop herself.

Karin Masters laughed. "Of course not."

Ana nodded. "Oh, okay."

"Just His teachings."

After the client had been walked out of the building and put into her car by Tara, the rest of them headed back to the conference room for a debriefing.

Bruce was the first to speak. "*Jesus Christ*, that was a good meeting!" he chirped, insincerely pumping his fist into the air. "Whooo!"

Ana was still stunned. "We're supposed to put the teachings of Jesus in the advertising? What the fuck, Bruce?"

He shook his head dismissively. "Don't sweat it. I think that's just bullshit to get us to do what they want. Our real problem is that they want the same crap they've been doing all along. Only slightly better-looking crap."

"Are we going to give it to them?" queried Adrienne.

Just then, Tara walked back into the room. She put her BlackBerry on the table next to her laptop, then said, "Why does a *It's a Child, Not a Choice* bumper sticker look so weird on the back of an S-Class Mercedes?"

This comment made Ana like Tara even more. One didn't much run into youthful exuberance with a side order of weltschmerz.

"Which begs the bigger question," said Ana, taking it a step farther. "Just what would Jesus drive?"

Adrienne jumped on it: "My Jesus would drive an Escalade. Murdered-out with smoked glass and twenty-six-inch black rims. My Jesus is a bad motherfucker."

"Interesting," said Bruce, leaning back and crossing his arms. "Because my Jesus does not believe in material wealth. He drives a Yugo. He just wants to get around in an economical manner. He's also Yugoslavian."

"You're partially right," said Ana. "Jesus is economical, but he has one of those cars that runs on french fry grease. My Jesus is Al Gore."

"Nope," said Tara, wagging her head and joining in. "Come on, you guys. My Jesus is totally Nascar. He's got one of those awesome cars with all the decals. It's why he had to call home Dale Earnhardt Sr. *Poor Intimidator.*" She spilled a little water from her bottle of Ice Mountain onto the carpeting for her dead homie, then flopped into her chair.

"Ugh," Ana said, the weirdness of the meeting catching up with her. "Can't that woman see that we're a bunch of heathens headed for eternal damnation?"

Bruce leaned back farther and lifted his feet up on the conference room table. He looked exhausted too. Ana couldn't imagine having to put on this kind of show for as many clients as he did.

"That's what makes us good ad people," he said.

"Why is she even here talking to us? What are we going to do, Bruce?" said Tara. Just then, she looked young and scared. This was the first account that she was running on her own and it was already a complete freak show.

Bruce said nothing for a moment. He scratched at the peppery stubble on his jaw. "I don't know what we're going to do. I sense that they feel as stuck with us as we do with them. It's not like anyone had a say in this . . . I'm sure they'd rather go to some Christian agency."

Ana made a face. "Does such a thing even exist?"

"There's a couple. Though I wouldn't trust them as far as I could throw them."

"Because they're Christian or because they're an ad agency?" said Ana.

"Does it matter?" Bruce checked his watch. "Look, I've got another meeting right now, but can you two hang out for a while tonight? Maybe we can figure out what we're going to do with these Christy knuckleheads."

Ana reluctantly nodded, then remembered that she needed to act more enthusiastic. But Bruce was already out of the room. The asking of the question was just a formality anyway—it was Bruce's way to telling them that they were going to stay late.

"These days just keep getting longer and longer," said Ana, stretching her arms over the back of her chair. Her mouth tasted like a Labrador soaked in Starbucks.

Adrienne eyed her sheepishly. "I can't stay tonight. I've got plans."

"What plans?"

"Just plans."

"*Just plans*? I have just plans too. I just planned to go home and have dinner with Joe and a boomba of pinot grigio, but that ain't happening. What are your *just plans*? You got a date?"

Adrienne looked down at the table and said: "I've got my shrink at six, which I've cancelled three times because of work. She just gave me the obviously-this-isn't-important-to-you talk because I cancel so much. And yes, I do have a date later. Anyway, it's kind of a date."

"Who?"

"You don't know him. I just met him at some ad thing last week. He's very nice. We've just gone out once, but he's got definite possibilities."

Ana was not used to this kind of talk from Adrienne. "Wow, a shrink and a nice date with possibilities. Sounds much more healthy than your usual cocaine-and-booty-call evening."

Adrienne flipped her off.

"Hm," said Ana, shaking her head. "Not a very kind thing to do to someone who you want to cover for you, lady."

"Please?"

"I'll just tell Bruce that you couldn't make it. Something came up. Okay?"

Adrienne patted her hand excitedly. "Thank you, Miss Ana. I'll cover for you next time."

"I know you will, cunt."

Ana received this e-mail at 5:10 p.m.:

A&A-
Will meet you in Main Conf Rm at 6. I'll have dinner brought
in. Hope Vietnamese is okay. Thanks for hanging around.
-B

Suddenly, Ana felt strange about being there by herself after hours with Bruce. It was almost always the three of them, but tonight it was just going to be her and Bruce for what was supposed to be a creative meeting but now felt more like dinner for two. Then she decided that was ridiculous since they were just going to eat in a conference room and toss around ideas for WomanLyfe.

＊ ＊ ＊

At 6:08 p.m., Ana entered the conference room to find Bruce sitting alone amid a bunch of open bags and Styrofoam clamshell containers. He raised his eyes from the box and noticed Ana just as he was shoving some noodles into his mouth. The noodles were very long and he had to shovel in more just to reach the end of them. His eyes kept getting comically wider and wider as he crammed them in. It was definitely the uncoolest that she had ever seen him. Ana couldn't help but laugh.

"Hungry, Bruce?"

He chewed for a long time, then swallowed. "I love these *bún* things, but they're a pain to eat."

"I can see that."

He wiped his mouth with a napkin. "Thanks for showing up. I'm a little hurt—I said six sharp and there's only one person here. I guess my word as a leader doesn't hold that much weight around this place."

"I'm sorry, Bruce. I would have been here on time, but I thought you meant, you know, CDT."

"CDT?" he said, confused.

"Creative-Director Time. You know how you guys always show up last to any meeting? Better everybody wait for you than you for them?"

Bruce leaned back and laughed. "You're learning fast, grasshopper. Where's Adrienne?"

"She had a late doctor's appointment that she couldn't get out of."

"Ah. Shrink?"

Why lie? There was no shame about it in the creative department. She nodded. They were all fucked up in the head.

"Oh well, sit down. I thought Tara was coming too, but she's on some conference call. Have something to eat. Looks like it's just you and me."

Ana sat herself down directly across from him. She was glad for all the bags and boxes between them. She picked up a container and chopsticks and helped herself to some green papaya salad.

"So how you holding up, Ana?"

She looked at Bruce, not sure what he was saying. "What do you mean?"

"I mean *this*," he said, raising his palms to indicate everything around them. "It's a lot of work, isn't it?"

Ana put down the chopsticks and slumped back in her chair. "Yeah."

He smiled at her as if he understood exactly how she was feeling, which she supposed he did. "Well, it's appreciated. Just so you know."

She smiled back at him.

At that moment, someone knocked on the open conference room door. Ana looked up to see a short, pudgy man with bleached-blond hair, the roots grown out black, wearing vintage seventies glasses. Her eyes were immediately drawn down his skinny jeans to a pair of glossy maroon high-top Japanese sneakers. It was Jerrod Amburn, senior art director and the agency's biggest gossip.

"Sorry to interrupt your intimate dinner, you two," Jerrod said, an unmistakable twang of sarcasm in his voice. "Bruce, can we show you some stuff in Jin's office?"

Bruce wiped his mouth and got up from the table. "Sure," he said, then turned to Ana. "Be right back."

At the door, Jerrod turned to Ana and gave her a brief sidelong glance that managed to combine both a sneer and an eye roll. Ana realized just then that people weren't thinking that Adrienne and Bruce had hooked up.

They thought it was *her* and Bruce.

17

The Imitation-Wood-Grain Nightmare

It was nice to be at the office by himself for a change. They had just put the week's edition to bed yesterday so the place was deserted. Ana had called earlier to tell him that she didn't know when she would get home. Joe figured that if he was going to be by himself, he might as well be somewhere besides the town house. He did like having his own office, such as it was. Compared to Ana's office, with her vintage Steelcase desk, shell chairs, and flat-screen TV, his setup was a complete hellhole.

Actually, it wasn't really even an office—it was more of a wide notch in the back wall—but it gave the illusion of being one by virtue of walls surrounding the occupant. There was no door, however, just one missing wall. Joe looked at the flimsy, turd-colored wood paneling. He could easily put his fist through it and had already been tempted to do so a number of times. Almost everything in the place was some sort of awful wood grain, either imitation or real-but-looked-imitation. The nicest thing on his desk was his first-generation iPod, which amazingly still worked. He had hooked it up to a pair of cheap speakers from Big Lots. Sufjan Stevens's *Greetings from Michigan* was currently playing, one of his all-time favorite albums. He examined his hand-me-down PC, the plastic stained amber with nicotine and age, as well as the lint-flocked coffee rings that covered his fake wood-grain Formica desktop.

With all that wood surrounding him, artificial and otherwise, when he leaned back in his chair Joe couldn't help but to think that his office had more of the feel of an open coffin. Not the most subtle of similes, he knew, nor accurate, since a coffin would probably be made of a fine cherrywood instead of quarter-inch pressboard paneling from the disco era.

Despite this, he still didn't want to go home because all the usual temptations would be there. He loved his friends, but there was almost always someone willing to go out for a beer. Those nights at the Midlands invariably ended up the same. One beer turned into six and he rolled into the house drunk, planting himself in front of the television where he would promptly fall asleep, only to wake up prematurely at five a.m. from a sugar rush of alcohol, feeling bloated, cotton-mouthed, and pissed at himself.

He did consider calling Chick to see if he wanted to go to a movie, but that was complicated because the two of them had such drastically different tastes in film. Though their tastes did intersect when it came to film noir and Billy Wilder and the Coen brothers, they had a difficult time at the local multiplex.

The best thing to do would be to see if he could get some work done. Some work that he could feel good about, not "Bead Shop Opens in Former Narcotics Anonymous Location." First, he nuked a couple of frozen burritos and ate them while reading the new-release reviews on *Pitchfork*. After that, he went into his bookmarks and pulled up *The Paris of the Midwest Is Crumbling*. On the front page, there was the headline: "Endangered Tikis." Joe clicked through to the piece:

The future of the Chin Tiki, the last of the grand old tiki bars in Detroit, is now in question. The place has been long-shuttered, but at least still standing. Those who have been inside the place, like myself, also know that many of its midcentury treasures remain there mostly intact, like some gauzy web-wrapped tiki tomb of Tutankhamen. Unfortunately, its demise now seems imminent because of its impending purchase by our own once-esteemed Pizza King, highly successful purveyor of cardboardish takeout pie from unctuous outlets across our fast-food nation, and now avid despoiler of historic buildings.

What happened to you, Pizza King? What evil alchemy overtook you? You are not the same man who once meticulously restored the old Fox Theatre, now the jewel of Detroit, back to its 1920s splendor, right down to the last gold-leaf Hindu deity and velveteen throne. It was, and still is, exquisite. Walking in is like entering the interior of a Fabergé egg. That was you, PK. You captured our love with that rarefied and glorious act of preservationist greatness. But what happened then? You lost interest in the restoration of old and elegant buildings. No longer Savior of the Past, you purchased edifices only to tear them down, often under cover of night to avoid adverse publicity. All under the shopworn rubric of "progress." O, Pizza King, where is thy victory?

Although there is still hope among local preservationists, lovers of Polynesian culture, and appreciators of buildings both iconic and ironic, that Pizza King will do the right thing, return to his restoration roots, and lovingly rehabilitate this exotic maiden, it has come to my attention that once the purchase is finalized, the building will most likely be slated for demolition, for yet another parking lot for the nearby sports arenas. Bravo, Pizza King! Thanks to your work, Detroit will soon have more parking spaces than actual citizens.

This was the first that Joe had heard about any of this. The "Pizza King" to which Brendan referred was a local billionaire who had been instrumental in the construction of both a baseball stadium and a football stadium within a mile of the Chin Tiki. Which meant that if what Brendan Sanderson said was true, soon all that would be left of the Chin Tiki would be a gravel lot where ragged men two steps from the street (literally and figuratively) would flag cars into empty spaces when there was a ball game or concert in the area. There would be little, if any, backlash. No one would express much concern about the destruction of an old Polynesian restaurant except a small group of preservationists and aging hipster tiki geeks. It was also happening just in time to put a damper on the annual Chin Tiki party at the Midlands.

Joe clicked on the photo of the Chin Tiki, its coved entrance resembling praying hands, and it led to pictures of the interior. Apparently, Brendan had gotten inside at some point and taken a lot of photographs. Joe wasn't sure if he'd done it illegally or with the permission of the Chin family, but he had definitely done it.

Every photo Joe clicked on led him to another and they were all pretty interesting, some of them rather beautiful. There were a few of the inside of the main dining room. Joe didn't know how Brendan got the light the way he did, but it seemed like the stone grotto was glowing as if from moonlight. There were a lot of shots clearly taken for posterity's sake—fancy Witco furniture, stoic Moai statues standing guard at the doorways, glass balls hanging from fishnets, the pattern of the carpeting, the grain of the wood paneling, the masks hanging on the walls. Pretty amazing stuff. He had to give it up for Brendan.

Joe clicked on the contact link and started an e-mail.

From: jkeen70@gmail.com
To: bsanderson@TPOTMIC.com
Subject: How did you do it?

Brendan- Just saw the photo spread on the piece about the Chin Tiki. Nice. How the hell did you get in there? -Joe K

Joe sent it off. Brendan must have been online because within two minutes, there was an answer in his inbox.

From: bsanderson@TPOTMIC.com
To: jkeen70@gmail.com
Subject: How did you do it?

I'm going back soon. Want to do that ride-along?

Without thinking about it, Joe wrote back.

From: jkeen70@gmail.com
To: bsanderson@TPOTMIC.com
Subject: How did you do it?

Yes.

The answer from Brendan came back in an instant.

From: bsanderson@TPOTMIC.com
To: jkeen70@gmail.com
Subject: How did you do it?

Righteous. Keep it under your hat.
Strictly on the QT Hush. Details to follow.

Joe had no clue as to why he had this sudden interest in tromping around an abandoned building, but there it was. Now he was committed. But why not? He was alone every night and practically every weekend. Maybe he needed an adventure. He could finally write that story about it. Maybe for the *Independent* or somewhere bigger than that. He could use a pseudonym or something, he didn't care.

Then there was that reason why he was alone most of the time: Ana. Even when she was around, she was not much fun these days. If she wasn't aloof and irritable, she was overwhelmed or worrying about work. Ana was now so wrapped up in her job that when he tried to talk to her about anything else, she would just nod at him until she could bring the subject back around to work.

He blamed it all on jobs. Yes, jobs were the problem. This is why he had avoided them for so long. Jobs were nothing but trouble.

It was almost ten when he got home. Ana was sitting on the couch with a glass of wine, half covered with an afghan. She looked very cute in her maroon velour tracksuit. The television was on but muted, some Food Network show.

"Hey," he said, leaning down to kiss her neck. She pulled her head back slightly as he moved in. She did this when she was stressed. "How was your day?"

"Okay." She glanced up at the ball clock. "Where have you been?"

"At the office. I was trying to get some work done." He dropped his messenger bag next to the couch.

"*Work* work? Or your work?"

He shrugged. "I don't know. My work, I guess. Wasn't terribly successful, but at least I was making an attempt." He decided to hold off mentioning that he had signed on for an illegal B&E.

"Why didn't you call?" said Ana.

He could tell she was annoyed. "You're never home, so why do I have to call to tell you that *I* won't be home?" He hadn't meant to say this in such a hostile way, but that was how it came out.

Ana pulled the afghan up around her neck. "Thanks. I needed some guilt because I'm already feeling so wonderful about everything."

Joe sat down on the arm of the sofa. "I'm sorry, I didn't mean to guilt you. But come on, you know I'm right. It's crazy. You're never here."

She pulled up her knees under the afghan and hugged them close to her chest. "I know, I know."

"Are you just going to keep doing this indefinitely? Working and working and working? Not thinking about anything else?"

"I *know*. I just don't know what to do about it." She squeezed her knees even tighter and closed her eyes.

"Are you listening to me? *Quit*. Find a new job."

Ana opened her eyes and held her head up. She was getting mad now and he realized that it was exactly what he wanted. He wanted to fight.

She stared at something in front of her. "I told you before that there are no jobs right now. No one's hiring. People are getting laid off. Times are bad."

"Times are always bad here," he said, feeling the flush of blood on the back of his neck. "Quit anyway. You can't just stay and be miserable forever."

"I am not going to quit. Who says I'm miserable? I like my job."

"No you don't."

"Don't fucking tell me what I like and don't like," she snapped. "I don't want to quit. This is just a busy time."

He leaned toward her. "Busy time, my ass. It was never this busy before."

Ana threw the afghan off her legs and pushed it onto the other end of the couch. "What do you know about any of this? This is the first steady job you've ever had and you're ready to bail, I can tell."

He hated when she thought she was reading his mind. "I am not."

"Yes you are."

He stood up. "I'm tired of this conversation. I'm going to read in bed."

"Why don't you go do that? I'm tired of listening to you bitch at me. Good night. I'll be up when I've had a chance to decompress." Ana unmuted the television midcommercial, and the sound of someone talking about toaster pastries cut through the room.

No you won't, thought Joe. And it was all he could do to keep from saying it out loud, but he was tired of fighting now. He stepped over to her, thinking that he might kiss her, then thought better of it. Instead he just said, "Good night."

Ana didn't look back up.

18

Knowing Your Enemy

The next night, when Ana found out she had to work late again, she decided not to worry about it. She simply texted *Working 2nite* to Joe's cell. It was the way to do it with the least amount of explanation and interaction. If he didn't like it, too bad. She was tired of his constant whining about her job. This was definitely not her ideal situation, but she was determined to keep her job and did not need him hounding her about it.

Tonight, they had to stay late to work on ideas for WomanLyfe. Thankfully, Bruce had told them not to worry about shoehorning the teachings of Christ into the creative, which made things considerably easier. Ana had also decided, and told herself repeatedly, that WomanLyfe was simply another one of the many weight-loss programs out there for women, just more comprehensive. Not only did they sell prepackaged nutritionally balanced frozen meals, but they also had a network of hundreds of franchised strip-mall fitness centers where women could complete a thirty-minute exercise circuit. It was a good, inexpensive workout, with aerobic, cardio, and weight training, all in a half hour.

Ana had even tried it herself and liked it. Okay, the truth was that both she and Adrienne had been forced to join WomanLyfe. On the positive side, she was actually exercising more than she had in years. Maybe she didn't exactly fit in at her local WomanLyfe center, since the crowd there was not what you would find at your typical health club, but that was what was good about the place. The women there were not Lycra-clad gym bunnies cruising for a health club hookup, but hard-working, unglamorous women wearing sweats and actually sweating in them. They were there doing the work, trying to be healthier, and she admired them for it.

Even Ana had to admit that it was all very well thought out, and aside from the Christian stuff sprinkled throughout (a tiny quote from Scripture on the back of chicken parmesan rigatoni?), it actually seemed like an effective way to get in shape. The fitness centers also sold books of daily affirmations and music CDs (a kind of Christian-lite, quasi-new-age music that Joe would have despised) to "strengthen the mind and spirit." It was all very positive, and surprisingly helpful, even to a heathen like Ana. She could see why women liked this program. Anything that promoted women joining together for the purpose of becoming healthier and happier had to be a good thing. Which allowed Ana to start feeling better about WomanLyfe. Until.

"Uh-oh," said Adrienne, perched in her usual place on the lime-green love seat that Ana had liberated from a retired SVP's office.

"Uh-oh *what*?"

Adrienne peered over her laptop. "Uh-oh, I just happened to find something about the intrepid founder of WomanLyfe. Some behind-the-scenes dude named Barry Jameson."

Ana was at her desk, half hidden behind her own laptop. "Gee, a man. *Quelle surprise*," she said, not looking up.

"Because who would ever expect a woman to be running a company that makes products for women? That would be crazy."

Adrienne's eyes skittered from her Mac to Ana, then back again. "You ain't gonna like this one bit, my dear."

It was not a big surprise that Adrienne had found something bad. Ana just wasn't sure that she wanted to hear it. "I thought we had decided to stop finding reasons to hate WomanLyfe and just try to be happy that we have jobs."

"I know, I know. I'm sorry. You're right. What's the point? We made our deal with the devil."

"Exactly. You can't just take a tiny sip of the Kool-Aid."

"Absolutely," said Adrienne, nodding resignedly. "Drink deep or taste not the corporate spring."

Ana was going to say something else, but then just sighed. "I guess you better show me."

"That's not a good idea."

"You know I have one of them computin' machines too. I could just use me the Google."

"Well, he's everything we feared he was, Ana. A real piece of evil. Money from the company goes to all the awfulest, craziest right-to-life organizations—even those crazy fucks who picket the funerals of dead soldiers."

"Jesus Christ," said Ana. "Wait, that's a weird thing to say. Sorry."

Adrienne snorted. "Take His name in vain all you want, lady. I don't care. My Jesus likes swearing. It's like a shout-out to Him."

"It's not funny. I was just starting to be able to rationalize all this. At least Karin, a woman, is in charge of the account. At least WomanLyfe is good for women. Helping them to become stronger and healthier—"

"While funding maniacs."

Ana shook her head and sighed again. "This is hard to ignore."

Adrienne fingered a lock of auburn hair. "Yeah. Even for me. And I'm very good at ignoring."

Ana felt nauseous. How could she keep doing this? How were they supposed to come up with ideas to sell this stuff when she couldn't even stomach the idea of what they did? She had to talk to Bruce.

For now, rather than continue working, they decided to go out for a much-needed glass of wine. Since the agency was located in one of the many generic suburbs that surrounded Detroit, they ended up at TGI Fridays. Ana hated chain restaurants, but neither of them felt like driving far, so it was either that or go home. And she didn't feel like going home yet. She didn't know if it was because Joe was right about all this—her being miserable about WomanLyfe, having more responsibility than she really wanted, feeling trapped by her job—or if it was something else. All she knew was that she didn't want to start the argument again. She was going to have a drink with Adrienne, try to relax, and hope that Joe would be asleep when she got home.

Adrienne took a long sip of her Shiraz. "That's nice," she said, setting down the glass. She leaned forward, rested her elbows on the table, and clutched each forearm. "So I didn't tell you. I nosed around to see if I could get to the bottom of this whole rumor business."

Upon hearing this, Ana felt yet another wave of nausea. So much for relaxing. "Oh god. What did you do?"

Adrienne puckered her lips, cocked her head, splayed the fingers of both hands in front of her like she was throwing some secret suburban white-girl gang signs. "I flew some heads, called in some markers, spoke to my sources on the street," she said in a *Joisey* accent that made absolutely no sense but was still funny.

Ana smiled through her queasiness. "I see. You have a Huggy Bear at the agency?"

"Exactly. An informant. My snitch."

"Let me guess. They think it's *me* sleeping with Bruce, right?"

Adrienne looked surprised and impressed. "How did you know?"

"I don't know. Something that shit Jerrod said made me realize it."

"*Hmph*. He doesn't have a chance to get with megahetero Bruce, so he's got to be all like that?"

"Did you find out who started it?"

"No, not really. Huggy Bear didn't come through with that information."

Ana took a sip of wine. It was spicy and lemony, and normally this would have made her very happy, but tonight it did not agree with what was going on in her stomach. "There's got to be some reason why this would happen."

Adrienne ran a finger along the rim of her glass, making an irritating high-pitched noise. "Probably not super surprising that they would think that."

Ana put down her glass. "And why is that?"

"I don't know. I've seen the way he looks at you."

"You have? He looks at me?"

Adrienne nodded gravely. "Oh yes. He's totally crushing on you."

Ana swallowed. "Yeah, sure."

"I'm telling you. He looks at you. When you're not look-ing, of course."

"Shut up."

"Hmm, I can't decide exactly what it is. Let's say it's part objectifying male gaze eye-banging with a side of boy who's lost his puppy. Sort of moony-eyed, little-boy lust."

"Ew, gross."

"I don't know how you manage to be so oblivious to it."

Ana thought about the night in LA in his hotel room. How he had looked at her then. "Why didn't you tell me all this earlier?"

"I don't know. I guess I thought it would freak you out or something."

"Yeah, well, you're right. It does."

When Ana got home, Joe was in bed with a copy of *The Wicked Pavilion* tented over his chest. She warmed at the sight of him there. It was nice to see him without having to listen to him. Ana picked up the book and leaned down to give him a kiss on the forehead, but before she could, he shifted and farted in his sleep. She stopped herself, placed his book-mark on the appropriate page, took off his glasses, put them on the nightstand with his book, then turned off the light and headed into the bathroom to wash up.

Ana was still buzzing from what Adrienne had told her, about Bruce crushing on her. She thought about how even as she was telling Adrienne that she was freaked out by it, she really wasn't. Hearing it actually made her feel good, better than anything had in quite awhile. She had sensed that Bruce had a little thing for her and she had ignored it. She would continue to do so. And while it was always nice to hear that you had an admirer, there was no need to get all schoolgirl giddy about it. *The captain of the football team likes me!*

Yet she liked hearing someone else acknowledge it. Was she that pathetic and needy? The truth was, Ana had learned a long time ago that certain types of conventionally attractive males like Bruce did not tend to go for gawky, bookish, bespectacled women like her, and she had always been fine with that. In high school, the kind of guy she usually attracted was someone not all that attractive to her. Vaguely good-natured, humorless boys who tended to talk too much about themselves (not uncommon for any of them), who weren't full-fledged jocks but played team sports, often not particularly well. They were nice enough, but she had not really cared much for them. They were the sensible boys who would become insurance agents, muffler shop managers, stalwarts of suburban communities. The sad thing was, she had gone out with those boys, they had even been her boyfriends and lovers, simply because they liked her and she had felt indifferent enough about herself to think that she didn't deserve anything better.

Then she had gone to art school and everything kind of swung the other way. She studied art history, she drew and painted, and suddenly she got a better glimpse of the woman she was and who she could become. She discovered artistic, interesting, funny, weird, crazy boys. She actually liked those boys and they actually liked her. She went to raves and parties and danced all night at the Leidernacht and fucked pretty much whomever she felt like fucking. Art school was everyone's chance to do just that.

Then came advertising, and then Joe, whom she now saw as a kind of amalgam of all those boys, somewhere in between the sensible and the wild. And the fact that now someone like Bruce was attracted to her? What did that say about her? What did it say about who she was now, who she was becoming? Was she changing in some way that she hadn't even realized? It scared her to think about it.

And was it just her, or did Adrienne seem upset about this whole thing?

The first thing Ana did when she arrived at work the next day was talk to Bruce's administrative assistant to get on his calendar. She had planned for Adrienne to join her, but had forgotten that she was at the studio doing steam-cleaner radio for Fanning.

When Ana walked into his office at 12:45, Bruce was eating lunch, a falafel from Sheesh. He had a container of hummus and a baggie of wedged pita in front of him as well.

He took a bite of his falafel. "Sorry to eat in front of you, Ana, but this is my only chance. I've got a meeting at one and I'm starving." He pushed the hummus and pita across the desk at her. "Help yourself."

Ana wasn't feeling hungry. Three glasses of wine on an empty, queasy stomach last night had pretty much done her in for today. The smell of garlic in the office was almost more than she could take. She was starting to sit down on one of the Bertoia chairs that faced his desk, then stood back up and closed the door behind her, knowing it would only set tongues to wagging. She didn't care.

"Closed door? Uh-oh."

Ana nodded as she scooted the chair closer to his glass desk and sat down. "Yeah. Uh-oh."

Bruce looked as though he'd been expecting this. He set down his falafel, wiped his mouth, glanced at his computer screen for a moment, and exhaled loudly. Steeled, he looked up at her. "Okay, let's have it."

"WomanLyfe is really bothering me. Have you researched them at all?"

"Yeah, I have."

"It's not good, Bruce. The guy that owns it? He, like, funds—"

"Terrorists?"

"No." Ana gave him an annoyed look, thinking that he was kidding around, but then realized that he wasn't. "Oh. Well, *yeah*."

He started wiping his fingers. "This is not as bad as you think. They don't really fund that *really* horrible group. The—"

"The 'God hates queers' group?"

"Yeah, them. That's just Internet bullshit, started by someone."

"Some pro-choice organization, say?"

Bruce picked up his falafel, stared at it, then put it down again. "Who knows? Some irate blogger. Those guys can put anything they want out there. What are you saying, Ana? Are you going to quit on me?" He looked vulnerable, as if he had really lost his puppy the night before.

"I don't want to quit, Bruce. I actually like my job, but I'm starting not to see any other choice. What's with us? Between these guys and Parnoc Industries, I don't know what's happening to this agency. Are we that desperate?"

Bruce held up his index finger and thumb an inch apart. "We've only got a *tiny* piece of Parnoc. It's interactive and you'll never have to work on it."

"Yeah, because I don't do interactive. If they decided to do, say, print directed to women, I guess I probably would have to work on it, wouldn't I?"

"That's never going to happen, Ana."

"Until they roll out Spring-Fresh Napalm or Lady Land-

mines or something equally vile. You didn't answer my
question. Why are we so desperate?"

"I wouldn't call it desperate. But things are not great.
And you know Edward. He doesn't care about political
stuff. A client is a client to him."

Ana thought about Edward, which she did not like to
do. He was an old-school ad guy, a remnant of the last days
of advertising excess of the eighties, where everyone was
still drinking a lot, but also snorting cocaine like it was going out of style, which it was. He was bloated, florid, with
a spare tire of crimson flesh around the perpetually tight
white collar that led up to his massive, balding, sun-damaged
cranium. Adrienne referred to him as the Big Red Guy. He
was once photographed for the cover of *Adweek* in his Armani
with a giant Cohiba (the cliché!) and his foot up on the edge
of his mahogany desk. When Ana saw it, she almost puked.
He couldn't have made the agency look stodgier. Even his
pose was offensive. Instead of the desk, Ana had pictured
the entire staff under that Bruno Magli, all being crushed by
the weight of his immense chateaubriand-engorged corpus.
The word around the agency was that he was notoriously
rude to restaurant waitstaff. She had heard a story about
him screaming himself even redder in the face at some poor
schlub who had dared bring him an eighteen-year-old single malt Scotch, instead of his customary twenty-five. As a
former waitress, she officially hated Edward's copious guts
after that.

"Isn't there something we can do?"

"Ana," said Bruce, his voice growing gentler, "this is
advertising. Sometimes we do work for products we don't
believe in. I know you have. You probably don't use half the
products or services of our clients, right?"

"It's different, Bruce. Not choosing to use a particular type of vacuum cleaner is different than being against everything that vacuum cleaner stands for."

Bruce shot her a hurt look. "So you're against vacuum cleaners now? Are you part of the whole hardwood-floor rebellion?"

Ana didn't find what he said all that amusing, but she appreciated the effort. She put her elbow on his desk, laid her head on her palm, and sighed. "It's really not funny. I don't know what to do. This is bothering me. A lot."

Bruce picked up a piece of pita and tore it in half. "I think you've trumped this whole thing way out of proportion. These people aren't *that* bad. Is their boss crazy? Yes, but whose isn't? They've got crazy Barry Jameson, we've got crazy Edward Cherkovski." He dipped the pita into the bowl of hummus and popped it into his mouth. After he swallowed, he said: "I think it would be a great idea if you met some of the people over at WomanLyfe."

"Oh god. No." Ana leaned back from the desk. "Karin was enough."

"Oh god *yes*, Ana. Excluding crazy Barry. Whom I've been told doesn't see anyone. I've never even met the guy, just his minions."

Ana shook her head. "Bruce. No. Don't make me go."

"Relax. Come on, you know how it is. Once you meet clients and get to see them as humans, it's much harder to hate them. That's the way it always is."

"No it's not." She was trying not to whine, but not succeeding.

"Once you get to know these guys, I think you'll feel better. They won't just be some faceless enemy. They're nice Midwestern people like us. Despite dropping her big ol' J-bomb into our meeting, Karin is actually very cool."

Ana had to nod in agreement. "Yeah. Before she did that, I really did think she was okay."

"See? In fact, I had a good talk with her this morning. We discussed the whole TV spots needing the teachings-of-Jesus thing."

Ana brightened slightly at this. "What did she have to say?"

Bruce snickered. "She's totally pulled back from it. Acting like she never even said it. Who knows? She may have just thought better of it. Or she may have thrown it in there just to get our knickers in a knot. Sometimes clients will do that, just to test you."

"Well, if that's true, it worked. I know my knickers were officially knotted," Ana said, immediately regretting it. Why was she talking about her panties with her boss? *Use your filter, Ana.*

Bruce just laughed it off. "Yeah, mine too. Look, I've got a meeting in Grand Rapids at eight a.m. on Thursday. What do you say we drive out there tomorrow night? You can be a surprise guest at the meeting. Besides, it'll be good for them to meet someone doing the actual work on their account. That way you won't be just some faceless creative either. Clients are always less likely to kill work when they know and like the person who created it."

"I guess that's true," Ana said.

"So plan on it. We'll leave work early if I can get out of a meeting or two."

"Okay."

Bruce wiped his fingers again, stood up, and put his hand on her shoulder, giving it a slight squeeze, then left his hand there. "Feel better?"

Ana noticed there was no wedding band there. "Yeah, I guess I do."

Bruce's hand left her shoulder, but Ana felt the warmth of it linger there.

"Good. And if you wouldn't mind, could you ask Adrienne to be more careful about her demeanor with clients? It occurred to me that she may have set Karin off at that initial meet and greet. If so, we need to put a lid on that."

"Of course."

Bruce smiled at her, one of those smiles that made you feel worthy of his attention. "I'm really glad we had this talk."

It wasn't until Ana was out in the hall that she realized what had just happened: she had agreed to go out of town alone with Bruce.

19
Heart of Tiki Darkness

Malcolm had asked him if he wanted to go see Satori Circus, a local performance artist who had a show downtown that evening at 1515 Broadway, and Joe felt weird having to lie to him. But he had promised Brendan that he would not talk to anybody about what they were going to do. So he told Malcolm that he was planning to stay in and work. Malcolm seemed perfectly cool with the explanation, but the whole thing still left Joe with a bad feeling.

Joe was standing in the foyer of their town house, looking out the window, waiting for Brendan to come pick him up. Was he insane to do this? He'd never even met the man before and now he was going with him to illegally break into a privately owned building? This was crazy. What if they were actually going to do a heist? What if he was being snared into some Tarantinoesque maelstrom of mayhem? Would there be heroin? Gunplay?

At first, he was glad that Ana was out of town, but now all he could think of was that she wasn't even here to bail him out if he ended up in jail. Joe thought of himself sitting in a big communal cell over at 1300 Beaubien, the ancient police headquarters. There he was—Joe and an assortment of gangbangers, crackheads, rapists, arsonists, and hard-core criminals. Good lord. He'd be someone's bitch in a matter of minutes. He took three deep breaths. *It's fine. Brendan knows what he's doing. He's a highly experienced urban explorer. He's done this dozens of times. His website's won awards, for Pete's sake. He's a Webby winner.*

This actually helped, at least for a few minutes. By that time, he saw what he figured was Brendan's Astrovan pulling up in front of the town house. It had to be the ugliest van he had ever seen. It looked like it had once been green and white, but was now covered with a grainy dark sheen of grime and rust and what appeared to be a viscous residue, as if it had been permanently parked beneath a pine tree that had bled out. When Joe walked up and opened the passenger door, his hand stuck slightly to the handle.

"Joe!" He was greeted from the driver's seat by a heavy-set young man with a burning bush of bright red hair that joined at the ears with a slightly darker, equally bushy red beard, of the sort that all the kids were sporting these days. (Yes, he had started calling them "the kids," first ironically, then it just stuck.) Brendan was wearing dark baggy jeans and a blue hoodie that looked as though he'd stolen it from a prison laundry. The effect was not unlike a giant, freckled, thuggish garden gnome of indeterminate race. "What up, doe?" he barked.

"Brendan?" Joe yelled over the music. Was this the same guy he spoke to on the phone? He didn't expect him to be so, well, young and colorful.

"Who the fuck you think it is, suburbanite? *What*? You think I'd be pushing a Benz coupe?" Brendan leaned over to grab Joe's hand in a thumbs-up seventies-style handshake.

When Joe clasped his hand, Brendan pulled him in for a makeshift bro clinch. Joe gagged a little from the smell of sandalwood and sweat and weed. The stereo was blasting the Dirtbombs' "I'm Through with White Girls."

"Good to meet you."

"Likewise, dog."

Slightly confused, Joe stared at him and started laughing. "Did you just call me dog?"

The mop of red hair flopped forward as he nodded. "I did indeed."

Joe cocked his head and nodded back. Apparently, he was a forty-year-old *dawg*. Cool. "Okay then, I guess. Good to be dog."

"It always is. You ready to bust out of your comfortable little neighborhood to hit the nasty old city and do some snoopin' around and shit?"

Snooping around and shit? Joe thought back to their phone conversation awhile back, Brendan talking about "the verity of decay." Was this the same guy? Feeling strangely energized, Joe settled into the spongy, collapsed seat, pulled shut the rattling van door. "Yeah, I guess I'm ready."

Before Joe could say anything else, Brendan grabbed his arm. "Lemme see your shoes." Joe lifted one of his old Doc Martens from the rusted floorboard. "Good man," Brendan said, handing him a half-toasted blunt that smelled of burned resin and sick-sweet strawberry. "You're gonna need this." Out of nowhere, he produced a flame and held it in front of Joe's face.

"Really?"

"Definitely."

Joe took a deep drag, trying to ignore the soggy-dog end of the blunt. Once the smoke hit his lungs, he started coughing like a consumptive.

"Let's do this!" yelled Brendan. He turned the music up

louder, now the Stooges' "No Fun," then hit the gas. "Classic fuckin' *Dee*-troit rock and roll!" he whooped, as the van stammered down the street with an asthmatic wheeze.

Joe took another toke and suddenly felt much calmer as they headed down Woodward Avenue, across 8 Mile, past the art deco apartment buildings of Palmer Park, past the burned-out husks of buildings next to the newly built strip centers of Highland Park, past the Boston Edison district, past Virginia Park where the Algiers Motel once stood, one of the flashpoints of the '67 riots (there was a Burger King there now), then down through the Wayne State campus.

"You nervous?" said Brendan, throwing his hand in the air to the music. Joe thought it was now Black Milk, a local rapper, but wasn't completely sure.

"Yeah, a little."

"It's gonna be interesting, I guarantee you."

"I believe you."

"So, you strapped?"

Joe looked at him, eyes wide. "You mean a gun? No . . . Should I be?"

"No, it's cool."

"Are you?"

Brendan smiled slightly. "Almost there."

After crossing over the Fisher Freeway, Brendan took a right on Montcalm down to Cass, where he parked about a block down the street from the Chin Tiki. There were closer parking spaces, but he assumed Brendan knew what he was doing. Meanwhile, the weed was making Joe's head reel.

"Come on," said Brendan as he threw open his door, which creaked so loudly, Joe considered scuttling the whole mission.

Joe got out of the van and pointed up Montcalm Street.

"Is that going to be a problem with the fire station right over there?"

"Yeah. Like those fucking guys care."

Joe scanned the area. There wasn't really anyone else walking around. Up the street, across from the fire station, he saw a couple of people going into a local tavern, the Town Pump. He turned to Brendan, who smacked him in the arm.

"Chill. It's no big thing."

"It is illegal, though, right?"

"Oh, fuck yeah it is." Brendan then grabbed the same arm and pulled Joe off the sidewalk. They walked through what was once the parking lot of the restaurant. On the brick wall next to them were the vestiges of an old painted billboard:

CHIN

TIKI

AUTHENTIC POLYNESIAN CUISINE

TROPICAL DRINKS

A giant tiki god was also painted on the sign that seemed to gaze down on Joe with a wide-eyed, thousand-yard Easter Island stare. Much of the painted surface had peeled off to reveal the brick beneath. Joe was suddenly fascinated by the tessellated pattern the bricks formed behind and around the tiki.

"Come on. We're going this way." Brendan led Joe along the perimeter to the very back of the building. There was debris all over the place—trash, papers, old pieces of fencing, and rusty objects that Joe couldn't recognize. Vegetation was growing up the back wall. "All right. Here we are," said Brendan as they stopped in front of a padlocked door.

"It's locked," said Joe, relieved they wouldn't have to do this now.

He watched as Brendan produced a key, inserted it into the lock, then twisted the base from the shackle.

"How did you—"

"Don't you worry your pretty little balding head over it. That's on a need-to-know basis." Brendan grinned and pushed open the door. "Welcome to the Chin Tiki." He grabbed Joe's arm, clicked on a long black Maglite, handed it off, and pushed him through the door.

"You want me to go first?"

"You have to. It's the only way."

"Says who?"

"*Go*. Just keep the light on the ground and watch where you walk. I'm right behind you. I'm going to stash the lock and shut the door."

Joe stepped farther into the building. The place smelled strongly of damp and must. He seemed to be in a short hallway, which probably led somewhere near the kitchen. Joe kept walking, continually sweeping the beam of the Maglite with each step, bouncing it off the glazed concrete floor, the gaudy floral wallpaper–covered walls, and the acoustical tile ceiling. He wasn't sure if he expected everything to be covered with graffiti or what, but aside from water stains and peeling wallpaper, the ceiling and walls were in decent shape. The floor, however, was thick with dust and covered with scuffs and footprints.

Brendan came up behind him. "Dude, you're making me seasick. Hold the light still."

"Sorry." Joe held the light directly in front of him until they reached the door to the kitchen area, which was more like what he had been expecting. The counters had been ripped from the walls, an old stove was tipped on its side, bare wires hung from the ceiling. Over in the corner lay pieces of scrap wood and bent metal. Joe stopped and waited for Brendan to join him. "What now?"

Brendan took the long Maglite from him. "First, no more psychedelic light show." He handed Joe a much smaller version of the same flashlight. "Then we get out of the most boring part of the whole place. Come on."

"What happened to the kitchen? Why's it so messed up?"

"Fucking Hollywood film crews. Idiots left things unattended while they were filming that Eminem movie. A lot of stuff got ripped off by scrappers. And if that wasn't bad enough, then the crew was plundering all the tiki stuff inside. You can tell there's a lot of shit missing now."

"Really?" Joe had heard something like that had happened while they were here shooting. Everyone was so thrilled that they were actually shooting an entire Hollywood film in Detroit (instead of just the ghetto B-roll that they usually came for) that they overlooked this small fact—the desecration of Detroit's last remaining temple of tiki.

"Fuck yeah." Brendan shined the light on all the debris.

"Assholes," said Joe. Then it occurred to him that he was here desecrating the place himself. He had just broken in. Or had he? How did Brendan get a key? Was it still illegal if you had a key? Probably.

Then Brendan grabbed his arm (he did that a lot), and Joe followed obediently, passing a few doors marked *He Tiki* and *She Tiki* that had to be restrooms, until the hallway opened into a dining room. The floor was carpeted now. Joe could discern gold tapa cloth patterns beneath the grime.

"Check it out," said Brendan.

"I've always wondered what this place looks like inside," whispered Joe.

"Now you know. Awesome, right?" Brendan shined the light on the room before them. Joe did the same with his smaller light. From what he could see, it was in fact awesome. The walls were covered with rattan matting, bamboo, and dusky tapa cloth. There were avocado-green leather banquettes along the wall and a long inlaid mural with bas-relief tikis, an oar and a tiki mask that seemed to smirk at the two of them. Dusty globes hung from the ceiling, where a leak had created a large hole in the acoustical tile.

They kept walking through what seemed to be a hallway, past the bamboo and rattan partitions that separated the various rooms of the restaurant. The two of them skirted around tipped tables and chairs, through powdery plastic foliage and clattering bead curtains, past dust-edged Moai figures that were almost as tall as Joe, huddled in corners. Then they entered what had to be the main dining room. Joe shined his light on the ceiling. It was covered with grass matting. Hanging from it were inflated blowfish lamps, wicker-shaded lights, and colored glass globes, suspended by fishnets and cobwebs. He was surprised that the nets hadn't rotted away over the years, then he tipped his flashlight downward and noticed the glass scattered on the carpet. Joe kept wishing he had that bigger flashlight back.

"Those are authentic Witco chairs," said Brendan, pointing his light on a group of high-backed chairs in the corner. Carved into the dark wood seat backs were the upper torsos of two large-eared natives, back to back, bisected only by a bright floral strip of orange, gold, and green vinyl that matched the seat cushion. At the top of the chair, the profile of one of the natives was serious, the other wore an ironic smirk like the mask in the other room.

"And check out these tables."

A group of them were pushed together and, without thinking, Joe reached over and ran his hand along the top of one. It was white with dust and possibly mold, but the surface felt silky. Where his fingers made contact, he could see foreign coins suspended in Lucite. The table was amazing, but he made a mental note not to touch his eyes or mouth until he got a chance to wash his hands.

"I'm surprised no one has taken this stuff," said Joe, thinking that a lot of it would be great to own.

"Nuh-uh. We don't do that. Take only pictures, leave only footprints."

Joe shined a light at Brendan's chest, just to see his face, to see if he was serious. "Really? So you're like the Sierra Club or something?"

Brendan nodded his head, as serious as Joe had ever seen him, though he had only known him for the past forty minutes. "Really."

"Cool. Why aren't you taking any photos?"

"I've shot it a couple of times. I wanted to travel lighter tonight. Plus, I'm carrying a rookie." Brendan grabbed Joe's arm again and started pulling him back toward the hallway. "Come on, you got to see the grotto. It's dope."

"Okay." Joe touched the back of a rattan chair, suddenly liking the feel of the dust and grime on his hands. He was excited now, he liked the whole idea of this, of the Joe who would do something like this, break into an abandoned building and explore. He liked Adventurous Joe. It occurred to him that he had never done much of anything outrageous or dangerous, and certainly nothing illegal. So it felt good

to be walking through a dilapidated building at night, especially while stoned. This was more like it! This was the Joe
he had been planning to be all along, before clearer heads
prevailed. (Who was he kidding? He had nothing to blame
but his own clearer head.)

As they approached the banister that led to the grotto,
there was a clanging sound. Brendan grabbed Joe's arm
again, only tighter this time.

"What was that?" said Joe.

"*Shhh!*" said Brendan, suddenly clasping his hand over
Joe's mouth. He shut off his big Maglite and covered the
beam of Joe's small one with his hand. It got very dark very
quickly. The only light came from between Brendan's glowing fingers. Brendan then took his hand from Joe's face and
placed a finger to his own lips.

Joe motioned at the back door and mouthed: *Is someone there?*
Brendan nodded slowly.

Joe mouthed: *Police?*

"What da fuck gon' on in here?" said a voice from the
back door.

"Probably some scrapper, after copper pipe," whispered
Brendan. "Shit."

Adventurous Joe was ready to run for it, but whoever
was there was at the door. There was nowhere to go. They
were stuck in this death trap of a building, with the only
open door at the other end. Joe's breathing quickened as the
footsteps got louder, heading toward them. Brendan took a
step. Joe grabbed his arm this time, but Brendan shook it
free and scuffed ahead silently.

"I kill any motherfuckers in my building!" shouted the
voice. Then there was laughter, which could only be described as diabolical.

Oh god, oh shit, thought Joe. *What's happening?*

Brendan turned off Joe's flashlight and handed it to him. "Keep this off and stay here," said Brendan, then reached under his hoodie and pulled out what looked to be a rather large blackjack. At least that's what Joe thought it was. He had never seen one before. "I'll deal with him."

Brendan took off, holding his Maglite like a truncheon in his left hand, with the blackjack in his right hand, leaving Joe in complete darkness.

"No!" whispered Joe, but no one answered. Brendan was gone. Joe was afraid to turn on his small flashlight, so he just stood there in the dark, not knowing what to do.

Joe heard what sounded like a fight breaking out by the back door. He turned the tiny flashlight on, keeping it close to the floor, and slowly made his way toward the back. From there, he could hear something get knocked over.

He heard the voice say, "Pull that shit on me, bitch? I'ma fuck you up." There was another crash, then a thud, then the sound of what might have been a head or body being slammed against the floor repeatedly. He heard Brendan scream.

He heard the voice repeat, "Motherfucker," with a strained emphasis on the "fucker," between blows. After a minute of it, there was silence.

Oh god. Joe stepped into the nearest dining room and slipped under a banquette table.

Then the voice again: "I know they's two of you. I'm comin' for *you*, motherfucker. Get ready to die like this white boy!"

Joe was paralyzed under the table. He didn't know what to do. He searched around for something to use as a weapon, but all he had was his measly little flashlight.

There was more diabolical laughter, but it sounded different this time. Then Joe heard two voices laughing and, before long, it didn't sound very diabolical. It was more hysterical. There was a flurry of footsteps and then Joe saw the beam of the Maglite.

"Hey Joe," Brendan yelled out between breathless guffaws, "it's cool! Everything's fine! We're just fucking with you, bro!"

Quickly, Joe tried to scramble up from the floor, but he bashed his head on the table. The beam of the flashlight found him. Joe looked up to see Brendan accompanied by a tall, thin black man with twists, wearing a peacoat. Both were laughing with delight at the sight of Joe squatted beneath the table.

"He may be the best one yet," said the tall man, in a voice that sounded different from the one he'd heard at the door.

Brendan finally stopped laughing. He wiped an eye. "Oh jeez. That is priceless right there. That is good stuff," he said, pointing at Joe. "Come on. Get up, playboy. We should go. We made a lot of noise."

"That's part of my process. The noise. The silence. And everything in between," said the tall man to Brendan. "You know I use The Method."

Brendan bowed at the waist to him. "Indeed. You are the Gielgud of psychotic crackhead scrappers. He held a hand out for Joe and yanked him up, then said: "I hope you understand, but we *had* to do that."

Joe just glared at him. What else was there to do? He stood up and started to brush off his clothes. He was filthy. This would be fun to explain to Ana if she were around.

"That's Malik," said Brendan.

Smiling broadly, Malik held out his hand. Joe didn't bother trying any fancy handshakes.

"Sorry about that, friend. It's a little thing we do. An initiation."

Joe brightened at the thought of not being the first person to be humiliated like this. "Really? Did I pass?"

Malik, trying not to laugh, just nodded. "Sure. You did fine."

Joe turned to Brendan hopefully.

"No you didn't," Brendan said, shaking his head. "He's just being nice. You sucked. You hid under a table. It's all right though." More laughter.

Joe sighed.

20

A Grand Rapids of the Mind

Bruce had gotten out of the office early, which meant that Ana had gotten out early as well. On the way out of the building, they had passed Jerrod in the hall. Ana gave him a big fake grin. He returned it, larger and faker.

"And where are you two off to?" he said, arching his brows like Myrna Loy. Ana had never heard that phrase sound so catty in her life.

"Client meeting for WomanLyfe, Jerrod," said Bruce, matter-of-factly.

"Wow. Late meeting for Grand Rapids!" There was no missing the faux surprise on his face.

"It's very early tomorrow, Jerrod," said Bruce. "Care to join us?"

Ana noticed that even Bruce sounded exasperated by this exchange.

Jerrod smiled again and shook his head while holding his palms up toward them. "Oh no, I wouldn't dream of it. Three's a crowd, after all."

Asshole, thought Ana, as he walked away.

"God, he's a dick," said Bruce.

"Oh yes," said Ana.

"He's lucky that he's such a good art director."

"Art director, yes. Person, no," muttered Ana on the way to Bruce's car.

Was it a surprise that Bruce had a beautiful car? A sleek black Jaguar, spanking new and gorgeous. She usually frowned upon conspicuous consumption. Her typical reaction to someone with a fancy car was the same as to someone with a perfectly sculpted body. *You're spending way too much time thinking about this. Maybe you should read a book now and then.* But as soon as she sat down in it and closed the door, she was cocooned in leather, burled wood, and Bruce's spicy scent. She tried not to think about what Adrienne had said last night. She was going to ignore it. Work was requiring her to spend time with her boss. She would do her job and forget the rest.

"Sweet ride, Bruce," was all she could think of saying. Then she felt like an idiot for saying it.

This made him chuckle. "Thanks. It's the first time I've ever gotten a car like this. Don't get me wrong, I love it, but it still embarrasses me a little."

"Really? Why?"

"I don't know. It's a little flashy." He rolled his eyes at his own comment. "Let's face it. It's *a lot* flashy, but part of me must have wanted that, I guess."

Ana waved her hand. "Oh, what the hell. We'll all be dead in fifty years anyway."

Bruce turned to her, half smirking as he pressed the ignition button. "There's a cheery thought." The car dreamily hummed to life like some internal combustion tone poem.

Ana laughed, realizing how it must have sounded. "I just mean, what's the difference? If you can afford it, why not drive a nice car?" She wasn't terribly sure where all this was coming from. She had driven the same Subaru for almost ten years. Joe's Volvo was almost twenty years old, but it had been eight years old when he bought it. (It was their not-so-secret shame that neither of them owned cars built in their hometown.) Perhaps it was just that this beautiful *objet* of an automobile appealed to the art director in her.

"Yeah, what the hell?" said Bruce, almost to himself. "I'm not a hollow man, trying to fill his life with shiny objects. Right?"

It was a weird thing to say. Ana spoke no more about the car.

The ride to Grand Rapids was uneventful. Bruce was on his Bluetooth for much of the two-hour drive. Ana had brought her laptop with her MiFi and personal hot spot, so she just caught up on e-mails while they drove. The seemingly hundreds of daily messages were the bane of her new job. She hated them, but today she was glad they were there. Even when the Internet coverage faded in and out, she still tapped away at drafts. It gave her an excuse not to have to talk to Bruce much. Not that it was expected of her. He seemed completely immersed in his calls, which was a relief. There was no overtly friendly behavior. Bruce was all business. They did chat a bit about some work done by her and Adrienne (who had found this arrangement to be suspect and told Ana to be careful) for WomanLyfe, but then Bruce got another call.

Ana had to admit, listening in on his side of the conversation, that she was impressed by the way Bruce was so knowledgeable about the various accounts at the agency. He was able to think strategically about them and their competitors, how that related to the work that he oversaw, while also knowing all the clients with whom he interacted, as well as the political ins and outs of the companies.

Once they pulled into Grand Rapids, they checked into the Amway Grand, then met in the lobby to go get some dinner. Bruce took her to a gastropub called the HopCat, where she discovered that he was a beer nerd. The place was all wood and granite, brick and brass. Beautiful European beer-advertising posters from the twenties and thirties were mounted on the walls and ceiling. Bruce started talking to the waiter about exotic beers with names like Delirium Tremens and Rochefort and Pliny the Elder. Beer wasn't Ana's beverage of choice, so she was going to get a glass of wine.

"Come on, it's a beer place," said Bruce. "You gotta get a beer."

Ana sighed, trying to be a good sport. She really shouldn't be drinking at all, considering how things turned out last time she had boozed it up with Bruce. And that was when Adrienne was there.

"I'm going to order you a lambic," he said, giving the second syllable a slight European accent.

"Sounds pretentious," said Ana.

"Come on. They have some really good ones here. You'll like it."

Bruce ordered something called a Final Absolution for himself, which made perfect sense to her, since everyone forgave creative directors for everything. He ordered some kind of Lindemans for her.

When the beer came, it was good, but she was surprised by the strong cherry flavor, not sweet, but very fruity. She wondered if this was traditionally a woman's beer, which made her instantly not care for it. She looked at the blackboard and made a note to order a bourbon porter. It sounded loathsome, but she was damned if she was going to drink girly beers.

"What's the plan for tomorrow?" she asked as she scanned the menu.

Bruce glanced up from his menu and, for the first time that day, really looked at her. "We roll into WomanLyfe at about ten to eight, have a short meeting with Karin and her people, probably a couple of hours, then hit the road. We should be back at the agency by one at the latest. Unless they want to take you on a tour. Then all bets are off."

Ana nodded.

"How do you like that beer?" said Bruce.

The lambic was actually starting to grow on her, but still she wanted to give Bruce some grief about it. "It's okay. For a chick beer." She didn't usually care for the word *chick*, but she figured that was what beer dorks called it.

"It's not a chick beer," he responded, surprisingly defensive. "I drink those. They're good for dessert. In fact, they're for the more discriminating palette."

Now she felt bad. "Oh, okay. Sorry. It is good, really."

Bruce smiled at her. "Nah, that's bullshit. Research shows that ladies love fruity beers." He shrugged and spread his palms out as if to say, *I cannot change what is unimpeachably true.* "Sorry."

Ana had to laugh. "Damn it!" she said, shaking her fist at him. "Well, I am a lady."

"Yes, you are." He touched her hand just for a moment before sitting back in his chair. "Sometimes we cannot help being exactly what we are."

"Hmm," she said, wondering if she was being pulled into some linguistic snare. "Who said that?"

Bruce looked to the left and the right, as if for imaginary tablemates. "Um. Me. Just now." He took a sip of his beer, then another.

"Really? It sounded like you were quoting someone." Ana gave him a playful frown. "How did you get to be so slick, Bruce Kellner?"

He winced, like she had just delivered a verbal blow to the abdomen. At first, Ana felt mean, but then she was glad that she possessed the power to hurt him a little.

"Oh, come on," she continued. "It's not such a bad thing. I don't mean used-car salesman slick. I just mean—" Now she decided to temper her comment. "I just mean you seem so good at your job, like you have it pretty much together. And you absolutely know it."

Bruce turned away for a moment and Ana panicked, fearful that she had both insulted and bored him at the same time. Then came a look in his eyes that she hadn't seen yet, a helplessness. "Yes, well, shall I give my ex-wife a call and ask her? I have a feeling that she'd have a different perception of me."

Ana made a face, a grimace that hopefully conveyed sympathy or concern or just said, *Sorry I peeled open that wound.* She drank her beer, thinking that she'd just shut up, but she did not do this. "How long were you two married?"

"Eleven years. We've got two boys."

It struck Ana as funny how people often attached the number of children they had when telling you how long they had been married. As if the offspring tally somehow justified or legitimized the collected years of matrimony. "Really? Wow, you're very good at keeping your personal life to yourself, Bruce. I had no idea you had kids."

He tilted his head, an abbreviated shrug. "Oh, sometimes people will bring theirs up, so I'll mention mine, but mostly work is work and home is home. Unfortunately, there was too much work and not enough home. Which explains why I no longer live at that home."

"Where *do* you live, Bruce?

"Eh, Bloomfield Hills. I bought a detached condo up that way. It's fine. Not far from my ex, so I see my kids pretty often."

"Yes, I'm starting to realize how work can get in the way of homelife."

"Really," said Bruce, leaning toward her to listen, as if she had so much more to say. She didn't, but his silence prodded her to continue, slightly against her wishes. Joe had taught her this old reporter's trick, of letting the silences hang uncomfortably until the subject went on talking, which was where the good stuff came from. Somewhere, Bruce had learned the same trick, probably with clients. Though she saw it for what it was, it didn't stop her from talking.

"My husband and I both just started new jobs and it's been really tough lately." (She had taken to calling Joe her "husband" in work situations years ago, after tiring of the constant explication regarding their living arrangements, as well as growing sick of referring to him as her "boyfriend.") Right then, when she might have expected a warm word of encouragement, a little *Buck up, it'll get better*, Bruce only nodded and seemed to take note of this fact. (*Why should he be encouraging?* she thought, given the way his own marital situation had gone.)

He rested his elbow on the table, then his chin on his hand. She again felt too much attention being paid to her. "How long have you two been together?"

"Fifteen years."

"Really?"

She didn't know how to read the astonishment in his eyes. "What?"

Bruce shook his head innocently. "Nothing . . . I mean, what, did you guys meet in high school or something?"

She tipped her head, peered at him suspiciously. "Come on, Bruce. Don't give me that. You know I'm not that young."

"Ana, I have no idea how old you are. I don't go through all the employment records of all the people who work for me. To me, you look like you're around thirty."

Ana tried very hard not to bat her eyelashes and say, *Really?* And mostly she succeeded, but she wasn't able to completely erase the smile from her voice, all the while remembering (and mostly rejecting) Adrienne's warning about revealing one's true age, about letting the perception be the reality. "Yeah, well. I'm not. Let's just leave it at that."

Bruce ran a hand through his hair. Ana thought it was the most perfect salt-and-pepper hair she had ever seen outside of Cary Grant. It was obviously well cared for by an expensive stylist. Then she caught herself: who the fuck cared about his hair? She took a sip of beer. The lambic was definitely growing on her.

"Yes, and the funny thing is, we're not even officially married. And we've been together longer than just about anyone I know. Almost everyone who we know who has been married that long is now divorced."

Bruce held his hands together palm-to-palm in front of his face, his elbows on the table. He was very good at studied poses that suggested attentiveness. The praying hands mostly hid his mouth too. "Hmm," he said, nodding. She watched him glance at the waitress (was he checking out her ass?), then he looked back at Ana. "No kids?"

"Nope." Ana had long ago learned to answer this question proudly, definitively, and most certainly not like an apology.

"Why not?"

"I like my life. I don't want to be a mother. When most couples have kids, it's the woman who gives up the most and does the most. I like having a career. I don't want it all. Having it all is too much."

"And he's fine with that?"

"Yes he is."

Joined palms shifted to interlocked fingers. "Why did you guys decide not to get married? You were obviously committed to each other."

Ana noted Bruce's use of the past tense and wondered what he meant by it. "We're still committed to each other," she said, more to be contrary than anything. "Getting the piece of paper didn't matter. It still doesn't. If you're committed, you're committed. A marriage certificate doesn't hold anything together." Then, before she thought better of it, she added, "As you well know."

A new beer appeared in front of Ana. *I have to have some food*, she thought, picking up the menu. She looked up to find Bruce staring at her. She smiled blandly, and then quickly buried her head in the menu.

Dinner was fine, though Ana wound up drinking too much. She did eventually try the bourbon porter, and it was so strong and so redolent of bourbon that it made her woozy, especially after the two lambics. She ordered a fancy buffalo burger with grilled onions and blue cheese, which basically undid whatever good she was doing by getting a burger of superlean meat. This happened a lot these days—starting off with good intentions, then having them mutate into some twisted justification for indulgence. Not long into the meal, she realized that she had the perfect opportunity to run some ideas by Bruce about the W2W division.

"I really think we have the opportunity to pitch some business that could actually be good for women and lucrative for the company. You know, maybe aim a little higher than WomanLyfe?"

Bruce took a bite of his burger (beef, of course) and nodded. "Like what?"

"I don't know. Okay, maybe not so much 'good for women,' but maybe get ahold of a small packaged-goods account, maybe something Michigan-made. There's a stand at Eastern Market called Farmer's Daughter. They make soaps and soy candles and natural cosmetics. If we took them on, kind of pro bono, maybe we could do something cool like that Dove Real Beauty work. Where instead of showing anorexic models who make women feel like shit about the way they look, they celebrated real women. Women who are beautiful, but don't have some sort of allegedly perfect fashion-model bodies that are impossible to achieve without starving yourself."

"Oh yeah. Those spots with the fat chicks."

Ana stopped dead and glared at him. "Are you fucking kidding me?"

Bruce bowed his head in pretend shame, half smiling. "Yes, I'm kidding. I'm sorry, I had to do something. You were being so earnest. Sorry. Go on. I know what you're saying."

Ana took a breath and resumed: "My big worry about WomanLyfe, along with their crazy allegiances, is the same as yours. That they're going to want the same crappy advertising but in a shinier package." Ana put down her burger, wiped her mouth and hands with her napkin. She rested her elbows on the table, assuming the same praying hands stance that Bruce had used earlier, then interlacing her fingers. "Ultimately, it's not really going to do us any—"

Just then Bruce leaned over and picked a sesame seed off her arm and put it into his mouth. He continued to nod at her, listening to everything she said, but it was such a completely strange thing to do, she could barely finish her sentence. "It's . . . it's . . . just not going to do the group, um, or the agency any good to have something, uh . . . bad out there," she said, now totally flustered. "Making us look . . . bad." She wondered if her face looked as flushed as it felt.

"I know what you're saying," said Bruce. "I agree. But we're backed against the wall with this client. We've had this talk before. We're stuck with them. It's going to be up to us, actually *you*, to sell them something that's better than what they've been doing. This is *your* job. To do something great."

Ana's speech had blown up in her face. She just sat there nodding way too avidly. She half assumed that she was close to being fired.

Then Bruce smiled at her, that beam of warmth radiating from him. He put his last bite of burger in his mouth, chewed it briefly, then nodded to himself. "I'm gonna get a calvados. Calvados?" he asked Ana. Before she said anything, he turned and waved down the waitress. "Two calvados, please." Within seconds, it seemed, a snifter appeared before her. Ana let it sit there, next to her half-full bourbon stout. She actually desired something stronger, but it was already nine thirty and the evening, while partially enjoyable, had already gotten way too weird, especially with the sesame seed incident.

It was one of the most curious invasions of personal space she had ever experienced; both random and silly, while so strangely intimate that her face still felt flushed. She supposed it was a kind of violation—but it was just a sesame seed. It wasn't like the time at her very first agency job when some old-school account executive who still drank his lunch every day came up behind her in the break room and honked her right boob. (Replete with sound effect.) She turned around and threw a steaming-hot cup of coffee right in his face. She was ready to kick him in the balls too, but he was already screaming and flailing around on the ground. Ten years earlier, the incident may have gone unpunished (or she would have lost her job for inflicting third-degree burns on a coworker), but luckily for her, it was right around the time that some of the first sexual harassment suits were starting to make the local news and the agency was terrified that the newbie junior art director was going to sue. It turned out to be the last straw for the AE. They had been looking for a reason to can his drunken ass and Ana was it. She did not feel bad about it in the least. In fact, she still regretted not kicking him in the balls.

It wasn't like that. But the sesame seed incident colored the whole evening in such a way that left her feeling absolutely unmoored. And, well, though she was kind of ashamed to admit it, a little aroused. Was it odd that, when she thought about it, she had kind of liked the intimacy of the gesture? Two fingers of Bruce (which sounded strangely like a seventies chop-socky film) touching her skin, plucking off a plump little seed, excited her in some inexplicable way. Now, finally capitulating to that calvados in front of her (Bruce on his second), the liquor burning away all concerns, the evening seemed to skitter off in a way that she was not sure she could control. Yet part of her couldn't help but to think that was just what she wanted.

Later, back at the hotel, they had a final nightcap. (Bruce was very big on the nightcaps, she realized. They'd had two "one last ones" at the HopCat. He clearly loved the idea of one last drink, as if that proclamation was some sort of inviolable rule. You could not have one more after that. Then when you did, it made that next nightcap, that next *one last one*, taste all the better.) In the elevator, her head muzzy with strange beer, strong apple liquor, and a final something at the bar (what was that?), when Bruce asked her to hit the 3 button, she realized that his room was on the same floor as hers. (He had headed for the lobby bathroom when she checked in.) Walking down the hall, she saw that her room was two doors down from his. Even then, drunk as she was, she wondered if it was too much of a coincidence, that maybe he had planned it; and when she stopped at her door, Bruce stopped with her. Not saying anything, he put his hand to her face (that hand now not feeling unfamiliar against her skin) and kissed her.

What happened next was a blur of sensations. Her pulling back for a moment (and it was only a moment) before she crushed her lips against his. Bruce's hands reaching behind her, against her back, grasping her waist, reaching up beneath the Western shirt she was wearing, his hand against the skin of her back, that part of her back that had not been touched by any other man in a long time. And it was that feeling of skin against skin that allowed her to allow Bruce to push her against the hotel door and hold his body against hers. Her hands were moving as well, one inside his shirt, one down along the front of his jeans. She felt the thickness there, heard him sigh deeply. Then his hand at the front of her jeans, moving hard against the seam, against her repeatedly, then up to her waist, tugging the metal button at its eyelet.

"Open the door," whispered Bruce after he undid the button, starting to slide the zipper down.

"All right," Ana said, actually managing to speak.

"Let's go inside." Yet another hand cupping her right breast. What were all these hands doing? Where were hers? Oh yes. *There.*

"I know you want to," he said, kissing the underside of her chin, a place not accustomed to the attention.

Someone thinking for her was not what she wanted, even though he was right and she did want to open the door. "Just a second," she said, her hands shaking, fumbling for the key card that she had slipped in her side pocket. Ana turned her back to Bruce while she tried to insert the card in the lock.

His hands quickly found their way back to where they were before, on her breast and at her zipper. She inserted the key card again, and the three small lights above the slot flashed red, then she tried once more. Red. Then again. Red. Red. Red.

"Hurry," said Bruce, his index and middle fingers brushing against her clitoris, making it harder for her to concentrate.

"I'm trying," she said, bumping back into his erection.

She kept her eyes focused on the tiny lights above the slot, and then inserted the card one more time. She waited for the three small lights to blink green, and when it finally did, she twisted down hard on the handle till the bolt made a loud *thunk* and pushed open the door.

At the sound, Bruce tried to move the both of them into the room, but just then she pushed him back hard, out into the hallway.

"I can't do this," she said, panting. She slipped through the slim opening she had given herself and quickly turned to shut the door behind her. "I have to go. Go away. I'll see you tomorrow."

Closing the door, she caught a flash of his face in the narrowing column between the door and the jamb. He was just standing there, looking at her in stunned disbelief. The boy with the lost puppy, breathing hard, face reddened with alcohol, suppressing something else entirely.

"Ana," he said to the closed door. "Come on, this is crazy." He banged on the door. "I know you want to do this."

Inside, she turned from the door and clutched herself, trying to stop shaking, knowing he was still there, knowing that she could get him back inside in an instant, and that a part of her wanted that. Then there was the other part that wanted to get away from what she wanted.

After a breathless minute, Ana finally heard his footfalls down the hallway and knew she was alone. She had never seen this side of herself before. Nothing like this had ever happened to her in all the time that she and Joe had been together. Not even close. She never thought herself capable of it. She was boring and monogamous and she liked it that way. She was too guilty a person to have an affair or whatever this was. Her conscience beat her up about everything. (Lately it had been knocking her around pretty good for being in advertising.) She knew she was going to think about this too much, especially given her lack of tolerance for infidelity in other people. You either commit or you don't. If you don't, fine, but don't act like you do when you don't. She had subtly cut people out of her life when they had revealed themselves to be unfaithful spouses or friends.

And now she goes and does this?

It wasn't so much what had actually happened (even though what had happened was plenty and she was still processing it right now, heart galloping, stomach churning, head spinning with alcohol, not to mention the unmistakable dampness between her legs), but that she would allow it to happen in the first place. It seemed like proof of what she had been thinking about last night, another sign that she was becoming someone she didn't even recognize.

After an uneasy night's sleep, complete with the bed spinning, a sweaty scramble to the bathroom to vomit (fumes of fruit and bourbon), and four thirty a.m. mind-racing spells of guilt, self-hatred, and fears of solitary nursing-home death, Ana got up at ten past six and pushed everything from her mind out of sheer survival: she had to get ready. She downed three ibuprofen, showered, dried her hair, put on makeup (extra concealer, please), dressed in the clothes she had brought for the meeting (a gray wool dress that she had loved, a totally overpriced indulgence from Anthropologie, now forever tainted by the memory of this trip), packed her suitcase, and quietly opened her door and rolled it down the hall, praying that Bruce would not hear her pass. Once in the elevator (superfriendly hotel employee engaging her in needless niceties; vague smile as she concentrated on the glowing rectangle of her iPhone as if waiting for an urgent message), she allowed herself some small sense of relief.

After checking out, stashing her suitcase with the bellman, and grabbing a nonfat latte from the weird German-style coffee shop (more hyperfriendliness from barista, people in Grand Rapids preternaturally cheerful; she hated it), Ana texted Bruce to let him know that she was downstairs and ready to head over to WomanLyfe. The meeting was supposed to start in an hour.

As far as she knew, they were about five minutes away

from the place, but she needed time to think. She could still not quite believe the events of last night. She knew she had been fairly drunk, but not *that* drunk. As she sipped her coffee, Ana allowed herself to think again about everything that had happened, and carefully constructed in her mind a hierarchy of worry.

First and foremost, she felt crushingly guilty for kissing Bruce. She hadn't kissed another man in that way since she had been with Joe. That said, she knew it had just been a kiss and she had stopped everything before it got completely out of control. Yet she was having a hard time reasoning away that simple kiss. Then she remembered that along with the kiss, there had been more kissing. A lot more kissing. *Oh, right.* Then there was the touching, which she hadn't really participated in, and had only allowed for a very short time. Oh, wait . . . yes, she had participated in the touching. Quite a lot of that as well. That had definitely happened, her hands far below the equator. Was it crazy to try to determine just how guilty she really needed to feel? On a one-to-ten indiscretion scale, was this maybe a four? Okay, maybe five, but it couldn't be much worse than that. The touching. The consensual touching. Did that move it up to a seven? Or even an eight? No, it couldn't be. There would have to be some form of actual sex before it got into the eight-point range. What was Joe going to say? Surely, he would forgive a kiss. Yet it was a lot more than a kiss. *If* she decided to tell him. Ana wasn't sure that was ever going to happen. Still, the idea of living with this made her feel sick inside. She was not this type of person.

Secondly, she was worried about how this was going to affect her job. She had no idea how Bruce would act when he came down. (Still no text back.) For all she knew, she would be summarily dismissed from her job. Then again, she better not be fired or the agency was going to get a massive surprise: she would sic a lawyer on Edward Cherkovski so fast he wouldn't know what sued him. So she'd probably get to keep her job. Still, Bruce could be a dick about the whole thing. Ana could be silently punished, demoted, given nothing but horrible jobs from now on, treated like shit so she'd want to quit. Yes, that was how things worked—they just made it bad for people they didn't want there. There were plenty of stories like that in every agency she had ever worked.

Even if none of this happened, things would definitely be weird. Right now, it felt like her best plan of action was to act like the whole thing never happened. Needless to say, she would never, ever go on a trip with just Bruce again. The whole thing was a huge mistake. She wouldn't even allow herself to be alone in a room with him. That meant she would have to tell Adrienne about this. She was not at all looking forward to that.

Which brought her to number three on her hierarchy of worry: All evidence seemed to indicate rather strongly that she had wanted what happened last night to happen. That she had enjoyed it. Telling herself that she was drunk was only going to work for so long. Adrienne always said that alcohol doesn't change people; it makes them more like themselves. This made her feel worst of all. She remembered now how much she had wanted to open that door and let him in.

Just how much did intention count? This was the question that worried her the most.

Her iPhone blipped with an incoming text: *On way down. CU in 5.*

* * *

Ana's plan to act as though nothing at all had happened was working surprisingly well. There was no mention of the previous night's occurrences during coffee at the hotel or on the walk to WomanLyfe. She and Bruce had merely gone over what they were going to talk about at the meeting. Luckily, there actually wasn't much for her to do. It was really more of a chemistry meeting for her. Her job was to be likable: "Hi! So nice to meet you!" Brisk handshake, direct look into eyes of shakee. "I'm Ana, one of the creatives who will be working on your account!" *Smile, smile, smile.*

So far, Bruce was not acting the least bit different than he had the day before. It was uncanny. But then, she should have known. He was a man. Thus, much better at acting as though nothing improper had happened, rather than acknowledging it, which could lead to discomfort of a physical or emotional nature. Denial was the psychological currency of the male. Acceptable anywhere, in any situation. *What? That never happened. Forget about it.* Still, it was eerie how easy it was for both of them.

The only tough part of the meeting was talking to Karin. Ana didn't know if the woman was tweaked about her and Adrienne at the last meeting, but she definitely detected a certain frostiness.

"What do you think the tone for the advertising should be?" Karin asked Ana, midway through the hour they were all to spend together.

It was the kind of question that felt like trouble, though she remembered Adrienne asking the same question to Karin back at the agency. Ana recalled some vague brand-oriented blather about *approachability*, which she could easily repeat, but she wanted to really answer this question. Whatever her answer, Ana sensed that she would be walking through a minefield.

"I think the tone should match your company," she began. "Caring, pro-woman, spiritual—"

"We're not pro-woman, we're pro-family," Karin snapped.

Okay, it hadn't taken very long to step on a mine. Ana considered the comment carefully. "Well, by caring about women, you are in turn caring about families. Because the women are generally primary caregivers for the families, right?" Ana saw some of the other people at the table nodding in agreement.

Karin's tone grew sharper. "But we're not some sort of feminazi organization that stands for all the wrong things."

First, Ana felt the heat rise in her ears, and then she realized that Karin was consciously baiting her. Just knowing that calmed her down considerably. She had fallen into too many traps in the past twenty-four hours; this was not going to be another one. Ana took a slightly theatrical breath, as though she was giving this query the utmost consideration, placed her elbows on the table, then pushed her palms together, looked away, then straight back at Karin. "Here's what I meant: Your organization wants to help women be healthier, happier, more spiritually aware, right? You want them to take care of themselves, so they in turn can take better care of their families, correct?"

"Of course."

"Well, you're being *pro-woman*, even if that phrase may have different meanings to different groups. And before we get into a big semantic argument, I have to say that we would never *use* that term. Besides, being pro-women isn't about how any group defines it. It's about how *you* define it. That's the reason you're advertising. To create your own definition out there in the marketplace of what it means to be a woman. But first you have to give women some hope that they can change their lives. The women we want to reach need an ally. They're overworked, underappreciated, and undernourished, physically and spiritually. They need someone that's pro-*them*. And that's your company."

Ana looked around. Everyone at the table was nodding like a roomful of promotional bobbleheads. Ana stared at Karin. The woman didn't look pleased, but she was nodding right along with them.

Later in the car, Bruce was in full boss-mode. Ana was relieved to have the meeting behind them and to have Bruce (and her) acting in an appropriate manner again. Hopefully, they could fill the entire trip home with work stuff. She remembered that she had her laptop and reached over to the backseat to grab her computer bag. It felt good to have it on her lap. She felt protected—not from Bruce, but from herself. She did not currently trust her instincts.

"That was good, how you avoided Karin's trap like that," he said.

Ana unzipped the bag, pulled out her laptop, and flipped it open. "Okay. So it felt like a trap to you too? I thought maybe it was just my paranoia."

A half laugh from Bruce. "Oh god, yes. It was a trap."

"Why would she do that?"

He shrugged. "I don't know. But I'm already starting to get used to it from her. Clients just do that sometimes, especially ad managers. Half of the time they're the reason we lose accounts. The ad manager ends up throwing us under the bus to save his own job. Even though they hired us for our expertise, they're constantly trying to prove that they know more than the agency. They want to set us up as elite snobs who can't come close to understanding the core audience better than them."

"Yeah, right," said Ana dryly. "We have that snobbish Detroit attitude. We're just like New York agencies, only worse."

He lifted a hand off the steering wheel and ran it through his hair. "Or sometimes people are just in a shitty mood, who knows?"

"Well, I'm sorry that she would feel the need to do that. I guess I always hope that women in business want to be supportive of each other."

Bruce tipped his head back and had a nice long laugh. "Ah, yes. Sisters sticking together, doing it for themselves. *You go, girl*," he said in a stiltedly sassy voice.

Ana felt embarrassed by his condescending tone, along with everything else she was feeling. "Yeah, kinda. Is that so bad?"

He smiled wistfully as he watched the road. "No, there's nothing at all wrong with that. But it's not really that way, is it?"

Ana hated to admit what she was about to say. "No, hardly ever. Most of the time it's like a big competition. Way more women in the business world treat me like shit than men. More backbiting, more bad behavior. It totally sucks."

"It's just something I've noticed in meetings and with the office politics. I mean, men do it too, but it's more—I don't know—more overt, more loud, more aggressive."

Ana shot him a glance over her glasses. "Yeah, I know what it looks like. I've been to the zoo."

"Touché," said Bruce, as he shifted his gaze from the road to smile at her.

Ana quickly looked down at the screen of her computer.

21

Out Come the Freaks

oe opened the front door of their town house and threw his keys and cell phone in the bowl on the prong-legged fifties table they had placed near the doorway. He had survived another soul-smothering day at the *Dollar Daily*. That afternoon, Terrance had him cold-calling area businesses to see if he could drum up ads for the newspaper. It had come to this; he was turning into a telemarketing Willy Loman.

Joe was hardly even writing for them anymore. Terrance just wouldn't relinquish any territory or let Joe do any of the things for which he had been hired. At first Joe thought that Terrance was one of those sadistic people who loved squelching others' talent because it made them feel better about their own lack of it. Yet he soon realized that the man wasn't evil, he was simply scared. Joe now believed that Terrance had sincerely planned to change the paper (it was how he could so convincingly sell the job to Joe), but the reality was that he was too afraid to do anything that might offend his precious "core audience," thus lowering profits. Which left Joe as the staff effigy, Terrance's walking compromise, his way to feel secure in the knowledge that something could happen should he desire to make it so. But it was never going to happen, Joe now knew that.

Of course, he still had "Rap Sheet," though Terrance had given him a talking-to for making it too funny.

"This is serious stuff, Joe. People turn here to find out what crimes are happening in their neighborhood. The *Detroit Free Press* tells you when someone's been murdered, but they won't publish a story about a break-in two blocks from your house. That's what we're here for."

Yes, spreading the news about someone's embarrassing DUI is a real public service, thought Joe. At that moment, he almost told Terrance to take "Rap Sheet" and shove it up his sanctimonious ass. Instead, Joe just nodded like the corporate toady he was. Except the truth was, he wasn't even a corporate toady. He should be so lucky. A corporate toady would probably make a lot more money. That was something that hadn't taken long for him to realize. Though his salary had sounded like a lot of money when he first took the job, it really wasn't. Especially compared to the money that Ana brought home as an SVP. He decided that she was just so elated that he would be contributing financially to the household that she'd neglected to tell him that he actually wasn't really making all that much. *Isn't that sweet? He's so proud of his little pauper's wage. I won't burst his bubble.* Joe felt embarrassed to think that, but it was probably true. Ana hadn't wanted to hurt his feelings.

Why had he chosen to do this? There were so many interesting things going on in the city right now and he was stuck writing about the vanilla suburbs. Still, who was he kidding? He was not one of the newly arrived swarms of twentysomething optimists and idealists, artists and upstart entrepreneurs (most of them recent émigrés from the suburbia to which their parents had fearfully fled in the seventies and eighties), riding their thrift-store bicycles on the deserted, litter-blown streets of the Cass Corridor, past once-grand Victorian mansions with trees growing through the moss-covered roofs, past stunned SRO residents, milling prostitutes, and the muttering homeless. Those kids were all looking to forge some new beginning, creating urban farms, quirky co-ops, quixotic start-ups and nonprofits, and hopelessly hopeful art projects. He had to admire their gumption.

Yet all of that sounded like a lot of work for a forty-year-old guy who had just gotten his first real job. But then, at least he wasn't like a lot of people his age who had fled the city long ago, holed out there in the massive, jiggling belly of exurbia among the homogeneous big-box stores and franchise restaurants, in a towering beige McMansion with matching patio furniture, waiting with trepidation for either the next promotion or the layoff that would make it all go away. He wasn't that either. What the fuck was he?

Joe lay on the couch, closed his eyes. He felt too exhausted even to get up for a beer.

When Ana came in through the door almost two hours later, Joe opened his eyes, feeling disoriented and logy. Apparently he had been sleeping. *Ugh.* He hated the heaviness of mind and body that he experienced after an involuntary nap. (For this reason, he did not like naps of any kind, whereas Ana could and would nap anywhere, anytime, especially if she was depressed.) He felt even worse when he remembered what he had been dreaming about.

Joe had been dreaming about being rich. Had he ever dreamed of money before? It felt perverse to him, like a wet dream that reveals the bizarre fetish of the dreamer. Yet, was it that surprising? He'd been thinking about money a lot lately. Fifteen years ago, all he thought about was writing and reading and music and art. Now all he thought about was making money. And in the dream, he had it. He was driving around in a massive chrome chariot, a gold 1971 Cadillac Eldorado, a real superfly pimp wagon straight out of a blaxploitation film, with the Continental kit on the back and the phrase *Sex Is My Hobby* hand-painted on the trunk. It was the kind of car that Joe had always coveted in a silly white boy way. In the dream, he was dressed in present-day clothes but he was loaded, a giant Detroit roll in his pocket, C-notes on the outside. He was copping a lean, one hand draped over the steering wheel, stopped at the light beneath the 8 Mile Road overpass where it was always dim and vaguely menacing. He remembered pulling out the wad of bills and handing money to some guy begging there. He was wearing dirty jeans and a torn T-shirt with a picture of Redd Foxx on it, emblazoned with the phrase, *You Big Dummy*. He peeled off some bills for the guy and said, "Here you go, broke-ass fool."

That disturbed him too. Joe would never, ever say something like that to anyone. He was too polite and way too afraid of getting beaten up. Nor would he ever use the term "broke-ass fool." (Maybe Brendan could pull it off, but not him.) Now the rest of the dream came to him: The Fred Sanford guy pulled out a gun and shot him three times right in the chest. After which, he was yanked out of the Caddy and left there under the bridge, in the middle of 8 Mile. In the dream, he even remembered staring up at the grime-caked girders of the overpass. Then came the truly bizarre part—suddenly he was driving the car again! Right out from under the overpass. He couldn't remember the face of the guy who had shot him, but there he was, Joe, driving the car right past the skeezy 8 Wood Motel, where there were always Good Humor ice cream trucks curiously parked in the lot.

Had he carjacked himself? Was *he* the broke-ass fool in the Fred Sanford T-shirt?

Joe hated dreams. He hated trying to figure out what they meant. Most of the time, he thought dreams didn't mean anything. They were just a collection of stupid incidents and things that felt like symbols but were really just a few random details he had seen in a movie or television show or read in a novel.

There was noise coming from the kitchen: a drawer opening and closing, the *thunt* of a wine bottle being opened. Joe peered up at the ball clock. It was ten past seven. He had been sleeping for quite a while. Even so, it was pretty early for Ana to be coming home.

"Ana," he called out. "Where are you? In the kitchen?"

Nothing.

Joe raised his voice, in case she was down in the basement. "Ana? You want to grab some dinner somewhere?"

Nothing for a moment, but he heard sniffling.

"Ana? Are you okay?" He sat up, still groggy and weary of dreams.

"Yeah," she said, her voice breaking. "I'm in the kitchen."

More sniffling. Joe got up from the couch. He found Ana sitting at the kitchen table, a glass of wine untouched before her. Her eyes were closed, arms wrapped around herself, slowly rocking. Joe walked over to her. "What's wrong, sweetie? Are you okay?"

Ana's eyes were red and swollen. She looked at him as if he could read her mind.

He kneeled next to her, laid his arm over her shoulders, trying to comfort her. "What's going on? Is it work?"

She shook her head, then turned away from him. "I don't know."

"Ana, I'm worried about you. You never used to come home so upset. Poor baby." Joe wrapped his arms around her from the side, inhaling her smell, a lemony sweetness that he never grew tired of. He didn't even know if it was something she put on, or just the smell of her skin. He kissed the hair above her ear, and then smoothed it out. "I'm so sorry you had such a bad day," he said.

Ana turned, put her arms around him, and squeezed hard. She started kissing his neck, kissing his mouth, her tongue darting across the edges of his lips, then diving inward. She then completely took him by surprise by sliding her hand down the front of his pants.

"Hey," he whispered into her ear, "not that I'm complaining, but I thought you were upset."

Ana took a deep breath. "Joe," she said, "let's go to bed."

It was the best sex the two of them had had in a long time. It was like it was when they were first together, before they moved into the same house. Joe wasn't exactly sure how it differed from their early-living-together sex, to the almost nonsex that they had been having lately, but this time he somehow recognized that newness, that eagerness, that fuck-each-other's-brains-out feeling again. It was like finding something that you hadn't realized you'd lost. It was the kind of sexual energy between two people that just naturally fades after a certain level of familiarity is achieved. Unavoidable, when you thought about it, and in many ways, just fine. That particular energy was supplanted by other things—less anxiety, laughter, the harmoniousness that came with a greater understanding of the other's pleasure—all of which made sex with that person an authentic act of intimacy, a joining of minds as well as bodies.

But this sex, this lovemaking, this fucking, had all of those feelings, it seemed to Joe. The newness and the closeness and the harmony, all at once.

"Was it just me," he said to Ana, lying there afterward, his side of the sheet rumpled near his feet as he tried to cool his body, still damp from exertion, his face and neck flushed pink, "or was that amazing?"

Ana lay still, her body covered with her half of the sheet, up to her neck, her arms under it as well, despite the temperate warmth of early spring. "Yeah," she said, leaning over to kiss him lightly on the mouth. "That was pretty wonderful."

Joe widened his eyes and gave a little shiver. "After-work sex. Unheard of in these parts." Ana curled into the space between his chin and shoulder. It wasn't helping him cool down, but was nice nonetheless. "What's gotten into you? We have to send you off to Grand Rapids more often. Is it all those Dutch Reformed conservatives? Is there some sort of funky atmosphere of repressed sexuality in the air?"

Ana moved closer to him. "I don't want to talk about Grand Rapids."

"Ana?"

"Yeah?"

"You okay?"

"Yeah, fine . . . sure. Just a little dazed."

"Yeah, me too."

She kissed him again.

"Ana, are we self-involved?"

She pulled her head away from where it was resting on his shoulder and peered at him. "This is odd postcoital chit-chat. I don't know. Probably."

"That's what my mother says, that we need to be less self-involved. That we're selfish because we don't have kids."

Ana rolled her eyes. "Mine says the same thing. I always tell her, *And making a tiny version of yourself* isn't *selfish?*"

"I don't get it. Are we really that bad, just because we don't want kids?"

"I don't know. If you stopped someone on the street and asked them, they might not call us evil, but they would probably say that we should have kids."

"Really?"

"You haven't figured this out yet? Wait, what are you trying to tell me? Oh god. Do you have baby fever?"

"Of course not, Ana. Which reminds me: I need to pick up some condoms. It's been so long since we used them, I forgot there was only one left in the box."

Ana fanned out the sheet and smoothed it around her. "Anyway, I know what you mean. I get this weird feeling from these women at work. There's like three of them that all got pregnant at around the same time. As if their bodies all got the idea simultaneously, like synchronized menstrual periods. They basically act like I'm a freak."

"I think maybe we *are* freaks," Joe said, readjusting himself under Ana's torso. His shoulder was falling asleep.

"They just have this smugness to them. They look at each other and it's like they're saying, *Isn't it so sad that she'll never know the joy of motherhood?*"

"Well, they do have a point. We never will know the joys of parenthood."

"True. And I'm sure there are many. But there are other joys to know."

Joe stretched his neck to the side. "Not to them. If they've got kids, they think you've got to have 'em too. They're like Jehovah's Witnesses or Deadheads. They're not happy until they've turned everyone on to Jesus or Jerry."

"Why? What do they care?"

"Having kids is just what you do. That's what everyone always says." He pushed back a dot of sweat on his temple with his finger.

"Is that why I sometimes feel like people are mad at us for not procreating?"

"I don't know, I feel that too. I think we all spend about 85 percent of our time talking ourselves into the decisions we've already made. *I did the right thing, didn't I? Of course I did.* Then when someone comes around who hasn't made the same decision, we look at them and say, *What's wrong with doing what I did? Not good enough for you?* Everyone wants people on their team. It's just natural. We do the same thing. Look how many friends we have who don't have kids."

After a short silence, Ana spoke up: "So, you ever think about what it would be like to have a kid?"

"Sure, how could I not? I've thought about it. I sometimes wonder what our lives would be like if we had kids. I know they would be a lot different than they are now. But not necessarily better or worse. Just different."

Ana took his arm and wrapped it around her, then covered the both of them with the sheet. "So I guess we're horrible people, huh?"

Joe squinted like a tough guy. "We're bad, baby," he growled. "So bad."

"Yeah," Ana said, her voice fading slightly. "I'm bad."

The next day, Joe noticed a difference in himself. Frankly, it was pathetic to see how much having sex improved his disposition. He didn't even mind making more cold calls that day at work and even managed to generate a couple of leads which were promptly intercepted by Terrance for further investigation. Joe was delighted to hand them over. He didn't want anything to do with them.

Happily, he had other things to do. That morning, in a fit of uncharacteristic enthusiasm (the sex again), Joe had actually convinced Terrance that publishing music reviews might help the *Dollar Daily* garner some media advertising. It was complete and utter malarkey, but it worked. The idea of big media bucks was more than Terrance could resist. So instead of making cold calls, Joe spent the rest of the day writing reviews of the new Iron & Wine (good), the new Grizzly Bear (really good), and the new Coldplay (meh). All fairly well-known stuff, but as he might have said to Chick, he was keeping it populist for now.

Joe loved writing music reviews and prided himself on actually writing about the music and not himself, like a lot of reviewers tended to do these days, and avoided overloading the reviews with intergenre comparisons ("haunting overtones of electro postpunk lo-fi Danish death-metal calypso swerving into Nuggets-era noirish Gothic Americana ye-ye-tinged soca psychedelica") or incessant references to other artists crossed with show-offy lists of their obvious influences ("It's as if Carl Stalling, Swamp Dogg, Clara Rockmore, Captain Beefheart, Lou Reed's *Metal Machine Music* album, Buddy Bolden, and Big Star all participated in a time space continuum–twisting fuck-fest that birthed a glorious Thalidomide flipper baby of sonic exploration"). Also, he tried not to pretend that he was Nick Kent or Hunter S. Thompson or Jacques Derrida, though he would have loved to have been either of the first two (except for the addictions and/or suicide). Anyway, it would probably all backfire on him when no new revenue followed the reviews, but he was hoping they might get a few glowing e-mails from readers that would turn the tide and make Terrance a little more amenable to actual culture in the paper, instead of yet another article like the one he had just finished yesterday: "Local Bakery Celebrates Anniversary with Cake!"

It didn't matter. He was in too good of a mood to care.

22

Semi-Infidelities and Interim Campaigns

Though Ana was dealing with it, the guilt lingered like a low-grade fever from a virus she couldn't quite shake. She would be seemingly free of it for a while, then it would pop back into her head at some inopportune moment, causing her throat to tighten and face to burn. For the past couple of days, Joe had been exceptionally sweet—and that couldn't have come at a worse time. Lately, he was full of lovey murmurings, bringing her coffee in bed, downloading music for her that he knew she'd like (Sarah Harmer and Laura Veirs, two of her favorite girly-girl folkies), and being so dear at the door when she would leave in the morning, telling her to "Be careful, okay?" before he would kiss her goodbye.

All this probably had something to do with the Return from Grand Rapids Sex. It had been pretty great, which made things even more confusing. Ana supposed that it wasn't too hard to figure out how and why that had happened. She comes back from Grand Rapids all hot and bothered and, for the first time in a long time, she and Joe set the sheets aflame. She hadn't planned to attack Joe the second she walked in, but it had just turned out that way. Whether it was residual lust or guilt or just that he was being so kind to her that made it happen, it was apparently just the sort of mind-emptying activity that she had needed at the moment. She also wanted to feel close to Joseph again, just to know that she still could. It was somewhat comforting to her that although the image of Bruce in the hallway occasionally flashed through her mind, that was definitely Joe with whom she was making love, not some sort of stand-in penis. Not that she hadn't ever fantasized about another man during sex with Joe, but it was usually some random dude she'd encountered at the library or the boho barista from the Limbus. Never anybody she actually knew. She kept telling herself that she hadn't done that much with Bruce, but it still felt like what it was: an emotional betrayal.

It wasn't much better at work. She even felt guilty for not telling Adrienne, though she was pretty sure that would not help anything. Besides, then someone else would know, which would make it seem all the more real and therefore worse. Was there any need to even talk about it? Especially when it had been so easy for everybody involved to act as though nothing had happened? To Ana, that now felt like the best course of action at the agency, where as always, the perception was indeed more important than the reality. It was Adrienne's dreamy twilight truth: *If you act like nothing happened, then nothing happened.*

Adrienne had required a short debriefing about the whole trip, but there wasn't even time to get into much detail. Ana filled her friend in on the meeting, the way Karin had attempted to trap her into looking like a liberal baby-killer who was trying to turn their audience into bra-burning, free-thinking, family-abandoning harlots. Adrienne high-fived her (semi-ironically) on the way she handled it, and that was that. Until Friday afternoon came around and Bruce called a meeting at six o'clock.

"What a dick-y thing to do on a Friday afternoon," said Adrienne, clicking shut her computer, which was balanced precariously on her knees. "Is it just me or is this happening more and more these days? The fucking six o'clock meeting—it's like no one is even supposed to consider going home at a normal time. Even that little shit Tara is doing it now."

"It's not your imagination. I think it has something to do with rising in the ranks."

"Really?"

"Apparently, the more important you are, the less important your free time is."

"Ana?" said Adrienne, turning to her, head cocked, eyelashes fluttering, her voice puddin' sweet. "My darling, supertalented, awesomely superlative, hyperbole-inspiring art director partner." It was never good when Adrienne laid on the schmaltz like this.

"*What*?" Ana said, as sternly as she could.

"I was planning to meet the man with possibilities after work."

Ana tried not to panic. "Can't you just push it back an hour or so? I'm sure it won't be a long meeting. Everyone wants to get home."

"Ana, please? Could you just cover the meeting for me? We were supposed to meet for happy hour after work."

Her throat felt like it was constricting. "I thought you were going to cover for *me* next time."

"I will. And the next time."

Ana pushed the breath out of her lungs, thinking that would lift the anxiety she was currently experiencing. "No."

Adrienne started to pout, which Ana hated as much as the sweet talk. But disappointment soon shifted to suspicion. Ana was usually an indulgent guardian. She knew her face was betraying her, revealing too much.

"I can't always be covering for you," Ana said, trying to sound uncaring, hoping it would lead to an argument, something she could actually handle right now.

"Are you okay?" asked Adrienne, reaching for her hand across the desk. "Is something wrong?" She clumsily petted Ana's fingers.

After this small display of affection, it became more difficult to dodge the question. "Nothing," she said, with little conviction.

Adrienne set her laptop aside, got up, closed the door of Ana's office, and sat back down on the love seat, perched on the edge, leaning forward. "Okay, you need to tell me what's going on."

Ana leaned forward in her chair. She took a breath and tried to settle her voice before she spoke. "Something happened with Bruce and me in Grand Rapids." She lowered her voice. "There was . . . *contact*."

Adrienne stared at her blankly, as though she didn't understand. "Contact? What are you talking about? Like what kind of contact?" Then the horrible recognition in her eyes. "Oh shit. You mean like *physical* contact?"

Ana nodded.

"Oh my god. Did you guys—"

"No, no. We didn't do that, I swear." Ana shivered. Avoiding Adrienne's gaze, she shifted her eyes to the computer screen in front of her. It had been a few minutes since she had touched the keyboard, so her screen saver activated and a personal photo had popped up on the screen. Of course it was Joe. It was a picture that usually made her smile, of a trip the two of them had taken up north to Mackinac Island. Joe in a cheesy souvenir store, wearing a big Dr. Seuss hat with dreadlocks attached to it. She hit the space bar and it evaporated, returning to a Photoshop layout for a possible WomanLyfe ad. The headline read in Gotham Condensed Bold type: *The life with time for everyone.*

Finally, Ana spoke. "It came very close to that. There was kissing and touching and feeling and rubbing and stuff. But I stopped it."

"Really? You kissed him? *You?* Are you kidding me?"

Ana looked straight at Adrienne and spoke deliberately: "I assure you that I am not kidding."

Adrienne stared at the floor for a moment, then up at her, visibly stunned. "I just can't believe it. You? Ms. Monogamy? I mean, what the what, Ana?"

Ana twirled her thermal mug, which had been drained of its contents hours ago. "Shit, Ade, I don't know. I messed up." She was a little surprised at this response by her friend. Somehow, she had expected her to be more sympathetic, more like Lady Talk, which was what they liked to call it when they were sharing information about men. Granted, Lady Talk was mostly Adrienne sharing information about the guys she had sex with, since Ana didn't care to divulge much about her and Joe (especially since she'd had so little to divulge lately), but it wasn't like that at all. "I'm sorry."

"Don't apologize to me. I'm just surprised." Adrienne sat back on the love seat, her fuchsia scoop T-shirt bright against the lime-green cashmere. "Did you tell Joe?"

"No, I didn't. Do you think I should?"

"*No.* Absolutely not. Do not tell him."

Hearing that brought back the full brunt of heaviness Ana had felt after it had all occurred, and she sighed.

"So what happened?"

"I don't know, it just happened." Ana didn't want to get into details. "All you need to know is that I don't want to be alone with him in the same room."

Adrienne gave her a look that she couldn't decipher—it could have been worry or disgust or anger or something else.

"What?" she finally said. "What is it?"

"You're in the market for trouble, missy. You're in the Big Mistake lot, kicking tires."

"I know, I know."

"Do you want to fuck him?" Adrienne said in a low voice. "Is that why you're so afraid of being in the same room with him? Do you want it to happen again?"

"Stop it. Don't say that." Ana rested her hands on her keyboard, stared down at them. Then finally, she said, "I don't know. No."

Adrienne took a breath and stared straight at her. "I'm going to give you the same advice you gave me: I think it's a bad idea."

While they were waiting for Bruce to show at the meeting, Adrienne didn't speak to Ana at all. Then Tara walked in and Ana realized that she hadn't had to say anything about any of it. *So stupid.* She watched as Adrienne sat there with her phone, furiously texting. Presumably, it was her after-work date, but Ana didn't dare ask.

When Bruce entered the room (6:14 p.m., Creative Director Time), clutching his titanium Mac, he looked tired and tense as he grabbed the chair just off the end of the long conference table. He did that a lot, Ana noticed, avoiding the seat at the head of the table, as if trying not to be the person in charge, though he indisputably was that man. He was always trying to be just one of the creatives. The only time she'd seen him sit at the head of the table at a meeting was a couple of years ago, and it was because all the other seats had been taken. Everyone had saved that seat at the front for Bruce. Jerrod, always looking for a chance to suck up, had said: "You're the head of the family, Bruce. I guess you get to carve up the ideas." Everyone had laughed, but she just remembered Bruce looking uncomfortable.

He opened up his computer and matter-of-factly started the meeting. "I just got off the phone with Karin at WomanLyfe and she informed me that they need new TV immediately."

Adrienne turned off the ringer on her cell and placed it facedown on the table. "Really. Just how immediate is she talking about?"

"Oh, like right now. If she could have them tomorrow, she'd still be mad that they didn't have them today."

Ana was shocked. "What happened? I thought we had time to work out a new campaign for them."

"Oh, we still do," said Bruce, clicking something with his touch pad, then closing the top of his machine partway. "She just suddenly decided that they needed what she called an *interim* campaign. Which is a nice way of saying that they want more of their shitty low-budget testimonials."

"I knew it," seethed Adrienne under her breath. "Those holy-rolling sons of bitches. Fucking cock-sucking, god-damn Jesus-in-their-advertising fucktards." It seemed like she was just going to continue this tirade, until she noticed Bruce glaring at her. Adrienne nodded curtly. "Moving on."

"We have to get going on this right now. I get the feeling that the company loves us, but that we're wearing thin on Karin."

Now this, thought Ana. She might as well get it over with. "Is it because of the 'pro-woman' thing, Bruce?"

He dropped his hands to the table. "Who knows? I thought we handled that well. Maybe she's just pissed that we didn't fall into her trap and expose ourselves as the bleeding-heart-liberal, abortion-loving atheists she suspects we are."

Bruce's use of "we" made her feel slightly better, as though she were not solely at fault for this. Then she thought, *Why would I be at fault? For having a brain? For daring to believe that women have a right to think for themselves? For not buying into all this subjugation of women for the sake of the Christian family? Fuck that.* She would do her job the best she could in order to keep this horrible account, but if they lost it, so be it. This was all getting to be too much.

"Just as a little refresher course," said Bruce, turning his computer around and tilting the screen up, "let's watch their old spots. I know we'll be able to do better than them, simply by using a professional director and a talent coach—"

Just then Tara perked up. "Oh, Bruce. I just got a message from Karin that they'll expect us to use the same crews they've used for the previous spots."

There was silence. Bruce put his elbows on the conference table, raised his hands to his forehead, and began massaging his temples. "Well, that's just fucking wonderful."

Tara looked like she wanted to hide behind her PC. "I'm sorry. But her exact words are: *We're very fond of the crews and they meet all our technical and spiritual requirements.*"

"What?"

"She also says that they have all the subjects chosen and ready to shoot." Tara's voice got higher. "I guess they were about to shoot a new set of spots when they got word that we were their new agency."

Another long silence. Bruce's eyes closed again.

"Bruce, why *are* we their agency?" said Ana. "It's obvious that we don't meet their requirements, spiritual or otherwise." She was going to say something else about the agency and WomanLyfe just not being a good fit, but she realized that Bruce was staring right at her with a very unhappy look on his face, a look that begged, *Please shut up*. So she did.

Bruce touched his upper lip with his fingers, obscuring his mouth as he spoke. "Find out if their crew is union. That might be a way to get some of our people in there. Tomorrow, call Karin and tell her that since the agency is a SAG signatory, we have to use union crews or we could all be penalized."

"I'm not entirely sure that's true."

"Neither am I, but check with Shonda in talent. Maybe there's something we can say that's close enough to the truth that will allow us to get people in there who actually know how to operate a fucking camera. And how to properly light a subject. This cannot be an embarrassment for the agency."

Tara was rapidly typing everything that Bruce was saying. Ana figured it was better than having to look at the bright rage in Bruce's eyes at that moment.

"You two," he said, now directing his attention to Ana and Adrienne. "Ana, think about how we can make these spots more visually interesting."

She remembered the original spots being static. "Maybe we can get away from the WomanLyfe facilities and shoot them with their families. Doing their favorite things. Or in a park, or at least someplace out in the world instead of in those dingy little gyms, or worse yet, in limbo."

"Yeah, that's at least something. Keep thinking about it." He turned to Adrienne. "Once Tara gets those subjects' stories from Karin, I want you to write scripts that we can get these people to read if their stories aren't compelling enough. Or if they can't put two words together properly."

Tara reluctantly piped up: "Karin says that they don't write scripts—"

Bruce turned back to her so fast, Tara flinched. "I don't give a shit *what* Karin says. We're writing scripts. Just don't tell her and we'll have them ready in case their new subjects are as verbally feeble as the people on their old spots." He shook his head, then leaned forward and reached around to his computer's touch pad. He hit the play button on a Quick-Time video, clicked to full screen, and they all watched the old WomanLyfe spots.

Ana had seen them once and had felt no need to view them ever again. They were heavy, sad, unhealthy-looking women standing in front of a green screen with the Woman-Lyfe facilities chroma-keyed behind them. The lighting was atrocious; some of the subjects had worn green, which made various parts of their bodies disappear into the background. The sound was bumped up almost into distortion and well beyond appropriate, not to mention legal limits.

And the performances. Oh, the performances. It was obvious none of them had ever set foot in front of a camera before, which wasn't uncommon for testimonial commercials. Usually, there was a certain technique involved with testimonials. You did multiple takes, with close-ups and wide shots so you had something to cut to. You put together all the least horrible bits into a tolerable testimonial. You didn't just do a locked-down shot of someone who could barely speak, key in product footage behind them, and call it a commercial. But that's what WomanLyfe had done. And it had made them a success.

4

23

Irony Loves Company

It was a full-scale turnaround from the night of the amazing sex. He had felt like he had gotten his old Ana back that night. Yet just as abruptly as the old one had appeared, the new one returned. It was disorienting. Even when Ana was around, she was distant, skittish, and easily annoyed with him. She was happier with her computer, taking care of work details. When he hugged her, she allowed it, but he could tell that she wanted to squirm away. He would have loved to have the communicative, nonworkaholic, active-sex-partner Ana around just a little longer. Would that have been so wrong?

Joe prepared dinner the evening before she left for her shoot in Chicago.

Something special for her last night in town—linguini with olive oil and aged Parmesan cheese, some fresh steamed green beans with slivered almonds, and an arugula salad with dried Michigan cherries and a balsamic vinaigrette. Pretty fancy for him. Sure, it had taken longer to shop than to actually prepare dinner, but still, he had wanted it to be nice.

After he served it, Ana had a few bites of the pasta, then her iPhone pinged for the third time since she had sat down at the table. She had taken to eating dinner with it there on the rare occasion that they actually ate together.

"Goddamn Tara," she said angrily. "Don't these people ever stop working?" She picked up the phone to read the message.

Joe couldn't help but to comment, "They're probably saying the same thing about you."

Ana took a dramatic breath and looked at him as if she knew he was right but there was no way she was going to admit it. She just started e-mailing.

"Good idea," he said, allowing a harsh edge to his voice. "You wouldn't want to accidentally talk to me or anything like that."

Ana's head fell forward. "Please don't do this, Joe." It was just the sort of thing that set her off lately.

"I'm sorry."

She kept her eyes on the plate of food before her. "I'm trying to be okay."

"What do you mean?"

A look of concern crossed her face. "I . . . I'm just trying to keep up. It's really hard."

After sending her e-mail, she pushed the dinner plate away and concentrated on the salad. She took a few more bites, then pushed it aside too.

"That was great," Ana said, before glancing away distractedly. It was like she couldn't keep her eyes on him for more than two seconds. She then moved her chair back from the table, picked up her phone and her glass of wine. "Look, I'm sorry. I need to go check on this. It's really important."

"Sure. Okay. Of course," said Joe, trying not to sound hurt.

"It was really good," she said, nodding. "Thank you."

"I wish you weren't going away."

Long pause. "Yeah."

She left the table and headed upstairs into the study.

Joe wanted to get mad, but wasn't really sure what to get mad about. She had been there physically, even said that she had enjoyed dinner, but that was it. There was nothing else.

The next morning, he got up extra early to see her off before she headed for the airport. She said goodbye, gave him a kiss at the door. He told her to be careful, and when he did, it looked like she was about to cry.

"Are you okay?" he said, taking her hand.

And then just as quickly, she was totally composed. "Yep. See ya." Then she was gone.

That evening after work, he texted Malcolm, Chick, and Todd to see if anyone wanted to meet at the bar.

Joe had forgotten all about Chin Tiki night at the Midlands. Until he walked in and saw garishly flowered Hawaiian shirts and muumuus all over the place, along with Gilligan hats, vintage sarongs, fezzes, clamdiggers, tapa-cloth cabana sets, grass skirts, and even a coconut-shell brassiere or two. There was something shocking about all that flesh that hadn't been exposed to the sun in months, suddenly out in the open. It was the kind of pale flesh that reminded him of a baby opossum he had once uncovered under the shed in his backyard when he was a child. He remembered it squirming and squinting at Joe and the horrible brightness he had brought into its world. Joe saw the same pinched expressions on some of the partygoers: pasty, doughy white people who had finally shed their parkas after an interminable winter, and were now exposing things that may have been better left covered.

There were occasional younger people sprinkled

throughout the crowd, but mostly, it was Chick's broken hipsters: graying goatees, shaved heads (make male-pattern baldness a statement!), flowered bandeaus holding in thickish waists (though not uncomely), pinup-style jet-black hair with bangs, and slyly arcane cultural references growing fainter with each passing generation. And Joe was one of them. This wasn't a problem, but it was interesting to see his peer group aging. Again, he had to wonder, was this healthy? Were people supposed to be doing this in their late thirties and forties and fifties?

Exotica music was blasting over the speakers. DJ Dave Detroit was spinning Martin Denny or Robert Drasnin or Arthur Lyman, he couldn't tell which. People were milling around in brightly colored clusters, holding tiki mugs or plastic cups filled with rum-potent zombies, daiquiris, and mai tais. Over in the corner, a man in a Gauguin shirt was carving a small tiki with a hatchet. Wood chips were flying as people stood by observing. It was fascinating, but Joe wondered if hatchets and alcoholic beverages in the same room was a good idea. Only time would tell.

It was actually a fun scene, the kind that usually made Joe happy, but tonight he felt disoriented. He had been hoping for just a quiet drink with his friends and now he was thrust into the middle of a Polynesian shindig. He wasn't even wearing anything vaguely tropical. (It was a vintage Pendleton shirt, for he had not made the switch to lighter clothing yet, though winter was long over.) Still, there was something about this music, about the crowd, that was lifting his disposition. He gave himself over to that, headed up to the bar, elbowed his way through, and ordered a zombie. Someone tapped him on the shoulder and he saw that Malcolm and Chick were right behind him.

"Hey. You guys want drinks?"

"Whatever you're getting."

Joe ordered two more, paid, and headed back through the crowd, carrying the drinks, carefully triangled in two hands, hoping no one would jostle him. For a moment, he couldn't see the guys. Then Malcolm rushed over to grab two of the drinks and together they walked to the giant papier-mâché Moai where Chick, in a bright yellow shirt emblazoned with thick-tongued orange flowers, had stationed himself.

"Ouch," said Chick. "Check out Bettie Page over there. *Hot!*"

Malcolm and Joe both said it at the same time: "Which one?"

"I don't even care," said Chick. "Damn it. I need to be more tiki. Or indie. Or alternative. Or retro. Or DIY. Or something. These girls won't give me the time of day."

"Why wouldn't they?" said Malcolm. "They're interesting women at an interesting event. You have things in common. You're both *here*."

"You're right," said Chick. "Fuck it, I'm going in." He walked off toward the Bettie Pages.

Joe watched him approach. It appeared as if Chick was complimenting the left Bettie on her tiki mug, which was a cross between an Easter Island head and Jack Lord from *Hawaii Five-O*.

"Look at that," said Joe. "Our little Chick, going off to pick up women."

"They grow up so fast," said Malcolm.

Todd walked up to join the two of them, carrying a very dark, strong-looking drink in a plastic skull mug. "Gentlemen."

"What are you drinking?" said Malcolm. "It looks heinous."

"A black mamba. I think it's dark rum, vodka, and black sambuca. And, for the record, it is heinous."

Chick rejoined the group.

"That was fast," said Joe, dryly. "You get the digits, *dude*?"

Chick shot him a look. "I'm going to ignore that."

Joe smiled.

"I see how it is. I'm out there, trying to make things happen, and you mock me."

"I'm sorry, Chick," said Joe, sighing dramatically. "So, how did it go with the young woman over there?"

"For your information, she found me quite entertaining. But she's not ready yet. I'm going to do a pop-in later, after she's had more mai tais. I'm extra amusing after numerous strong tropical drinks. Then I'll make my move." Just then, a middle-aged couple walked by, each holding one hand of a small Asian boy, about six years old. They were all wearing matching gardenia-print aloha shirts. Mom and Dad, who were not Asian, were each holding a zombie in their free hand.

"Pretty darned cute," said Malcolm.

Joe nodded. "Yep, even to evil childless people like us."

"Really? Why are we evil?" asked Todd.

"Oh, I was just kidding," said Joe, caught off guard by the comment. "I was just having this conversation with Ana the other day about how we're so bad that we don't have kids." He had tried not to make air quotes around the words "so bad," but did it anyway. There were too many concepts and actions and phrases whose old meanings had been commandeered and bullied into newer, ironic, or cynical meanings.

"I think I've had that same conversation with Gina," Malcolm said. "Our decision to not breed has not been a popular one."

A moment passed. Todd held up his hands. "Well, don't look at me. Ain't gonna happen here."

"Nice," said Chick. "You're all barren. Shooting blanks. Wonderful."

"It is odd," said Malcolm. "Four men, all in our thirties—"

"Don't forget Grandpap here," said Chick, pointing a thumb at Joe.

Joe shot him a stiff smile.

Malcolm continued: "And none of us have children? That's a fairly rare occurrence. Go to a bar most anywhere and I bet you'd be hard pressed to find four men in our demographic who aren't dads many times over."

"Well, what's wrong with us?" said Joe.

Todd looked vaguely annoyed. "What's *wrong* with us? There's nothing wrong with us. I just don't want kids. No thank you. It's been done. Ultimately, what's the difference if I have children? We're all dying from the moment we're born, so why pull more people into this mess?"

Chick reeled as if the breath had been punched out of him. "*Jesus.* That's harsh. What a fucking nihilist."

"I'm not saying my opinion doesn't have consequences," said Todd pointedly. "It's why I broke up with Dorinda. She suddenly decided that she wanted children. I didn't. Hard to find a compromise there."

"You could've gotten one of those hairless dogs," said Chick. "Looks like a baby, but you don't have to send it to college."

Everyone ignored Chick, except Joe. "Trotting out the B material, are we?" *Zing.*

"How about you?" asked Malcolm.

Joe shrugged. "I don't know. Just never felt the calling. It just seems like something that you should really want." He paused to take a sip of his drink. "It's totally life-changing. I guess for me, I figured it would keep me from doing the things I wanted to do—"

Chick interrupted: "Like what, Keen? Being a poor beatnik writer?"

Joe didn't let on that Chick had zinged him back.

"Let him finish," said Todd.

"I don't know. Almost everyone I know who has children has let go of their dreams. They end up transferring them all onto the kid."

Malcolm, happy to serve as moderator, chimed in: "Maybe that's okay. We're not all going to achieve our dreams. Sometimes our dreams are ridiculous things that we don't even deserve to achieve. We just *want* them."

Joe kept talking: "You're right. But is it that bad to consider yourself when it comes to *your* life? I used to get so mad at people when they said childless people are selfish, but now I'm starting to think that they're right. I *am* selfish."

"It's true," said Chick. "You are obsessed with yourself. As evidenced by the self-pleasuring incident of a few months ago."

"I think we're all forgetting the genetic imperative," said Malcolm. "We're supposed to procreate. Animals don't think about it. They keep the species going. So we, who don't procreate but could, are considered freaks."

Joe tried hard not to look shocked that Malcolm used the very same word that he and Ana had used. *One of us. One of us.*

"I'll give you that," said Todd, obviously anxious to jump in. Joe had never seen him so passionate about one of their conversations. "But we're also the only animals that know we're going to die. That's a reason why having kids is actually selfish. You have kids, so in your head you get to live on after you die." He snorted disdainfully. "Deal with mortality, people. It's here. You're still going to die. Oh yeah, and so are your children."

"Listen to this fucking guy!" bellowed Chick. "It's like I'm in a Bergman flick. I'm at a luau with Death."

"Sorry if you can't handle reality," said Todd.

Joe continued, "I just think a lot of people do it because they think they're supposed to. The world makes you feel that way. *When are you two going to have kids?*" he said in a high-pitched voice. "We've heard that from my folks forever."

Malcolm, who had been married for nine years, rolled his eyes. "Same with Gina and me."

Joe went on, trying not to get too worked up, "After a while, they didn't even care if we got married. We had complete permission to pop out a little grandbastard. I'm sorry, but that's no reason to reproduce—to shut your parents up. But I think a lot of people do it because of the pressure. Ana finally told her mother that it wasn't going to happen, so she better get used to the idea."

"What if Ana suddenly wanted one?" said Malcolm.

Joe exhaled loudly. "Jeez. It would be a surprise. What about Gina?"

"She says no, but I guess it could change. Who knows?"

Joe thought for a moment. "Honestly? If I was absolutely truthful with myself, I'd have to say that if Ana suddenly wanted a child, I'd probably cave."

Chick threw his hands up. "So everything you just said is total bullshit? You hypocrite. You have no sack. Why wouldn't you stick to your guns?"

"Because I love Ana and because I'd like to stay with her?" said Joe, a little meekly.

This infuriated Chick. "So you'd have a kid just so your woman wouldn't leave you? Great. Not very fair to the child either. A father who hates his guts."

Malcolm cut in: "Joe would be fine. Lots of guys wind up being fathers even when they think they don't want to and they're good dads who love their kids. You just rise to the occasion."

Todd shook his head adamantly. "Wrong. Not everyone rises to the occasion. Lots of awful parents out there fucking up their children with repressed resentment over their own bad choices."

Incredulous, Chick wagged his head. "Man, you're a cookie full of arsenic. I'd hate to take a bite out of you."

Joe smiled at Chick, recognizing the quote from *The Sweet Smell of Success*, one of their shared favorite films.

Chick waved his hands at them, disgusted. "Fuck all you guys. I can't wait to be a dad. I love my nephews and nieces. They're so fun. I get along with them great."

"Do you all sit at the kids table?" said Joe.

Chick shook his head again. "You're all dead inside. I pity you. Just wait, you'll be sorry. Unlike you monsters, I'll have someone to take care of me in my old age."

"Ha!" said Todd. "Are you kidding? By that time, you will have long since alienated all your children."

"Yes," said Malcolm, laughing. "They'll have spent everything they have on therapists."

"They'll be fighting over your Hollywood fortune as you

lie gasping in a nursing home," said Joe, enjoying it as they all piled on Chick.

"Oh really? Whereas you guys will die in some *independent*-living senior apartment." Chick chuckled spitefully. "Yeah. You'll be so independent, no one will even know when you're dead. Oh, that's right—your neighbors will know, when the smell gets bad enough."

"Just a reminder," said Todd, "I won't care. I'll be dead."

Chick shook his head as if they were making the mistake to end all mistakes. "Suit yourselves. You guys are putting the last nails in the coffin of intelligent America. Not enough smart people are reproducing. And if they are, it's just one little prodigy with a quirky name, that's it. Next stop, art school and homosexual experimentation."

Joe had to laugh. "Damn it. Chick may be right. All the people we complain about? Stupid America? They're the ones doing all the reproducing. Creating smaller, dumber, ruder versions of themselves."

Chick drained his zombie and belched. "Yes. Thank you. I hope all you godless child-haters are pleased with yourselves."

They all stopped talking as an obese, sweating, red-faced man in a pink aloha shirt walked past, wearing a tall furry blue hat with horns sticking out of the sides.

"Was that a Loyal Order of Water Buffaloes cap?" said Chick. "From *The Flintstones*?"

"I think so," said Todd. "That's really . . . something."

Suddenly distressed, Joe addressed the group: "Do you guys ever wonder why we like all this stuff?"

"What stuff?" said Malcolm.

"I don't know. All of it. This."

Chick seemed confused. "What's *this*?"

Joe shrugged, held his hands out in front of him. "I don't know. *This*. This party. The idea of this party. What is it? Is this how we define ourselves? We're here at this tiki party, listening to goofy music that someone's playing from weird old record albums. I'm seeing people dressed like they're from a sixties cartoon show, or wearing Mexican wrestling masks. I've already seen tattoos of Sid Haig, R2D2, a unicorn puking a rainbow, a cross-dressing Bugs Bunny, Peewee Herman, a gay Batman and Robin, and then there's the sixteen Bettie Pages walking around—"

"Amen to that," said Chick.

"You mean ironic appreciation of junk culture?" said Todd, nodding. "What's bad is good, what's wrong is right? Enjoying crap and mediocrity? Blithely snickering at everything from a safe and superior distance?"

"Yes. Exactly," said Joe. "Just what makes us like these things? What the hell happened to us?"

"We're victims of our generation."

"I think low culture is interesting," said Malcolm. "Especially when it's mixed with good stuff. Pastiche and such."

"Ugh, don't you start getting all postmodern on me," said Todd, holding up a fist. "So help me, I'll slug the first person who mentions Michel Foucault."

"Who?" said Malcolm and Chick, at the same time.

Joe continued: "I mean, I'm the first to admit that I love this stuff, but when is it going to end? This worshipping of ephemera? How long will our generation be obsessed with the past, with stuff that barely meant anything when it happened? That's remembered only because it's old or bad or weird or kooky. I mean, come on, *I'm* making fun of socalled stupid America? I'm at a fucking luau in Detroit."

"Christ, what is *with* everyone tonight? I'm out," muttered Chick, as he headed off back to the Bettie Pages.

Just then, across the bar, Joe noticed a group of twentysomethings. A reedy, tattooed urchin girl in a knitted cap and a seventies-glasses-wearing boy with a giant beard and a multicolored hoodie and a few others. The whole group was hoodied and skullied and kaffiyeh'd, conspicuous by their age and lack of Polynesian apparel, looking around and laughing with what seemed to Joe like amused indulgence. He pointed them out to the others. "Look at that bunch. You think they're into this? They're laughing *at* us. At this."

"Or they're laughing at something equally trivial," said Malcolm. "Have you ever listened to a group of people in their early twenties? It's painful."

Joe cupped a hand to his mouth and yelled toward the group, "Better not smirk too much, kids! It won't be long before your version of irony will be hilarious to the next generation!"

"Your tattoos will represent everything they don't want to be!" added Malcolm, laughing.

As far as Joe could tell, the twentysomethings didn't hear a word that he said. He was glad, because saying it all made him feel like a bitter old man.

24

The Irish Car Bomb

na had never been part of a television shoot like this before. Tension buzzed through the air on the soundstage like a cloud of angry blowflies. There was always stress and anxiety—shoots were inherently tense situations—but never like this. Since Karin Masters had complained to Edward Cherkovski about the way WomanLyfe was being treated by the agency, everyone was trying very hard to make her happy, while swallowing back the bile welling in their throats. The result was an angry obsequiousness that resulted in many tight-lipped smiles and kind words spoken with unkind inflection.

Certainly the complaint was a black eye for the newly formed W2W division. The whole account should have been completely overseen by Ana and Adrienne by this time. Instead, simply to make Karin happy, Bruce was forced to attend a low-budget TV shoot in Chicago that could probably be handled by a couple of juniors and a midlevel producer. Along with Bruce, Ana, and Adrienne, the agency had also sent a senior producer, an account executive (the recently unpromoted Tara), and the new account supervisor, Tara's boss, Trish Roncelli, whom Ana loathed, after once overhearing the woman tell a traffic person that "creatives are like fifth graders, and should be treated accordingly."

Adrienne described the whole affair as "a clusterfuck of Hindenburgian proportions." Ana was inclined to agree. Even though she was not pleased about Bruce's presence for her own personal reasons, she was glad that he was there in his capacity as executive creative director. He would also be around later to absorb some of the blame, which would normally be divvied between the overseeing associate creative directors. Namely, her and Adrienne.

In one way, the number of agency people present was a good thing. For this shoot, the WomanLyfe client was a collective of four. Karin and three other women, each one dowdier than the next, all of them wearing capri pants, and each in their own way casually contributing to this atmosphere of chaos, anxiety, second- and third-guessing, and insecurity. Currently, all were perched on the frayed edges of canvas director's chairs at the Video Village, a small scrimmage of seats semicircled before the video playback monitor.

For the Capri Pants (Ana quickly came to think of them this way, for she could never remember all their names and did not care enough to try) huddled around the monitor, nothing was ever quite right. They would rotate the complaints, each taking a turn. That day alone, Ana decided that she had heard every known euphemism for "problem." It was an endless litany of concerns, nitpicks, worries, challenges, nif-naws, quibbles, tweaks, snags, holdups, and glitches, each needing to be acknowledged and given due diligence by the agency.

Wardrobe:
Capri Pants #1: We don't like what the subject is wearing.
Ana: Um, you approved it at the wardrobe fitting.

Capri Pants #1: We don't like it.

Ana: What are you thinking of for her?

Capri Pants #1 (Looks to others): Maybe some capri pants?

Talent:

Capri Pants #2: We want the subject to speak more clearly.

Adrienne: I'll talk to the director. (Speaks to director, comes back. More takes are shot.)

Capri Pants #2 (Looks to others): We still can't understand her.

Adrienne: The problem is that she can barely speak English. We told you that it would be a problem when you chose her. (Long silence.)

Capri Pants #2: We want the subject to speak more clearly.

Catering:

Capri Pants #3: We would like some Twizzlers on the craft service table. Could you please have someone from the production company get some?

Ana: Of course, right away. (Speaks to line producer, who sends a runner out for Twizzlers. They appear within twenty minutes.)

Ana: Here's your precious Twizzlers. Kindly shove them up your ass. (Unspoken.)

It didn't have to be this way. The process could have been, if not easy, then at least fairly simple. Drag the subjects in front of the green screens (the first battle that the agency lost to the client) and let them tell their stories off the tops of their heads. (Absolutely no scripts: the second battle that the agency lost.) Repeat with varying camera angles (multiple takes at different angles: the sole battle that the agency won), then everything gets supposedly, magically repaired in postproduction. Ana had never been on a shoot where the phrase "We'll fix it in post" was uttered so frequently that it felt like a mantra.

The one saving grace was the ten subjects themselves. Most of them seemed like genuinely nice, down-to-earth Midwestern women who had actually achieved good results with the WomanLyfe program. A couple of them related heart-wrenching stories about how WomanLyfe had helped them to lose weight, get in shape, and feel better about themselves for the first time in their lives. For Ana, it allowed her to believe (at least enough to get her through the shoot) that WomanLyfe actually did help some people. Nice to hear, especially after recently finding out that she would indeed be working on the agency's newest and most odious account, Parnoc Industries, manufacturers of war machinery.

By far, the best subject was an African American woman in her forties (who looked pretty damn good, Ana was happy to note), dressed in a close-fitting, short black dress, who told how she had once been over three hundred pounds. When prodded by Ana to share more of her story, she revealed that she had also been an alcoholic with an abusive husband. WomanLyfe had helped her lose the weight and given her a sanctuary, a place to go to feel better about herself. She was sober now and out of the bad marriage. The woman was articulate and told her story candidly and compellingly. A testimonial like this was like manna from heaven. Ana and Adrienne and Bruce all looked at each other at the same time, thrilled that they had someone with such a moving, emotional, personal story. After they finished shooting her narration in both close-up and a medium shot, Bruce, Ana, and Adrienne excitedly approached Karin.

"She's awesome," said Bruce. "She's the star. This will be the real keeper of the campaign."

Karin shook her head vehemently. "No, we're not using her. Her story is too depressing. We don't want to talk about anyone being an alcoholic or in a bad marriage. That's not our brand. Plus, she's dressed like a trollop. That dress is way too short."

"Karin," said Bruce, with an impassioned sharpness to his voice that Ana had never before heard him use with a client, "her story is *inspiring*. It will help other women come to WomanLyfe who are in similar situations. I guarantee you. It's just the sort of thing we want for the brand. Letting women know that here is a way that they can change their lives." He paused and lowered his voice. "And she happens to look great in that dress."

Karin glanced blankly from him to Ana and Adrienne, and then said, "We're not using her. We always bring ten women when we do a shoot, then we use our favorite four. She is not one of our favorite four." She then walked away toward the craft service table and helped herself to a napkin full of Peanut M&M's.

Bruce just stood there. Finally, he squinted, took a deep breath, and slowly exhaled. Even though she felt crushed herself, Ana actually felt bad for him.

Adrienne muttered under her breath. "I fucking hate that bitch."

Bruce turned to her and said curtly, "Don't say that about our client."

Adrienne lowered her eyes and walked away.

"You okay, Bruce?" said Ana.

He looked at the ground and nodded once, more to himself, it seemed, than in response to her question. "Yep."

The rest of the day proceeded in much the same manner. Bruce stood with the "director," a video production guy from Grand Rapids who, though vaguely competent, did everything that Karin asked for, and nothing that Bruce, Ana, or Adrienne asked for. Still, Bruce stood there, acting as if he were working with a real director, though real directors almost always defended the creative.

Ana and Adrienne sat at the Video Village, trying to make conversation with the Capri Pants. It soon became apparent that these women had no power, they were simply Karin's lackeys. At which point, Ana and Adrienne gave up.

After Subject 4, Adrienne gave Ana the eye, then a tilt of the head, to indicate a move over to the craft service table. Ana got up without a word and followed Adrienne over to the coolers filled with bottled water and pop.

"Fuck this," said Adrienne. "I've got to get out of here. Let's step outside. I have to get away from these idiots."

"Shouldn't we stay here in case Bruce needs us?"

"Has he needed us yet?"

Ana shook her head.

"Then let's go. We're not going to leave town, just get some air. Unless you can't bear to be away from Bruce." She headed toward the soundstage door.

Ana said nothing and just followed. In the two weeks that had passed since they got the word that the agency would be producing WomanLyfe's interim campaign, Adrienne had been chilly with her. Ana had tried to talk to her, told her that there was nothing going on with her and Bruce, but things had been definitely strained between them.

They walked through a short padded hallway to get outside. Adrienne pushed open a heavy, metal-clad door, let Ana out, and then shimmed a doorstop into the jamb so it remained open just a crack. They walked out to a large alley behind the soundstage. The sun stung Ana's eyes after being in dim light for so long. A headache was brewing. She put on the vintage Jackie O sunglasses that she'd had fitted with her prescription and regarded the building. It was fairly plain for a place that had been built in the twenties. Supposedly, it had been Charlie Chaplin's soundstage before he moved out to Hollywood for the better weather.

Adrienne sat down on the open tailgate of a truck that was currently unoccupied. She pulled out a pack of Marlboro Lights, plucked a cigarette from it, stuck it in her mouth, and then fished around in her purse for a lighter.

"Since when do you smoke?" said Ana.

"I like to smoke sometimes," Adrienne responded, cigarette bobbing between her lips. "Especially when I'm stressed. It feels good. You should try it."

"No thank you. I have enough bad habits."

Adrienne continued to claw through her bag. "You're telling me."

"Come on, Ade, what does that mean?"

Finally, Adrienne found the lighter, sparked it, and lit her cigarette. "You know what it means, Ana." She took a deep drag, exhaled. "When he talks to us, he's actually talking to you and I'm just standing there. You're always going to be his favorite because of what happened. That's the way it works around here."

"Why are you being this way?" said Ana, unhappy to

even be speaking indirectly of these matters. "Anyway, not all that much really happened." Even saying it didn't make her believe it.

"Fine, let's say that's true. Do you know what that makes you?" She pointed a finger at Ana. "You're The Unattainable."

"What does that mean?"

"It means just what it means." Adrienne let out a derisive snort. "Anyway, don't you know? Even though you two supposedly didn't do it, it's like you did. Everyone thinks you did because of the way he acts around you."

"They do?"

"Of course they do. You think Jerrod isn't spreading that shit all over the agency? It's a done deal. You may as well have fucked him."

"He is such a little bitch."

"Ana, is he that wrong? Really?"

"Yes, he's wrong. Nothing happened."

Adrienne rolled her eyes. "Oh, I'm sorry. That's right—no penetration." She delicately held up her hands like a little girl. "So *nothing* happened."

"Jerrod was spreading those rumors even before—" Ana stopped herself before saying something she had avoided admitting to herself.

"Please, is it really all that different since it allegedly wasn't actual sex?"

"Would you be quiet, please?"

"There's no one around here but us, Ana." Adrienne took a deep drag of the cigarette. "You know, maybe it was just heavy petting. If it was actual sex, Bruce might be more discreet with his ogling. Now he's all full of longing."

"Just shut up, okay?"

"Dude, you're never going to get fired now. No matter

how bad things get in this city, you'll always have a job at the agency."

"What?" The word came out high-pitched, almost cartoony. "That's ridiculous. Why would you say such a thing, Adrienne? Why are you saying any of this?" Ana suddenly remembered the look on Bruce's face after she pushed him away. She realized that it had been anger. As if to say, *Why would you deprive me of this?* "I actually rejected him," Ana said, trying not to stammer. "Eventually." She wasn't sure where she was heading with this, but she was going to go with it. "He could've made my job a living hell after what happened. He still could."

Adrienne tipped her head and stared blankly at Ana. "But he hasn't, has he? No. Far from it. He just looks at you with his little sad face." She stuck out her tongue halfway and made a gagging noise. "It makes me fucking sick."

This was hard to refute. Ana had noticed the same thing: when she would suddenly turn to face Bruce, she would catch him looking at her. He would immediately turn away or talk to someone else, but she saw it. It confused her because she still liked it, even after what had happened. But the idea that other people noticed it bothered her enormously. "And why would it make you sick?"

"It just does."

"Why, Adrienne? 'Cause he's looking at *me* that way and not you?"

"Fuck you." Adrienne threw her cigarette to the ground and walked away.

Ana stood there, not even sure how any of this had happened. She didn't really believe that Adrienne was jealous of Bruce's attention. Adrienne seemed to hate Bruce these days. Ana had just wanted to say something cruel. And she had succeeded with a silly, spiteful comment that would have better suited a mean high school girl. Now her partner, who was her closest friend, was seriously angry with her.

As much as it bothered her to admit, it appeared that in Adrienne's mind, Ana had really done something wrong. Ana did not think of it that way: Even if Bruce was currently paying a bit more attention to her, nothing had really changed. She and Adrienne both still had jobs, as unpleasant as they may have seemed at the moment. Also, not that Adrienne cared, but Ana had narrowly escaped cheating on Joe. (Though she was still not quite believing that herself.) Either way, what right did Adrienne have to get so upset with her?

Everything felt wrong these days—Ana's job, her relationship with Joe, Adrienne. *She* felt wrong. She thought about leaving the shoot, catching a cab to the hotel, packing her suitcase, and heading for the airport. She and Joe would figure something out if she weren't working. Maybe she could be the happy-go-lucky freelancer for a change. Or maybe she would just actually fuck Bruce. Apparently, in everyone else's mind, Ana had already done the deed. So what was the difference?

She decided that she better get back inside. But when she pulled at the metal-clad door to return to the soundstage, it wouldn't open. She pulled again to make sure. It was definitely locked.

The fact that there was a weekend splitting up a four-day video shoot was ridiculous. Thursday, Friday, Monday, and Tuesday. This might happen on a real commercial shoot, but on this kind of rinky-dink production? *Please.* Ana soon discovered that this schedule was specifically designed so the WomanLyfe clients could have a shopping weekend in Chicago. Extra days in a nice hotel for them—*that* was what they were willing to pay for, not a real director or production company. Thankfully, the client did not expect to be entertained over the weekend, at least by the creatives. They were staying at a different hotel with the account people and no one would see them again until Monday.

It was also a lucky break that Bruce was needed at the agency over the weekend, so he had caught a Friday-night flight back to Detroit, not to return until Monday morning. That made things easier for Ana. The prospect of a weekend with Bruce in yet another city was something that had worried her. Especially since Adrienne was not being a cooperative human shield these days. Nor was she being much of a friend. Ana had called her on Saturday morning about breakfast, and then later for dinner. Adrienne was not answering her cell.

Ana ended up spending the entire Saturday in her room, moping around, eating room service food, watching television, reading, working, and playing Snood on the computer. She didn't even let the cleaning staff in to straighten up. (How many clean towels does one woman need?) Sad, when she had a big, beautiful city out there to explore. (There was so much of Chicago that reminded her of Detroit, yet without all the abandoned buildings.) She could have asked Joe if he wanted to drive in for the weekend, but since he hadn't called once, she was pretty sure that he was mad at her, along with everyone else.

Except Bruce, of course. Which was its own odd situation. She had been surprised how he'd kept his distance during the whole shoot, only speaking with her when it had to do with work. Maybe it was because all eyes were on him to save this fast-sinking dreadnought of a client, especially since it was Cherkovski's pet project, but Ana continued to be amazed by how thoroughly one man could erase an incident that had felt like such a big thing to her. Was he just trying to be professional? Was he waiting for another chance? She tried not to think about it one way or the other, except she just kept thinking about it.

On Sunday, she got out of the room finally, hit the treadmill in the workout room, then cleaned up and went for a walk down Michigan Avenue. She strolled in and out of some places, but they were all the same generic mall stores. She noticed that everyone sort of looked the same too: so many apple-cheeked Caucasians, all holding a cup of Starbucks, pushing around gigantic baby buggies, and wearing one or more articles of North Face clothing. It all depressed her enormously until she found the Garrett Popcorn store, where she bought big bags of both caramel and cheese corn. So delicious. She ate half of the caramel corn walking back to the hotel and felt better. Cheese corn and pay-per-view movies sustained her through the rest of Sunday. She didn't leave the room again until their seven thirty a.m. meet-up in the lobby.

On the set, everyone was there, but there wasn't much conversation. Which was just fine. The client, sated after a weekend of shopping and dining, was too tired to create many new problems. Besides, they had bonded heavily with Trish the account supervisor. They were all laughing and rehashing all the fun and shopping and meals they had over the weekend. Ana hated all of them. Adrienne was staying away too. Bruce as well. It seemed like everyone from the creative department had given up trying to turn the spots into anything good. WomanLyfe would just get whatever crap they wanted.

At the end of the shoot day, no one had drinks together at the hotel. Everyone just disappeared back to their rooms. Ana thought about calling Joe, but why hadn't he called her? Did he somehow find out what happened? Did he hear something more from Malcolm about the rumors? Maybe he knew about the whole Bruce situation and had decided that now was the perfect time to graduate from virtual to analog MILFs. The idea of this disturbed her deeply.

That night, after consuming the rest of the caramel corn, Ana fell asleep watching television, until a jarring dream awakened her at 4:43 a.m. She dreamed that Joe had been in a car accident. His Volvo had flipped and he couldn't get out and she couldn't get to him. The smell of dripping gasoline was so vivid to her, so real, that she was practically crying when she woke up. Ana seriously considered calling Joe, but she stopped herself, knowing that a late-night call would just scare the wits out of him. And what if someone else *was* there?

In the morning, Ana just focused on getting through this last day of shooting and heading home the next. That was all she wanted. As the day wound down, she started to feel better. The final two subjects had gone well. She just had to oversee a photo shoot for print and online. Even with that to do, it seemed like they might wrap early. She was starting to think that maybe she could even catch a flight home to Detroit that night.

Then, of course, something had to happen. Ana was standing not far from Bruce and Steven, the agency producer. The two of them were having a hushed, obviously tense, probably budget-related conversation, when Karin walked right up and interrupted them by saying: "So, where are we having our wrap party?"

"Wrap party?" said Steven, forcing a smile. He blinked at least ten times.

"Of course. We always have a wrap party after our shoots. Where are we going?"

"Well, Karin, we don't really have that in the budget—"

Karin's face stiffened into a death mask.

Bruce stepped up. "I'm sure we could go somewhere nice for drinks."

Karin's voice lost all color and tonality. "Topolobampo at seven. We'll meet in the bar. We'll be expecting a nice dinner."

She then walked away leaving, the two of them just standing there, looking at each other, as if to say, *This agony isn't over yet.* Ana turned and headed to the craft service table so they wouldn't see that she had witnessed their humiliation.

Ana had found that wrap parties for commercial shoots were pretty much a thing of the past. Maybe agencies on the coasts still had the bloated budgets that allowed their production companies to pay for such old-school luxuries, but most agencies in Michigan sure as hell didn't. Everything was budgeted to the bone. No one in their right mind would have ever expected such an extravagance on a low-tech, low-ball production like this one.

Except WomanLyfe. Ana watched from the craft service table as the two men continued their conversation, voices still hushed, gesticulation even more pronounced. She knew that if Adrienne was there, she would say something like, *Damn. Karin has officially made this agency her bitch.* And she would be right.

* * *

As far as Ana could see, it was going to be the worst wrap party for the worst shoot for the worst client that she had ever encountered in her entire career. Yes, that was about right.

Yet dinner was very good, an amazing modern Mexican meal, and Steven made sure that the good wine and top-shelf margaritas kept flowing—but could all that alter the fact that everyone hated each other? Ana wouldn't have thought so, yet before long the atmosphere resembled that of a group of people who actually seemed to tolerate one another. Karin was being downright nice—but why shouldn't she be? She had won the war along with most of the battles. The Capri Pants were flushed and friendly, all flirty with Bruce, as if now that their jobs were done and their god-awful commercials in the can, they could relax with the cool kids from the ad agency.

Bruce was being his charming self, regaling the WomanLyfers with stories of other shoots, of directors he had worked with. There were some A-listers mentioned, and though Ana was impressed, she was pretty sure that the Capri Pants didn't have a clue who any of them were. There were also star-studded tales of going to Cannes for the commercial film festival. The irony of telling stories about an international advertising competition in France to a Grand Rapids client for whom you just shot a series of insanely bad video commercials was not lost on Ana. Every once in a while, she would glance over at Adrienne, hoping for a split-second eye roll. Yet when Adrienne did actually look back, Ana would immediately avert her eyes, fearful for the angry glare she assumed was coming her way. When they did finally make eye contact, Adrienne gently raised her brows in an expression of extreme boredom. Ana smiled tentatively at her and hoped that perhaps this signaled that Adrienne was no longer quite so mad at her.

After dinner (when Bruce ordered calvados, Ana couldn't help but cringe), the client was still not ready to call it a night. So the whole slew of them walked down the street to an allegedly authentic Irish pub constructed from pieces of actual authentic Irish pubs dismantled in Ireland (apparently they no longer needed authentic Irish pubs there), where the drinking continued. Although part of Ana felt like poisoning herself into a complete state of numbness, the other, stronger part of her pulled back from the group and stayed on the sidelines. She noticed Adrienne doing the same. Strange, since Adrienne was usually at the epicenter of fun, never wanting to miss anything. Ana would usually be nearby, unable to be the extrovert but still absorbing the raucous behavior through Adrienne via osmosis. Tonight, Ana was feeling too sensible. Aside from the Bruce situation, it just seemed prudent to stay in control, what with all these clients around. She was also thinking of approaching Adrienne again, wondering if there was some way to win her back.

When Bruce started in on the shots, Ana felt like she was watching the consul from *Under the Volcano* crack open a bottle of mescal, knowing the night would now most assuredly tailspin into the abyss. Ana would have never thought for a moment that Bruce could get a group of middle-aged dowdies from Grand Rapids to first down shots of Bushmills, then Irish car bombs (shots of Baileys dropped into pints of Guinness—*ack!*), but he was doing it. Ana realized that not only was Bruce drunk, he was now in full-on client entertainment mode. He was creating a night that they would all remember (mostly) and talk about—but most importantly, he was building a relationship with them to keep the account. This was where all the movies and TV shows about advertising got it right: this was where the real work was done—not in the creative department. One thing Ana knew: she did not like this Bruce. He seemed hollow and ridiculous and insincere with all his hooting and yelling and slamming down of glasses. At one point, he put his arm around Karin, squeezed her toward him, handed her a shot, and chanted her name until she drank it. Sure enough, she drank it.

It was getting loud. Ana wondered when they were going to hear from management about the noise. Then again, with all the money they were throwing around, it would be a long time before anyone said anything. Ana was managing to act like she was having a good time, smiling at the high jinks of Bruce and Karin and the Capri Pants. She was sitting next to Tony, the line producer for the production company. Every once in a while, he would lean over and try to make conversation. Mostly, she just nodded at him.

Then he asked her, "Isn't it nice to get out of Detroit?"

Maybe he didn't mean to imply that Detroit was a hellhole and anyone in their right mind would want to escape, but that's sure how it sounded to Ana. Even though it often *was* nice to get out of Detroit, considering the perennially dire situation there, she certainly wasn't going to admit it to him.

"Actually, I miss it," she said. And she truly meant it.

"Really?"

"Yes. And there's no need to be so surprised," she said, not bothering to hide the anger rising in her voice. "I love where I live."

"Oh, I didn't mean it that way."

Ana smiled coldly. "I'm sure you didn't." There was no more conversation after that.

She was seriously considering quietly slipping away to catch a cab back to the hotel when she saw Adrienne heading outside for a smoke. Ana grabbed her purse (her Coach from the outlet mall) and followed her out. She paused at the door while Adrienne moved to the curb with an unlit cigarette between her fingers. Ana walked up behind her as she lit up, trying to make just enough noise so she'd know someone was there.

Adrienne turned around. "Hey," she said.

Ana just started babbling. "Look, Ade, I'm so sorry about everything. That was a stupid thing that I said. I was just mad. I'm just so fucked up lately. I don't know what's wrong with me. I think it's this fucking job." Adrienne kept looking at her. Ana felt self-conscious about saying any of it, all of it. But she kept talking. "I just want you to forgive me. Please, I miss you. I miss us being friends."

Adrienne just looked at her, not in a hostile way, but neutrally. Still, no response. Before she could say anything else, Ana started crying. It was bad. It surprised her the way it rose so quickly and unexpectedly in her.

Adrienne tossed her cigarette into the gutter and gathered Ana, now sobbing, in her arms.

"I hate this job, Ade."

"I know, sweetie. Me too."

"I have to get out of there. I don't like *me* anymore," Ana said between sobs. "I don't know what happened. I turned into a bad person."

Passersby were now staring at them, Ana blubbering and hugging Adrienne.

"Come on, Ana. Take it easy. I can feel your nose running on my frock."

Ana laughed because she was right, her nose was running on Adrienne. She opened her purse to get a packet of Kleenex, then blew her nose and immediately needed another tissue. After she blew her nose a second time, Adrienne spoke.

"I slept with him," she said.

"What?"

"I slept with Bruce."

Ana didn't know what to say. "You slept with him? When?"

"That night in LA. After you dropped me off at my room, I went back to his room."

"But you were so drunk," Ana said, no longer feeling at all like crying. "You didn't even know what you were doing. That's practically rape."

Adrienne gave her a look. "Come on, Ana, I knew what I was doing. So did he. Sure, we were both really drunk. It was not a good idea." She paused. "I'm not saying it wasn't pretty good, though."

"Why didn't you tell me?"

"I don't know, I felt stupid. I knew you'd get mad at me. It was so unprofessional. I didn't want to fuck up our work thing. I was afraid I already had. So Bruce and I acted like it never happened. Man, is he ever good at that."

"God, I know."

"But when you told me what happened—"

"You got mad at me?" Ana said, voice rising. "That's total bullshit—"

Adrienne held her hands up. "I know, I know, it's bad. It's totally my fault. I shouldn't have gotten mad. I'm sorry. I just was so pissed at everyone—you and Bruce, especially me for wanting the attention of someone who obviously doesn't give a shit about anyone but himself."

"What a fucking creep. Why didn't you tell me to watch out?"

"I did, Ana. Repeatedly. And it's you we're talking about here. I never thought you'd do anything like that. You and Joe are . . . well, you and Joe. You know, *together*. I make fun of you two, but I'd love to have that. I couldn't believe it when you told me about Bruce."

Ana thought about having to go back to the agency, working with Bruce again, editing these awful commercials for the next month, having to work late and never be home, all for this horrible account and these horrible people. She rushed over to a nearby trash can, almost getting there before her expensive dinner came gushing out. Some jackass passing by in a cab whooped at her.

"Oh shit," said Adrienne, running up next to her, putting her hands on either side of Ana's face, tucking a few little curls of hair behind her ears.

Ana's hair was nowhere near long enough to puke on, but the gesture was comforting. After another torrent, she took the tissues that her friend offered and wiped her mouth. Ana turned from the trash can and caught her breath.

"I'll be right back," she said to Adrienne.

Ana walked back into the pub, toward where Bruce and Karin were sitting a table away from the Capri Pants. They were laughing. Bruce had his hand over his mouth, obscuring it, a gesture that Ana now understood. It was as if he didn't want God to see him lying. Then she saw a glance between Bruce and Karin, her hand on his knee under the table. Ana knew that they would hook up tonight. As she approached, Karin's hand gently slipped back into her lap.

"Hey, Ana," said Bruce, turning toward her. "What's up?"

Ana spotted an almost full Irish car bomb that had been

abandoned by one of the Capri Pants. She picked it up and poured it over Bruce's head. Over the splash of milky stout, she heard the *thunk* of a shot glass as it connected with his skull.

"I quit," she said.

25

Attempted Dinner

Ana surprised Joe in the morning by showing up before nine, just as he was about to leave for work; he hadn't been expecting her until evening. Ana simply walked into the house, threw her bags down on the floor, left her rolling suitcase standing there with its handle extended, and announced: "I'm going to bed." No greetings, no niceties, no *God, am I exhausted*.

"Aren't you going to work?" Joe said. "I figured you'd come back from Chicago and go right there."

"Nope."

She seemed different. Relaxed. "What's going on? Don't you have editing and stuff to do for your commercials?"

Ana walked up to him, smiled slightly, put her hand on the side of his face, and then gave him a light kiss on the mouth. She continued to rub his cheek for a moment longer. "I'm just going to bed. I'm tired." Then she walked out of the room.

A minute later, he could hear the shower running in the bathroom. He stared at her bags still there near the front door. He wasn't sure what to do. She obviously didn't want to talk, but she seemed okay. Better than her last trip. So he picked up his messenger bag, opened the front door, and headed to work.

* * *

If Ana hadn't wanted to talk in the morning, she sure wanted to talk when he got home. Fairly apparent by the way that she said, "We have to talk," moments after he walked in the door. It was a phrase that still chilled his vitals when he heard it. He had come to assume that when a woman said, "We have to talk," it was never anything good. It was something he had found out with some frequency from girl-friends of many years ago. He could not remember any "We have to talk" talks that had turned out well.

"Okay," he said. What choice did he have?

He did notice that Ana looked beautiful, better than she had looked in months. Her eyes were clear, the circles beneath them were gone (makeup, no doubt, for no amount of sleep in one day could erase the dark moons that had lately settled beneath her gray-green eyes), and her voice sounded lighter. She was even walking differently, all the tightness she had carried in her upper torso seemed gone. There was a languid quality to her movements that he hadn't seen in months. It aroused him.

"Come on, let's eat," she said. "I made some dinner."

"You did?" She hadn't made a meal in ages. It was mostly her late hours, but he also worked late on Wednes-days, when they were putting that week's *Dollar Daily* to bed. Consequently, one or the other were always making sandwiches or microwaving frozen entrées. Not the most nutritious of choices, he knew, but they were both too tired when they got home.

Tonight, Ana had made pork tenderloin with a crust of coarse salt, pepper, and chopped rosemary, a side of rata-touille, grilled polenta, and a bowl of mixed greens. Judging from the work-intensive menu, she must have been cooking all afternoon. As wonderful as everything smelled, this in itself ratcheted Joe's anxiety up a notch. He knew that Ana liked to cook when she was feeling stressed or worried. She poured him a glass of wine, a really nice Sancerre, the kind of wine they only had when they were feeling prosperous.

"Ana, what's going on? You're scaring me." Joe sat down at the table, trying to decide whether they were celebrating something or *talking about* something. He could discern nothing from her face. It was pleasantly blank. She seemed to be working up to something and it wasn't exactly whetting his appetite.

Ana poured a rather full glass of wine for herself, and then sat down across from him. "So," she said, "I quit my job yesterday."

"You did?" Joe felt vaguely relieved, but not as much as he might have expected.

"Uh-huh."

"Wow. Really?" He placed his hands flat on the table, not sure what to do with them. "Well, that's great. I'm really glad."

"You are?" She still looked like there was something else bothering her.

"Yes, absolutely," he said, meaning it absolutely, at least for that moment. Yet seconds later, he started to feel anxious. It was the thing that he had hoped for, even asked her to do because it was hurting them, but now it hit him that he was the sole breadwinner in the family. He would be hopelessly and indefinitely trapped at the *Dollar Daily*. He wasn't going to mention this, of course, yet he couldn't help but think it. "What made you do it?" he said, trying to keep things light. "What brought on this sudden spell of sanity?"

Ana shrugged stiffly. "I don't know. I just got fed up.

With the whole place. All the bullshit. That stupid client and their horrible politics. And they were just so mean." She took a breath, then a sip of wine. "The shoot was an absolute nightmare. Worst I've ever been on."

"Was it that Karin woman?"

"Yes, I really couldn't stand her. And there was nothing to do since that company was all in bed with Cherkovski, that fucking piece of shit."

She was very upset. Ana was just as likely as he was to swear like a longshoreman, but she usually didn't do it about the people she worked with. So to hear her go off on Cherkovski, who as all signs seemed to indicate was indeed a fucking piece of shit, was surprising.

"I just kept thinking it was going to be okay."

"I know you did." Joe leaned across the table to take her hand and noticed tears welling in her eyes. "It's okay. You did the right thing. I'm really glad that you're out of there. It was sucking the life out of you."

Ana sniffed, then stared down at the table. Joe thought she was going to be all right.

"Yeah," he said, "when I didn't hear from you, I was wondering if things were going badly."

Ana looked up at him. "Joe, why didn't you call?"

It was his turn to stare at the table. He studied his plate, which was still empty. "I don't know. You seemed so distracted before you left, I didn't want to bother you . . . I guess I was mad at you."

"Why?"

"I don't know, I just was. You were so caught up in work while you were here, you just didn't seem to care about anything. And once you were gone, it was sort of a relief. I'm sorry."

"No, you're right."

"Well, it doesn't matter anymore. I'm glad you're here now." His eyes widened in excitement. "*So*. What did Bruce have to say after you quit?" he asked, not bothering to hide his glee.

Ana raised her head and took a long, aching breath. "There's something else, Joe."

He didn't know where to go, what else to do, after she told him the real reason why "we have to talk." Ana told him everything that had happened with Bruce: the kissing, the touching, the fondling, the unzipping, the unbuckling, the pawing away of clothes, and finally, finally, *finally*, her actually doing what she should have done in the first place: saying no. As much as he wanted to tell himself that Bruce was the aggressor in all this, that Ana was some kind of a victim, he knew it was not true. Ana was as responsible as Bruce was for what happened. She said as much.

He could not stop running it through his head over and over, as if forever stuck on digital repeat. The two of them outside of some fancy hotel room in Grand Rapids, dry-humping like a couple of horny high school kids.

"We did not have sex, Joe," she had said, like the Bill Clinton defense was somehow going to comfort him. "I swear it."

He could not even look at her at that point. "Oh, that's wonderful, Ana. So it was just the hand job?"

"No, it wasn't anything like that."

"No, just you two necking, and grinding, and groping each other and all up in each other's junk."

Ana's face was a mess at that point; all the color had drained out. The nice meal she had prepared sat there ignored and getting cold, the smell of the pork tenderloin starting to sicken Joe before long.

"It just got out of control," she kept saying. "I had drunk too much."

"Out of control? It got *out of control*? Are you fucking kidding me? What? You only meant to peck him on the cheek instead of grab his cock? What does 'out of control' mean?"

"I didn't mean that. I just meant—"

Joe hit the table. He hit it hard with the flat of his hand. His glass tipped over, spilling the wine all over the salad. He was glad. He had wanted to make noise, break something. It was the first time in all their years together that he finally understood how a man could strike a woman. He had been taught all his life that this was never supposed to happen, but tonight he understood how it could. He hit the table again.

"Why did you stop, Ana? Seriously, at that point, you might as well have just fucked him. I mean, what's the difference? That's what's so insane about all this. Seriously, why did you stop?"

She stared at him, her eyes red and glistening, as if she were deciding whether or not to tell him. Finally, she said it: "He told me what to do. He told me what I wanted and I didn't like that he did that. It shocked me into realizing what I was doing and that I didn't want to be doing it."

At that moment, everything felt so painfully and irredeemably true to Joe. He knew that this was indeed exactly what had happened. This was so like Ana, who never liked to be told what to do or what to think. "Even though you wanted to do it," he said.

"I can't lie, Joe. I came very close to wanting to do it."

All that violent energy suddenly whooshed out of him.

He shook his head, now exhausted. "I don't even know what that means."

He felt collapsed inside. He just got up and walked out of the kitchen. Ana sobbing and running after him, telling him how sorry she was, that she hadn't meant it to happen, that it just happened. Why didn't this feel real? Why did it feel like he was stuck in some mumblecore indie flick?

Him just stopping at the doorway and saying: "Sounds to me like you wanted it to happen."

Her crying. Him crying. Him leaving. Not sure where he was going to go, only knowing that he could not be in their place with her for the time being. Now him drinking by himself at the Midlands, feeling so numb even after only a single sip of the pint of Two Hearted in front of him with the untouched bump of Knob Creek next to it. It had just felt like the thing to do. He assumed that's what men in Detroit had been doing for the past century after hearing bad news, only they didn't have microbrews or fancy bourbon. The only thing he knew was that he wasn't going to get drunk. If he got drunk, he would only feel much worse.

He just didn't know what had happened. When he and Ana first got together, they were well matched. But little by little, Ana had grown out of his league. He had noticed that of late, but had conveniently ignored it. While she had gotten more successful, gradually climbing the ranks in the agency world, winning awards and promotions, he seemed to flounder more, growing increasingly aimless in his writing and work habits, searching for some nebulous and ever-more-elusive creative project, finally ending up at the *Dollar Daily*, which now felt like a sadly appropriate place for his dubious talents. As he started to lose his hair and thicken around the waist, she had actually gotten more attractive. Her success and the confidence it had given her had made her more beautiful. The money she pulled in hadn't hurt either, especially when it came to clothing and personal grooming. Even though he was forty now, he still pretty much dressed like a twenty-three-year-old in Chuck Taylors and jeans and thrift store shirts and T-shirts with the names of stupid bands on them, bands that most people hadn't heard of, which allegedly made them cool.

Joe thought about the stares he and Ana got when walking into a nice restaurant. Men looking at Ana (because they did still look at her and she was well worth looking at), then their eyes shifting over to Joe. He now understood what they were thinking when they saw the two of them. They were thinking: *What is* she *doing with* him?

Is it any wonder that Ana was attracted to a successful, good-looking, charismatic asshole like Bruce Kellner? What was probably most surprising about this whole thing was that it hadn't happened sooner.

His cell phone rang. It was Malcolm. He muted it. Joe did not want to talk to anyone at the moment.

He heard a voice behind him: "Well, I guess I know how I rate."

Joe turned to face a smiling Malcolm, holding a beer in one hand and his iPhone in the other.

"Oh shit. I'm sorry, man," said Joe. "I just kind of wanted to be alone."

Malcolm stopped smiling and put his hand on Joe's shoulder. "You okay?"

He was not sure if he wanted to talk about any of this, but he couldn't seem to stop himself. "Something happened. With Ana."

Malcolm sat down on the stool next to him. "I heard about her quitting. Quite the performance."

"What? What do you mean?"

Malcolm was obviously confused by his confusion. "She didn't tell you that she dumped a beer over Bruce Kellner's head in Chicago right in front of the client?"

Joe sat back on his barstool. "Really? No."

"Oh yeah. I guess Adrienne quit today too. I don't know what was up with her, but there goes the whole W2W division." Malcolm raised his hand and waved. "So long, ladies. Everyone at the agency is all abuzz. It would have been gone anyway. I heard we lost WomanLyfe too."

"Really?"

"Yes, some nonsense about not respecting their wishes about putting Jesus's teachings in the advertising. Really it's just because they want all the footage and content we shot for their commercials and website. They'll just put it all together themselves. This way, they don't have to pay an agency and they can do anything they want. I guess they're pretty notorious for that sort of thing."

"Wow. Nice business."

"Pretty standard stuff, actually. Good riddance. It was a crap account."

Joe took a pained breath. "Mal?"

"Yeah?"

"Did you ever hear anything about anything going on between Ana and Bruce?"

The long pause that Malcolm took before answering told Joe everything even before he spoke.

"Look, you hear all kinds of stupid things floating around an agency. Mostly it isn't true. I had heard stuff about Adrienne and Bruce too. Anytime anyone gets promoted and someone feels slighted, people will gripe about it, especially if there are women involved. There are people who practically do nothing but go from cube to cube spreading rumors."

Oh, what the hell, thought Joe. "The reason I'm asking, Mal, was because, uh, there *was* something going on there."

Malcolm inhaled sharply. "Oh shit. I'm sorry."

"It's okay. It's not exactly what you'd think, but almost what you'd think. If that makes any sense."

"I'm not sure it does, but that's okay. We don't need to get into it."

"Thank you." Joe took a sip of his beer.

"What are you going to do?"

"I don't really know yet."

"Well, whatever was going on with Bruce is obviously not going on now. And at least she told you. If she didn't care, I don't think she would have done that."

Joe nodded. "I know."

"Don't do anything that you'll—oh god, you know what I'm saying." Malcolm took a breath and started again. "Look, I know this isn't the guy thing to say at a time like this, I know I'm supposed to call her a fucking bitch or something, but we both know that's not true. Maybe she just . . . made a mistake."

"I know."

"You want to talk more?"

Joe shook his head.

"I'm really sorry about this." Malcolm gripped Joe's shoulder again, then let go. "I'm going to take off."

Joe grabbed his arm to stop him from leaving. "Before you go, could you do me a favor?"

"Sure, of course. What do you need?"

"You know how you have your talent? How you can tell someone's secret truth?"

"Yeah," said Malcolm warily. "That was mostly bullshit. I was probably drunk when I said that."

Joe could tell that Malcolm didn't like where this was headed. "I need you to tell me mine."

"What? *No.* Absolutely not."

"Seriously, man. I think I need to hear it. I need to know my truth or my fear or whatever. I think it will help me. I really do."

"No, I don't think about that stuff with my friends. I wouldn't know."

"Yes you would. Just give it a moment and it will come to you."

"Quit it, Joe. I'm not going to do that."

He watched Malcolm, who now looked very uncomfortable. "You've already thought of it, haven't you?" There was another long silence and Joe knew he was right. "Please? I know you think this isn't the right time for it, but I really think it will help."

Malcolm peered skeptically at him. "Are you sure? Are you going to hate me after this?"

"I don't think so, but I can't guarantee it."

Malcolm's gaze shifted to the back bar, where he idly examined the bottles. He took a long breath. "You're afraid that there's nothing real inside of you. No pain, no craziness, no brilliance. You think all great artists are fucked up and you know you're not. You're ashamed that you're a nice guy, that you're pretty normal. You think it means that you're not *authentic*. So you hide behind other people's accomplishments. You see greatness in other people's work, but instead of inspiring you, it paralyzes you. You're so afraid that you won't create something great that you don't create *anything*. So you've talked yourself into believing that knowing about things is as important as doing them. It's just easier for you."

Joe nodded, as if to say, *Keep going.*

"You drop names and make references. You talk about songs, but rarely does a song speak to you. You laugh at cleverness because you recognize that it's supposed to be funny, not because it is funny. You know about things for the sake of knowing about them, because you think you're supposed to, because you're afraid of being left out, not because they interest you. You're a dilettante, a potterer. You simply stopped trying to be anything more."

"I'm a coward," said Joe.

"And then there's that," said Malcolm, exhaling.

"Thank you," whispered Joe.

26

The Exterminating Angel

The fact that their town house was only 850 square feet made it difficult for them to avoid each other. Yet that was exactly what she and Joe had been doing for the past week. He had been spending much more time at work lately. At least Ana assumed he was at work. He would leave in the morning and not come home until nine or ten at night.

When Joe did come home, he just went up to their study and stayed there, either on the Internet, reading, or watching DVDs with his headphones. On the night of their talk, he had shut himself in the study where he blew up the air mattress that they used for overnight guests. Ana was in their bedroom with the door closed, feeling numb as she listened to the whistled huffs of Joe's breath as he inflated the mattress. It went on for at least twenty minutes. She wanted to get up to talk to him, but worried that it would start all over again. She wasn't sure what she feared more—ultimatums or silence.

Since that night, he had slept in the study. That room was his area now, Ana supposed, and the bedroom, their old bedroom, was hers. The kitchen and the bathroom were the demilitarized zones, where both could tread, albeit warily, but they were hardly ever in the same room at once. Ana didn't know what Joe's future plans were and she was afraid to ask. Walking up to the bathroom one night, she did peek into the study and saw that he was looking at apartment listings online, which did not bode well.

The strange thing was, Ana suddenly had all this spare time, most of which she was devoting to regret, depression, and slumber. She didn't much leave the house, spent a lot of time in bed, sleeping twelve to fourteen hours at a time, but there were still the other ten to twelve hours of the day to account for, so she tried to busy herself, filling them with trivial tasks. Like putting all her music, photos, and personal files from her work computer onto a separate hard drive. After that, she wasn't quite sure what to do with the computer, since no one had contacted her about it yet. Ana assumed that she'd eventually get a call from the agency's IT department, but still hadn't heard anything.

At first, she planned to transfer all the files to the home computer, but then thought better of it. She did not want to upset the delicate balance by invading the small territory that Joe had taken for himself. Anyway, it was probably better if she had her own computer. So Ana actually left the house, braved the mall, and bought herself a new Mac laptop. She rationalized the purchase by telling herself that she would need it to put together a website for her portfolio if (and that was a big "if") she decided to try to get another advertising job, though that was not something she was even thinking about yet.

The money for the computer wasn't a problem. Money wasn't a problem at all, and wouldn't be for quite some time. Ana had been saving since well before her promotion, and she hadn't really done much of anything besides work for the past five months. There had not even been time to buy anything. Basically, she could comfortably afford to not work for at least a year and probably more like two. Here was the shameful truth: she actually had a savings account. It was one of those quaint Midwestern things about herself that she didn't necessarily share with other ad folks because they would find it, well, so quaintly Midwestern. She wasn't sure if women in their twenties could even grasp the concept of having money and not spending it, but this woman recently arrived in her forties had always felt the need to save. It was her Fuck You Money. Ana had always loved that expression. Amazingly, she had never used the money until last week, when she said fuck you to Bruce Kellner.

The computer turned out to be a good idea. Besides getting her out of the house, setting it up occupied her for a good three days, helping to keep her mind off everything. Except when she transferred her photographs and got caught up in the vacation shots—she and Joe in Austin, she and Joe in Guadalajara, she and Joe in Amsterdam, she and Joe up north, and so on. The subsequent meltdown put her in bed in a depressed, somnolent state for an entire afternoon.

The next day, she was still recovering when she got a call from Sue Smithick, the agency's human resources director (a.k.a. "The Exterminating Angel," as Joe had dubbed her after Ana had told him about her blandly sweet face, and how she coolly and efficiently oversaw all hirings, firings, and layoffs at the agency like some death-camp commandant).

Ana's initial reactions were those of a dutiful corporate citizen. *Why would Sue be contacting me? Am I in trouble? Was it the computer? What did I do?*

Then Ana remembered that she was no longer a corporate citizen. What a relief.

How could she be in trouble? She had quit. *Fuck you, agency.*

"Ana, I hope you're well," Sue said, all cheery and cordial. "Getting some much-needed rest, I bet?"

"I'm great, Sue. Fantastic." And just saying it made her feel fantastic, or at least closer to it.

"Good. Glad to hear it. Look, I was wondering if you'd be willing to come in. At your convenience, of course, for a little exit interview."

It sounded ominous at first, and Ana again wondered if she was in some trouble. Why would they want to conduct an exit interview with her? What would they have to gain? What were they trying to find out? Why was Sue being so nice? They shouldn't even want to talk to her. She had disgraced a CD in front of a client. Then the truth of it jabbed her in the ribs like some sharpie from a thirties screwball comedy: *Wise up, sister! They're shiverin' in their boots!*

"Um, that would be fine, Sue. I'd love to. How about today?"

"Wonderful. Is three p.m. okay?"

"See you then."

For the first time in the past week, Ana felt strong. She was actually able to motivate her moping, depressed, excessive Food Network watching, compulsively oversleeping self. So Ana closed up the computer, turned off the television, pulled herself off the couch, showered, applied makeup, then donned her black D&G meeting pantsuit that she had scored at the Neiman outlet last year, to go talk to The Exterminating Angel.

In the car on the way there, all the stories about Bruce came back to her. Everything she had conveniently suppressed when she was infatuated with him, all the stories about the young art directors, the rumors of quietly settled sexual harassment suits, the vaguely inappropriate jokes at which she had blankly smiled, all the hands on the shoulders, not to mention the fact that he'd had relations of some sort with both her and her partner. All of it came back to her, and just thinking of how stupid she was made her face burn. Yet it also made her crave revenge.

She soon found herself clicking across the marble threshold of the agency. (She had decided to wear heels, even though she had always found them painful and slightly ridiculous, but today she wanted to be as tall as possible.)

The first person she saw: Jerrod Amburn. He smirked right up to her, well into her personal space. Ana had never seen someone look so self-satisfied.

"Well, looky here—look who came to visit," he said disdainfully. "Guess the chickens have come home to roost."

Ana didn't know if it was the suit or just the fact that she no longer cared, but she glared at him and pressed a finger into his chest as hard as she could. She was glad when he flinched. "Why are you so mean, Jerrod?"

He looked bewildered by this statement. "I'm not mean."

"Yes you are. You're very mean. Do you know that no one likes you because you're so mean?"

He inhaled dramatically. "That's not true."

"It *is* true. People just act like they like you because they're afraid of you. They're afraid that as soon as they walk away from you, you're going to say something awful about them. Because you do. They gossip with you about everyone else so you don't gossip about *them*. That's the only reason anyone talks to you."

The smirk fell away and she saw that Jerrod knew she was right. He was a person that no one trusted.

"I'm sorry," he said, in almost a whisper.

"You should be sorry. It's no way for a person to be. You make me sad."

Then she was done. Jerrod walked away much less buoyantly. Ana strolled up to Alethea the receptionist, who was trying very hard not to smile.

What happened after that wasn't exactly the high point of Ana's life as a contemporary feminist, but it sure was fun. She spilled hard to The Exterminating Angel. Not all of it, of course; she left out the trip to Grand Rapids and anything else that implicated her as being actively involved. She even used some terminology that Sue would find familiar, re-calling it from the company's annual workplace-sensitivi-ty course. Ana alluded to a "hostile work environment," a place of "inappropriate" comments, not to mention Bruce's leering and touching, etc. Oh, such glee to watch the Angel squirm, lips tightened and flattened to her teeth, head flut-tering with tiny, almost indiscernible hummingbird nods. This was all Ana wanted: to make the agency, as personified by one of its executive-committee toadies (sad that it had to be a sister), very uncomfortable. Ana then went in for the coup de grâce with "My attorney finds it all quite interest-ing." She hadn't really planned on what happened next.

Sue Smithick took a long, silent look at her. Sue had to know that it was all true, but she may also have known that something happened between her and Bruce. (And Adri-enne!) Still, did that really matter? To them, it was only the perception that mattered. Would the agency want to risk a scandal? "Head of Women's Marketing Group Sexually Ha-rassed" was not a headline any agency wanted to see flash up on the daily *Ad Age* e-blast. Or worse yet, on *AgencySpy*, the mud-slingingest of them all. No, definitely not.

That was when the packet appeared.

* * *

Feeling shaky, but better than she had in quite some time, Ana decided to call Adrienne from the car. (Joe had dispassionately relayed the information from Malcolm to her that Adrienne had quit the day after she had, bless her heart.)

"Hey lady," said Adrienne. "I was wondering when I was going to hear from you."

"I just had my exit interview. Have you had yours?"

"Oh yeah. They got an earful. I told them that they were lucky that you didn't sue their asses."

"Well, that explains a lot." Ana told her what happened with Sue Smithick.

"What did you do when she pulled out the compensation packet?"

"I took it and ran."

"Damn right. That's some serious cigarette-and-pantyhose money." A pause on the line. "I'm really sorry about everything, Ana."

"Forget it," she said, remembering why she loved Adrienne. "Just think about where you'd like to go for dinner. Somewhere *fancy*."

After hanging up with Adrienne, the high started to fade and Ana thought about what had happened. Was this fair? She had signed up for all of it. She had put up with the jokes, enjoyed the attention, and had even stupidly allowed, perhaps encouraged, what had happened with Bruce. No, it probably wasn't fair that it would turn out this way. Did she care? In a word: no. As far as she was concerned, the agency had it coming for what they put her through.

As fun as it was death-gripping the desiccated testicles of Edward Cherkovski (Adrienne's words), it was still cold comfort because of what was happening with Joe. How long would this go on? Were they already split up? Were they together? For right now, she was glad that they were still living under the same roof. It made her feel that things were not completely and irreparably severed. It all seemed sadly appropriate to Ana. She was part of a couple that was not quite married. She had not quite been unfaithful to Joe. And they were not quite broken up over it. It was so like the two of them. She hoped they could ride this out.

Ana knew she wanted that, and that she still loved Joe, but that was all she knew. After a week of not working, her mind was just starting to clear. Leaving an agency job felt like easing from the depths of Stockholm syndrome, swimming upward to the blinding, rippled surface of sanity. She was still decompressing, but could feel a new calm rise within herself, even with all the worrying and crying and sleeping and fear of not knowing what would happen.

It was a sense of release, a feeling of being let go.

27
The Verity of Decay

After his embarrassing display at the Chin Tiki, Joe was surprised when Brendan invited him on another one of his "field trips." Joe certainly hadn't planned on ever setting foot in an abandoned building again. Yet he was torn. Did he really need to do this again? This was no gentle avocation like philately or tinkering together a schooner in a jug. It was illegal and dangerous and scary. At the same time, Joe wanted to try it once more and was not sure why. Perhaps a shadowy activity based on the exploration of broken things seemed sadly apropos to his state of mind these days. He'd felt so adrift lately, a floating fugue of sadness and anger and ennui, where he was always about five seconds away from a crying jag.

That state of mind was probably why Joe agreed to participate. He woke up Sunday, feeling like crap after another night scooching around on that goddamned air mattress. It didn't help that Malcolm had talked him into going to a gallery opening in Hamtramck, then to see the High Strung at the Lager House that night. His ears were still ringing. Joe thought about showering, dismissed it, pulled some clothes out from his to-be-washed pile, threw on his Doc Martens, and left the house, not worrying if he woke Ana or not. After picking up coffee and a hot salt at New York Bagel, he drove down Woodward Avenue to meet up with Brendan at the corner of Park and Bagley downtown.

They were walking on the street in front of the building and Joe was already nervous. He had read somewhere online that the old United Artists building had a charming history of dropping bricks onto cars and passersby. He tried not to think about it. The front doors of the place were sealed with weathered plywood, encrusted with gnarled and welted hip-hop posters for Esham and Trick Trick. Over two of the doors, someone had painted giant pink polka dots. Probably an acolyte of Tyree Guyton, who on Heidelberg Street had painted polka dots on old buses, car hoods, trashed kitchen appliances, and a sparsely populated block of mostly abandoned houses—crazy vibrant splashes of color and life and energy in a neighborhood decimated by crack and blight, a ghetto theme park. Joe had interviewed him once for the *Independent*.

"C. Howard Crane," proclaimed Brendan, as they did a reconnaissance lap around the building. He paused before one of the dotted doorways and adjusted the camera bag slung across his chest.

"What?"

"Dude designed this theater in the twenties. He designed a shitload of theaters in Detroit back in the day. All over the place. He did the Fox, the Majestic, the State. C. Howard designed theaters like a motherfucker."

"Really?"

"Hells yeah."

Somehow Brendan could say things like *hells yeah* and make it sound all right. If Joe had ever said anything like that, he was pretty sure that he would sound like a complete ass.

"Remember I told you about this place, the way it looked a few years back?" Brendan continued. "A few graffiti artists had taken over the whole joint—Joy, Gram, Coupe. Most every window had a painting on it. Mayan hieroglyphics and shit. Looked so sick."

Joe had researched it and found a couple of photos online. He did know what happened, but he wanted to hear Brendan's version. "Yeah, it really did look great. What happened?"

"Just before the fucking Super Bowl came to Detroit in 2006, the owners had the place secured, then painted all the windows black. They hung a banner on the side of the building for 'development opportunities' or some such shit to trick everyone into thinking that the building was going to be renovated. Nothing ever happened. It's been empty ever since."

Joe looked up and saw the banner now, stained and rag-torn, flapping in the wind against the side of the building. "Did you say secured?" he said, experiencing a slight tightness in his chest. "So this isn't like before, where it was so easy to get in?"

"Oh no. This a bitch to get inside. It's gonna take some *work* to get up in this piece."

"Oh boy."

"Not to worry, cuz. I got a plan."

As it turned out, Brendan's plan was to scare the *hells* out of Joe. It was not pleasant. Walls were scaled, video cameras ignored, and advice like, "Whatever you do, don't look down," was dispensed. Once they were in, it was an incredible mess: broken glass, giant sloughed flakes of paint, plaster, dirt, rags, and trash everywhere. Joe was eerily conscious of the crunch all that debris made beneath his shoes, like some toxic breakfast cereal. Once their eyes adjusted to the light, Brendan gave Joe an LED flashlight headband.

"Put this on."

Joe started to tighten the band to put around his head.

"No, no. Like this," said Brendan, as he hung his around his neck like a pendant. When he turned it on, the area around both their feet was illuminated. "So you can always see where you're walking."

"Cool," said Joe. He did the same, then pulled from his messenger bag the big blue Maglite that he had purchased specifically for this adventure. He would not be caught with the little flashlight again.

Brendan nodded approvingly, and then held up his hand. "Okay, now let's just be quiet for a minute."

"What?"

"Just listen."

The two of them stood there, not saying a word. Joe didn't hear anything but the occasional pigeon and the far-away sound of traffic. When the sound of automobiles faded, there was only the hiss of silence. At one point, Joe shifted a foot in the rubble and Brendan shot him a look.

After what seemed like a couple of minutes, Joe finally spoke: "What are we listening to?"

"History," said Brendan. He closed his eyes for another ten seconds, then opened them. "Okay, let's go."

"Wait a sec," said Joe. Now that he knew what they were listening to, he wanted to stand there a little longer.

"Come on, let's hustle."

"What's the big rush?"

"You'll see."

Brendan tugged at the sleeve of Joe's Carhartt. Joe followed, now a little concerned. Where were they going?

Were they rushing to another hilarious thespian ambush by Malik? Whatever it was, Joe was suddenly happy to get away from where they were standing, its strong odor of dust and mold, along with a rotting, fetid smell that he could not place, as if the walls and inner structure of the building were decomposing.

There in the murky grime and shuddering half-light (from unseen windows, unknown fissures, from the Maglites they carried), Joe glimpsed flashes of random images as they marched through the detritus: a mosaic of shattered glass here, a pile of bricks there, a broken chair with half a metal film canister leaning against it, a room filled with dozens of empty gallon jugs of Seagram's Gin, another room where someone obviously slept—a swelled and tattered human nest of yellowed newspapers. It made Joe think of the Irving Penn photographs from an old coffee table book he had reviewed ages ago for *Out of the Attic*. The book was called *Passage*, and in it were photographs of refuse—crushed cigarette butts, stomped-on paper cups, discarded rags, disintegrating lost mittens, and other objects found in the street. The photographs were eerily beautiful, stark black-and-white, flecked and folded with textured filth, the warp and weft of decay. Joe found himself wanting to stop and take some photographs, but Brendan kept rushing him along. He weaved the beam of his Maglite across the cluttered floor and walls as they traversed a hallway covered with graffiti, mostly names: *Slack, Mo B, Mosh, Gray*, ABYS*. It occurred to Joe that these were people who wanted to be heard, to offer proof that they existed, but came to a deserted, half-dead place to do it. He didn't know why that made sense to him, yet it did.

Finally, after a few turns, they reached an area that felt

like a side chamber of a theater. The lowness of the ceiling reminded Joe of certain claustrophobic anterooms of other old venues, places he had seen shows—the Masonic Temple or even the Fox, where you felt the compression of space, which then allowed you to feel relief when you entered the grand space of the auditorium. (C. Howard knew what he was doing.) Joe studied the swollen stucco as they passed. They ended up in what Joe believed was once the round main lobby of the theater.

The floors of the rotunda were covered with debris, even more than where they came in—paint and plaster, brick and statuary, a flokati of dried sludge and curled silt. You couldn't really say the walls were bare, because mostly there were no walls. Two of the three Gothic arches on one side of the rotunda were now stripped clean—the elements and the vandals were sloughing the place from the inside out, revealing the tessellated cinder-block bones of the building. Where there were walls, you could see remnants of gold-leafed ornamentation gone to chalk, traces of intricate designs, petroglyphs of lost grandeur.

Eventually, Brendan allowed them to pause for a moment to take in what they were looking at. Near them, Joe was stunned by the sight of a relatively unscathed gray-white wall, its ornamentation still intact, a two-story art deco Indian maiden in plaster bas-relief, her face placid and all-seeing, her towering headdress curving against the vaulted ceiling, the sleeves of her gown stretching almost to the ground, the intricate, fruited folds of it deeply engrimed, dotted with black mold, but still exquisite. The only desecration was where someone had written at the bottom of the wall, not in graffiti style, but in a clawed marker script: *My Heart Is Missing.*

"Wow," said Joe, gazing up at the tableau in front of him. It was a silly thing to say, he thought, but it was what he said.

"Yeah," said Brendan, smiling. "Wow. I don't know why the vandals haven't trashed this one. There used to be six of them."

Joe stared up at the maiden, not sure what he was feeling—it was strange to encounter this beauty in the middle of such carnage.

Brendan pulled out his Nikon, set up the small tripod he'd slung over his back, and took some photographs. The light from his flash unit hurt Joe's eyes.

Joe took a few shots as well, using only the available light, which wasn't much.

Then Brendan was ready to leave again. "Come on, let's keep moving."

Joe was starting to understand why he didn't want to stay in one place too long. This was a lot to take in, an assault on the senses. He was feeling overwhelmed. Joe followed Brendan up a flight of side stairs. Somewhere beneath Joe's feet, under the grime and gnarled paint and disintegrated plaster, was softness, a fleshy memory of carpeting. He held his light pendant as they scurried up the stairs to keep himself from getting dizzy. The two of them surfaced onto the mezzanine for a full view of the theater. They stopped again.

Brendan turned to him. "The view's better from up here. And it's safer."

Joe needed to catch his breath, not just from sprinting up the stairs, but also from what was laid out in front of him. He stared out at an immense palace of ruin. Sunlight had indirectly found its way into the auditorium from ceiling fissures and hidden smashed-out windows, giving the place a brownish-gray cast. It was the color of the doves that he could hear roosting somewhere. The giant room smelled of damp and guano and rust and rotting plaster and moldering fabric, as if the two of them had slalomed up the alimentary canal of some behemoth to its vast bloated stomach and were now examining what it had eaten before it died. Joe thought of climbing through the Trojan horse in *The Dream Life of Balso Snell*. Then he noticed that leaking in from somewhere high above them was the fresh smell of spring air.

Forty-foot-long tatters of curtains hung over what was once a stage. Flanking the stage were the jagged mammoth remnants of broken Gothic filigree where the pipe organs were housed. Above them, giant cone-shaped sconces snugged the ceiling. Traversing the sconces were X-shaped light vents now crushed or dissolved by water. On either side of the balcony were shattered vestiges of the Indian motif. A small bas-relief of a face much like the one of the maiden peeked at Joe from high, too far up for the vandals to smash.

"Goddamn," Joe said. At that moment, he couldn't help but wish that Ana were there to see this. Was she capable of appreciating something like this anymore? He didn't know, yet he had a feeling that she would.

"Take a look at that proscenium," said Brendan. "It's still incredible."

Joe was surprised by how tranquil he felt in this place. The two of them just stood there looking around. He wasn't even sure for how long. It may have been a half hour for all he knew.

"It's strange to think about all the people," Joe said, when he finally spoke.

"People?"

"Yeah, the thousands of people—the millions—who probably walked through here over the years, just going to the movies. Seeing *Doctor Zhivago* or *Shaft's Big Score!* or *I Am Curious (Yellow)* or whatever." He took a breath. "Just standing here, you can feel that people *lived* in this place. They laughed and applauded and cried. They met future husbands and wives. They brought their kids. They threw popcorn and drank pop and broke their teeth on jujubes."

Joe felt stupid after he said it, but Brendan didn't laugh. "It's beautiful," Brendan said.

It surprised Joe that Brendan should see it too. Then he realized: *Of course he saw it.* It was why he had been rushing here in the first place.

"Yes it is," Joe said.

"I knew you would understand. Not everybody does."

"You know, what I don't understand is how this place could be beautiful? It's horrible, really. This incredible old building left to fall apart."

"I don't know why. It's totally fucked up that this would ever happen to a building. This should never happen anywhere. But I see something like this and I want to try to find the beauty in it, make some sense of it, give it a reason, to fill it with something. Meaning."

Joe raised his camera to his eye and scanned the great room. He took a lot of photographs. He wanted to remember this.

"It looks different through the lens, doesn't it?" Brendan said.

"I don't know why. It just makes more sense this way. It's easier to take in."

"Uh-huh. Sometimes what I'm looking at is too intense

for me to understand without a filter, a way to view it. The camera helps." Brendan leveled his camera at the stage and squeezed off a shot.

"Why is this so magnificent? What's wrong with us?"

"I told you," said Brendan. "The verity of decay." He reached into the pocket of his flannel shirt and extracted a loose joint and a purple plastic lighter. He lit the bent end of the cigarette, took a long hit, then passed it to Joe.

"I still don't get you," said Joe, taking a small hit. He had to have his wits about him if he was going to walk out of here without sustaining injuries. He passed it back to Brendan.

Another massive toke, smoke held in for many seconds, then exhaled through tightened lips. Brendan closed his eyes, then opened them. "This building is the truth about us all, forced right in our face. Look at the fuckin' world out there. Everyone loves to surround themselves with the newest and the shiniest and the brightest. The newer, the better. The farther out in the suburbs, the better. It makes us feel safe, yo, like we're going to live forever." He paused, then took another hit and held it in. His head tipped back after exhaling. "This building is what's going to happen to all of us. That's why it's so fucking hard to look at, but why we can't look away. It's why some people hate this city and it's why other people are still drawn to it and keep believing in it. The fear and the fascination. Monk called it *ugly beauty*. The same reason we look at car accidents and horror films. We want to be reminded. Something in us still seeks the truth, even though it's easier to hide behind the lies and the shiny surfaces." Brendan stopped; the joint had gone cold between his fingers. "Things die. This building is dying. Yet we need to look upon it. Bellow said that death is the dark backing a mirror needs if we are to see anything. The death helps you see the life. But you have to be willing to see it all."

"You think not everyone sees it all?"

"No, I don't."

"Yet somehow I don't feel so special right now," Joe said, starting to reel from the view and the toke and an encroaching paranoia.

"It's not about feeling special. It's about the knowing."

Brendan relit the joint, took a hit, and passed it to Joe, who didn't know what to say anymore. *Fuck it*, he thought. He just nodded and took a long drag. He started to cough, then couldn't stop coughing. Finally, he gathered enough saliva in his mouth to soothe the burn. He swallowed and caught his breath.

"Come on, bird lungs," said Brendan, laughing. "Let's bounce. I'm getting too high to be walking around in this crazy shit."

Joe was already there.

28
Attempted Dinner, Part 2

That afternoon, Ana decided to cook. Even though there were still the remains of almost an entire dinner in the refrigerator. It was the one she had made over a week ago, the night that she had told Joe about quitting her job and everything else. Neither of them had touched the meal that night, so she had wrapped it up in foil and plastic containers (except for the wine-soaked salad, which she pitched), all while sobbing over what had occurred. Even then, she realized that most people would have just left the food on the table, but she couldn't do that. So she had cried and wrapped the food, cried and put it away in the refrigerator, cried and cleaned up the table. Emotional anguish apparently made her more efficient. This was something her bosses at various advertising agencies had probably figured out a long time ago.

Since that night, neither she nor Joe had eaten any of the leftovers. They had been in the fridge all that time, perfectly edible but tainted by the circumstances of the dinner. So today, she opened the container of ratatouille and dumped it into the garbage bin under the sink. She did the same with the foil packages of pork loin and polenta.

Ana started again. It wasn't going to be much of a dinner, but it would be something. It would make her feel better. There was a jar of homemade pesto in the fridge that she had made a month ago on a rare Sunday off, but it was still perfectly fine. In the pantry, there was a box of linguini. In the depths of the crisper were some carrots that she could peel and sauté. A frozen garlic bread in the back of the freezer. It would do.

After a while, she did feel better. Just the activity of preparing food had that effect on her. She had already sautéed the carrots in butter and a little orange juice. They just had to be reheated. The water was simmering. All that was needed was to put in the pasta. The oven was on at a low temperature to defrost and slowly bake the garlic bread and the kitchen was warm and fragrant. She was sitting at the kitchen table drinking a glass of wine, flipping through *Atomic Ranch*, hoping Joe would show up, when she heard his key in the back door. It was about four thirty and she realized that she had no idea where he had been all day. The thought saddened her.

"Hey," she said as he walked into the kitchen.

Joe made a noise that may have been a greeting or just a grunt, then looked at the set table, the pot of water bubbling on the stove, ready for the pasta. He went to the refrigerator and pulled out a bottle of Ghettoblaster ale, went into the silverware drawer for the bottle opener. She noticed that the sleeves of his Carhartt and one of the legs of his jeans were really dirty.

"You hungry?" she said. "I made dinner. I just have to drop the pasta. It'll only take a few minutes." She just wanted him to sit down with her. She didn't know what her plan was after that, but it would be a start.

Joe opened his beer and looked at her. "No, I'm good. Thanks."

He started to leave the kitchen. Ana grabbed his arm. "Joe, please. Stay and eat with me, okay? Please?" She could see that he was considering it, rejecting it, considering it again.

"No, I'm going up to the study." He pulled away from her.

"Joe. When are you going to start talking to me again?"

"I'm talking to you right now."

"I mean *talking*. Like we're us again."

He set his bottle of beer on the table. "Are we us now? When have we been us lately? Seems like we haven't been *us* for a long time."

"I know. And I want to fix that."

He placed his hand on the beer bottle, his thumbnail digging into the label, tearing it. "I doubt if you can."

"Let me try. Come and have dinner with me, please?"

He lowered his head. "Why do you think dinner is going to help so much?"

Ana let out a small breath. "I don't. I just—"

"Then stop trying to lure me to the table with food. What do you think I am? Some dumb man that you can win over with a hot meal?"

"No, of course not." Ana leaned back against the kitchen counter and crossed her arms tightly against her stomach.

He stared at her. "Look, I think I found a place to live. I'll find out tomorrow. I'll try to be out by the end of the month."

It was news that she had so hoped not to hear.

"Don't cry," said Joe sternly.

"I'm not crying."

"Yes you are. Stop it. I don't care if you're crying."

He didn't need to say it, but she could hear it in his voice: *This isn't going to work.* It wasn't why she was crying.

Ana hated it when she cried. She had never tried nor wanted to control men with her tears. (Yet she now realized that Joe was right: she had been trying to tempt him with food into loving her again, so oblivious was she to her own intentions.) It was just this whole time catching up to her. She had felt so bad this week, then she felt strong, and then she went right back to feeling bad. Stupid and bad and wrong.

"Damn it, Ana. Stop."

"I can't stop," she said. "If I could stop, I would. Just get out of here if you're so anxious to go."

"Fine."

Ana followed the sound of his footsteps up the stairs and into the study, where he shut the door, not so much with a slam as a firm, airtight *whomp*. Ana turned off the boiling water, then sat down on the kitchen floor, pulled her knees up to her chest, leaned back against the cupboard doors, and wept until she fell asleep.

Ana's throat was sore and dry and she reached around for the bottle of water she kept next to her nightstand, but couldn't find it. She coughed hard when she tried to breathe. Her stupid alarm would not shut off and it was so annoying. Finally, she opened her eyes and coughed again. Her face was stuck to the floor. This was obviously not the bedroom. It seemed as though she were awake, but somehow lost in the middle of some bizarre dream sequence or a flashback from a movie where everything was soft-focus and hazy. Then looking around, her eyes finally focused in on what seemed to be the source of the haze. Two feet from her, smoke was streaming out from the sides of something and rising in coils to the ceiling. It reminded her of the stage at a Slayer concert that some jerk took her to in the eighties. Fucking hair metal. How could she have liked it as much as she did? Ana now decided that this was perhaps not a dream, yet if it was, it had just shifted to her kitchen. Then there was Joe standing over her, his eyes red and streaming tears. He was holding a vintage striped dish towel over his mouth.

"Ana, Ana!" He was shaking her, rather roughly. She didn't like him doing that.

Ana coughed, then coughed again. Then she couldn't stop coughing. "What?" she finally said, still drowsy and very uncomfortable. Her leg was asleep. Her eyes hurt. Her throat was so sore.

"Are you okay?"

She was coughing as if she wanted to bring something up, but nothing was coming. Joe stood up and opened the kitchen window over the sink. Cool air entered the room, dissipating some of the smoke, which was still billowing out of the oven. She heard a faucet run for a moment, then stop. The alarm was still blaring, though now she could breathe a little easier. "What is that noise?" she said, after she stopped hacking.

"It's the smoke detector, Ana. It went off upstairs right next to the study. How could you not hear that?"

"I heard it."

"Did the downstairs one go off?"

"I don't think so." Her voice cracked as she spoke. She tried to clear her throat.

"Are you all right?"

Joe had his hands on her shoulders (it felt good now) and was helping her to sit up against the bottom cupboard. He handed her a glass of water and fanned away some of the smoke.

"I think you left something in the oven."

She coughed again and tried to stand up.

Joe held her down and handed her the dishcloth. "Just stay, okay? I'll get it."

Ana had another sip of water, covered her mouth with the dishcloth, and tried to breathe. Her lungs hurt. Her eyes stung. After a few moments and another rush of smoke into the kitchen, Joe kneeled next to her, coughing, holding a small flat ingot of black matter between two oven mitts as if he were displaying the carbonized result of some lab experiment gone terribly wrong. There was still smoke rising from it. It smelled awful.

"Garlic bread," croaked Ana.

Joe tried to twist his face into some semblance of anger, then just started to laugh. "You idiot."

Ana began laughing too, which made her start coughing again. It hurt, but she didn't care.

"It's not funny," said Joe, half scolding the both of them as he set the smoldering plank up on the windowsill. "I thought you were dead." The alarm finally stopped.

Ana took a sip of water, then looked at him. "From garlic bread smoke inhalation?"

"I'm sure it's happened," he said. "Somewhere. Italy."

"Do they even make garlic bread in Italy?"

He shrugged. "I don't know. But it would definitely be the stupidest way to die ever." He fully gave in now to his laughter. "Jesus, Ana."

It was the first time they had laughed at anything together in what felt like a year. Ana set the glass of water down and awkwardly leaned forward to put her arms around him. "I'm so sorry, Joseph."

Joe rested her head against his neck and shoulder. "Shhh," he said.

5

29

A New Sincerity

Malcolm had called to see if he wanted to have a beer. Joe wasn't sure if he wanted to, wasn't sure if he should. They had just gotten home from a weekend trip up north to Traverse City. Ana was unpacking her suitcase in the bedroom and getting together a few loads of dirty clothes for the wash.

"Hey you," said Joe. "Feel like getting a drink with Mal and Chick instead of doing laundry? I could do that tomorrow."

"Yes, you could. You'll screw it up, but you could do it."

"All right then, fine. *You* can do it tomorrow."

Ana thought for a moment. "Eh, you just go. Go see your friends, it's okay."

Joe touched her arm, tilted his head toward the door. "Come along."

She kept sorting clothes in separate piles on the floor. "I don't want to keep you guys from having your man conversation or anything like that."

"What the hell do you think we talk about?"

"I don't know," she said, tossing a black T-shirt in a pile of darks. "I guess sports." Joe could see that she was trying to keep from smiling as she said it.

He played along. "No, not a lot of sports talk, I'm afraid."

"Well, if it's not that, then it's got to be pussy." Ana didn't even look up when she said it.

She could still surprise him. Smiling, he said, "I'm sorry to disappoint you, but we are sensitive gentlemen of refinement. The female pudendum only occasionally enters the conversation. And even then, it's commented upon with much respect and dignity."

Ana gave him a deadpan look, and then shook her head. "I forgot that you guys are barely men."

Joe laughed.

She peered at him from over her glasses. "Yes, well, it's funny because it's true."

He had missed *this*. Ana could always make him laugh. For a while, he had forgotten how funny she was. It seemed like she had forgotten it too.

Ana dropped a pair of white socks into a pile of lights. Then she walked over and kissed him.

At the bar, Chick regarded the two of them as if they were out of their minds. "So you *both* quit your jobs? Now you're both middle-aged slackers?"

Joe nodded, then Ana.

"Sweet baby Jesus. I cannot believe this. So have you decided which mother's basement you're going to move into? Or are you going to alternate? Joe's one week and Ana's the next? I can see the two of you down there now, half-blind and pale from lack of light. Sweaty albinos subsisting on Funyuns and Mountain Dew, too fat to get up off the couch, playing Halo online with the rest of the stay-at-home senior nerds. For fuck's sake, Keen. I thought you had at least grown up a little."

Joe cast his eyes downward in pretend shame. "I thought so too, Chick. But I guess not."

"He's really wound up tonight," said Malcolm to Ana.

Chick was fun to watch when he got like this. It was all part of the act, but Joe was wondering if there was a scintilla of sincere indignation in there somewhere. It was hard to tell. He was just so good at ranting.

Then Chick started in on Ana: "And you! Lovely Ana. I thought you would have known better. Him, I expect it from." He jerked a thumb back at Joe. "But you? Oh, Ana."

"I'm sorry to have disappointed you, Chick."

"You have. Profoundly. Please know that." Then he started back in on Joe: "What did you do to her, Keen? How did you ensnare her? How did you weave your evil spell over her? You dragged beautiful, employed, mature Ana down into your abyss of joblessness, irresponsibility, and, and—"

"Morning bong hits?" said Joe, finishing his sentence.

"Yes!"

"Are you done?"

"Almost. My only regret is that I won't be here to witness the inevitable descent into complete and utter sloth. I won't be able to find you two huddled in a gutter somewhere and say, I told you so."

"Wait. What?" said Joe. "Why won't you be able to find us in the gutter? And FYI, it will probably be under the 8 Mile overpass."

Chick gestured at Malcolm. "Didn't this bum tell you?"

"I thought you'd want to tell him yourself," said Malcolm.

"I'm leaving for the coast next week. I got a gig. I sold a script and they want me there to rewrite. And then they'll probably fire me and hire some other asshole. I'll be an official Hollywood hack instead of a Motor City hack."

Ana walked up to Chick and gave him a hug. "Congratulations, Chick. I think it'll be good for you."

"Well, it's only for a couple of months."

"That's what everyone says," said Joe, shaking Chick's hand.

"Let me have my fantasy for a while, Keen."

"Next time we see you, you'll be all tan and talking about colonics."

"And up to my eyeballs in poon!" Chick sheepishly turned to Ana. "Sorry, Ana."

"I wouldn't expect anything less of you, Chick."

"That's probably not really going to happen anyway."

"Probably not."

Chick went over to the bar to retrieve his almost full pint when Todd walked into the bar. He had a stunned look about him.

"What's up, Todd?" said Joe.

"They tore down the Chin Tiki. They're finishing up right now. I was just down there. It's gone."

"Are you kidding?" said Chick, his voice getting louder. "It's Sunday night. They don't tear things down on Sunday night."

"Of course they do," said Todd, shaking his head. "It's when no one is looking."

"I thought that place had historical status," said Malcolm.

Todd shook his head again, slowly and wearily. "If it did, it doesn't matter now. It's gone. It's just a mound of Polynesian rubble."

"What happened?" said Ana. "Why'd they tear it down?"

Todd flagged the bartender. "Why else do they tear anything down in Detroit? For a parking lot."

Joe didn't say anything. He was sorry to hear about the Chin Tiki, but it was no surprise. Brendan had been right.

A chain-link fence had mysteriously appeared around the place a few weeks back and that was always the first clue. Every once in a while, it meant that they were rehabbing a building, but mostly it meant that it was going down. Joe was glad that he'd gotten a chance to go inside, even if he had made a fool of himself there.

In a way, he was fine with the place being gone. Maybe it was time to stop plundering the past for everything that was amusing or silly or ironic about it. He was getting tired of detachment, of things being funny for all the wrong reasons. It felt like business for the young. Irony in one's forties seemed, well, not necessarily sad—it just felt as though perhaps one's remaining time could be better spent. Maybe that was something he could write about. *Confessions of a Broken Hipster: One Man's Aimless Journey from Cynicism to Sincerity.*

Meh. Then again, maybe he would keep thinking.

In the meantime, he would still laugh, of course, but he would try to laugh less at the earnestness of others, at good intentions gone astray, at ill-placed irony, pretentiousness, and ignorance, at the bad masquerading as good.

Oh, who was he kidding? Those were the best things to laugh at. Yet it wasn't hard to figure out why he was feeling this way. While everyone was talking about the Chin Tiki, he glanced at Ana, who was standing over near Todd. Finally, he caught her eye. She walked up to join him at the bar. They both turned away from the others for a moment. Ana stood next to him, her shoulder pressed tightly up to his, and raised her glass of wine. He raised his pint glass and touched it to hers.

What they hadn't told anyone and probably wouldn't for some time, until they were ready to have a party, maybe in the fall, was that they had gotten married.

When Ana proposed to him shortly after they got back together, it had finally seemed like the right thing to do. And really, what was the difference, one way or the other? They had talked about it in the past, went back and forth on it, with each of them having taken turns supporting or opposing the idea. They had never meant not getting married to be some sort of statement. They had just never felt the need to commit in that manner, until they finally did. And when they did, it had felt good to do something sincere.

After they left City Hall in Traverse City on Friday afternoon, they'd each called their parents. Was it really a surprise that everyone was thrilled?

"Finally, finally," they had all said. Joe and Ana tempered the whole experience by telling them that they had also both quit their jobs and were going to travel for a while. Joe was going to write while Ana was going to figure out her next move. They could practically hear the eyes rolling over the phone.

"That's all right," Joe's mother had said. "You just take a little break, and when you get back—"

By that time, Joe had hung up.

Acknowledgments

I'd like to give special thanks to these people for their help and continued support:

Rita Simmons, my best friend, whom I can't imagine a life without, who helped me finally break the nine-year curse between novels.

Keith McLenon, Nick Marine, and Tim Suliman for the inspiration, the laughs, the IPAs and stouts, and, most importantly, the friendship.

DeAnn Forbes for coffee talks, for offering to help before I even know what I need, and for being the first badass woman I met in advertising.

Tim Teegarden for the slow rolls and the meticulous notations.

My sister, Susan Jane Summerlee, for overall wonderfulness.

Doug Blanchard (for the cool covers), Donna McGuire (for unerring eye and tall insights), Luis Resto (for bass, keyboards, and melodica), Doug Shimmin (for oud, shamisen, and bouzouki), Dave Toorongian (for the exotica), Jim Dudley (for perseverance), Jeff Edwards (for aloha shirts), Doug Coombe (for photographs), Dave Chow (for the Chin Tiki; please forgive my liberties), not to mention true-blue ad pals Eric Weltner, Holly Sorscher, David Bierman, Terry Hughes, Barry Burdiak, Gail Offen, Duffy Patten, Cristina Lorenzetti, John Roe, Nancy Wellinger, Dave Colucci, Lyn Webb, Michelle Andonian, Sue Fiorello, and longtimers Andrew Brown, Jim Potter, Tony Park, Mark Mueller, and Michael Lloyd.

Sandra Dittrich, Debbie Karnowsky, Mark Simon, and Cindy Sikorski for being my favorite CDs.

Michael Jackman, Walter Wasacz, Geoff George, and Travis Wright for their expertise and technical guidance.

The memory of Christopher Towne Leland for still being an inspiration. (Hey, guy!)

Jud Laghi for the excellent representation.

Sally van Haitsma for still being in my corner.

Ibrahim Ahmad, Susannah Lawrence, and all the folks at Akashic for their patience and for being so great to work with.

Claudia Tarolo and Marco Zapparoli at Marcos y Marcos for their belief in my work.

Cary Loren of Book Beat and all the dedicated booksellers in the US and abroad who have supported me over the years.

The local artists whom I shamelessly name-checked in this book: Little Bang Theory, Satori Circus, White Stripes, the Dirtbombs, Sufjan Stevens, the Detroit Cobras, the High Strung, Black Milk, Richie Hawtin, Esham, Trick-Trick, and the Stooges.

To the Emory, Ferndale, and Detroit: my favorite hangs.

Speramus meliora; resurget cineribus.

ALSO AVAILABLE BY MICHAEL ZADOORIAN FROM AKASHIC BOOKS

BEAUTIFUL MUSIC

Michael Zadoorian
author of *The Leisure Seeker*

Beautiful Music

A NOVEL

"Danny Yzemski tunes out a dysfunctional family with Frank Zappa and Iggy Pop, shaking his countercultural fist at The Man in this eight-track flashback of a novel set in 1970s Detroit."
—*O, THE OPRAH MAGAZINE,* ONE OF *O's* TOP BOOKS OF SUMMER

"*Beautiful Music* is a sweet and endearing coming-of-age tale measured in album tracks."
—*WALL STREET JOURNAL*

"For Danny, cracking the seal on a fresh piece of wax and dissecting cover art and liner notes are acts of nigh religious experience that unveil to him a community of fellow rockers across Detroit . . . It's in these small moments—a lonely boy experiencing premature nostalgia—that Zadoorian shines."
—*WASHINGTON POST*

"Michael Zadoorian has captured an era when Detroit simmered with anger and fear while it simultaneously reverberated with the joyous noise of rock and roll. *Beautiful Music* eloquently evokes the beauty, confusion, and power of that late 1960s/early 1970s milieu."
—DON WAS, GRAMMY AWARD–WINNING PRODUCER, MUSICIAN

"The story of *Beautiful Music* is painted with rich, exquisite detail and all the painful hyperawareness of growing up in a culture of mixed signals, confusion, and loss. Salvation comes through music. A miraculous safe place in which to belong."
—NANCY WILSON, SINGER/GUITARIST, HEART

"Like Nick Hornby or the great Nick Tosches, Michael Zadoorian is the rare novelist whose prose crackles with the energy of the best rock and roll. *Beautiful Music* is a beautiful bildungsroman that does the sounds and spirit of his beloved Detroit proud."
—JIM DEROGATIS, AUTHOR OF *LET IT BLURT: THE LIFE AND TIMES OF LESTER BANGS*

"Popping with Detroit cultural landmarks, *Beautiful Music* wraps a disturbing yet humorous tale of beleaguered adolescence in 1970s Motor City around the A-list rock music that made the dingy landscape an aural playground." —STEVE MILLER, AUTHOR OF *DETROIT ROCK CITY*

www.akashicbooks.com
AVAILABLE IN HARDCOVER, PAPERBACK, AND E-BOOK WHEREVER BOOKS ARE SOLD.